Strictly Legal

Strictly Legal

ANDREW FITZPATRICK

authorHOUSE®

AuthorHouse™
1663 Liberty Drive
Bloomington, IN 47403
www.authorhouse.com
Phone: 1-800-839-8640

First published by AuthorHouse   10/21/2011

ISBN: 978-1-4670-0786-3 (sc)
ISBN: 978-1-4670-0787-0 (ebk)

Printed in the United States of America

Any people depicted in stock imagery provided by Thinkstock are models, and such images are being used for illustrative purposes only.
Certain stock imagery © Thinkstock.

This book is printed on acid-free paper.

Thanks to all my family and friends for their support through my life. Thanks also to the people and poetry of south west Dublin. You are my muse, my soul, my everything—and the only true paradise on God's green Earth.

The Thoughts of Dosser Doyle (Volume One)

I clasp my hands as I spring out of bed and I smell the sunny Saturday air flow through the open window. Saturday mornings are where it all begins, the clasping of hands, the smelling of air and the death of dozens and dozens of our winged friends. I look at myself in the mirror and remark the obvious increased muscle tone of my abdomen. I have to admit that my work out regime is achieving remarkable success in a very short space of time and this brings to mind the overrunning of the low—countries and France back in '40. I affect a pistol shape with the thumb, index and fanny-fingering finger of my right hand and slowly draw the corporeal toy gun from my side and aim it at the head of my reflection. I do the same with my left hand and then rotate my finger-pistols inwards and pretend-shoot my head in a ghetto-gansta style. I then revert to a more orthodox, Caucasian style of gun-holding and empty both imaginary magazines into a phantom convertible which speeds off into the far off nowhere behind my reflection's back. I blow the smoke from both barrels, before replacing the pretend guns in my imaginary holster and then chastise myself for concluding the performance in such a trite and clichéd manner.

I get dressed while listening to Eminem's "The Way I am", pausing only to turn up the volume when I hear my sister screaming at me to turn it down. I then head to the bathroom and take a rather unpleasant defecation. It smells so badly that I actually retch while still sitting on the jacks and get a little bit sick into the wash hand basin. I subsequently wash my teeth thoroughly but decide against flushing the jacks as I can hear my sister humming outside the door as she waits for me to finish my morning ablutions. As I walk out the door I just mutter "I'd give that a few minutes if I were you" but my sister is now talking on the phone on the subject of

1

what I'm pretty sure is fake-tan, and my sagacious counsel appears to go unheeded. I go downstairs and the waft of smoky rashers makes my mouth water. My mother and father are just finishing their respective breakfasts and sit listening to the radio as I check underneath the grill for assorted bowel cancer-causing pork products (as I like to call them). I then shake the teapot in order to ascertain the remaining volume of tea inside and squeeze the butter to determine its spreadability.

The radio seems to be airing an interview of one presenter by another presenter (shock horror) and I begin to feel rather indignant about the proliferation of such conversations across all forms of media. My musings on the cosy journalistic cartel who prop each other up in a self-sustaining industry of banality are interrupted by the sound of my mother's voice. "Were you drinking last night?" My mother routinely asks me this question every weekend. Every weekend I have been using some form of life enhancing substance (although not in the way that you may imagine but I'll explain all that later) and every weekend I give the same answer followed by a concocted story to explain the previous night's tardiness. "Of course I wasn't drinking mam; you know I won't break my pledge until I'm eighteen. A few of us just went to the cinema and got some chips afterwards." My mother raises an eyebrow indicating that further testimony is required in order to convince her of my sobriety. "Oh yeah, now don't get worried or anything but we had a bit of hassle at the bus stop. We were waiting for the last bus and these travellers came along and they had sticks and dogs and stuff and they started asking us for change for the bus. So we just legged it. I think a couple of them chased us for a bit but we managed to lose them. We had to walk all the way home then cause we missed the bus." "Oh my god, did yis not ring the guards?" "Ah sure what's the point in ringing the guards, there's no dealing with them knackers. Bastards are outside the law, always have been and always will be." My father lifts his head from his newspaper to deliver his diatribe and saves me from having to explain myself any further. He has his prosthetic leg, leaning against the wall beside him and he is airing his stump while resting it on a nearby stool. My mother's anxious curiosity is quelled by my father's timely interjection and I liberally spread the malleable butter on virgin-white bread.

My sister comes into the kitchen, slaps me over the head and calls me a disgusting pig. My parents seem completely oblivious to both the physical and verbal assaults on my person as my sister sits down to eat something which I don't actually recognise as food and can't be bothered asking her to find out what the fuck it is. I construct a hideously large breakfast sandwich and make a point of eating it in the noisiest and messiest way possible. I intentionally smother the beast in tomato sauce so that it mixes with the butter and runny egg yolk, and a continuous flow of the viscous substance trickles on to my plate which I then lick like a kitten drinking milk from a saucer. My sister pretends not to notice my rather uncouth breakfast etiquette. This is a tactic which she has been employing in recent weeks and one which I must admit is beginning to irk me somewhat. I then feel like a complete sad bastard for being annoyed because my sister seems to be winning our psychological sibling war and quickly move into the front room. I have two episodes of "Generals of the Third Reich" recorded and halfway through the first one which is about General Paulus, my phone rings and it's Tarzan.

"Dosser you lazy prick, are you up and ready?" Tarzan is my friend, business associate, confidante, comrade, trusted lieutenant and fellow poet/philosopher. He's obviously at least a quarter black but this is never officially recognised or spoken about as both his parents, grandparents and the rest of his family are Procol Harem's one hit wonder. He got the name when some idiot kid in primary school called him by it as an early attempt at a racial slur. Of course everyone laughed because they were just thinking: Tarzan, jungle, monkeys etc. As we weren't particularly friends at the time, I felt no need to point out what seemed to me the very obvious holes in the basis for such an insult, so I just chuckled along with everyone else. I pause the video just as Zhukov's strategy for entrapping the 6th army is being diagrammatically illustrated on the screen. "Tarzan you kiddie-fiddling paedo, of course I'm ready. Meet you in the killing fields at 1200 hours. Have you amassed an ample arsenal?" "Not as ample as your ma's bleedin arsenal, what?! Or your sister's tits!" I obviously set Tarzan up to make a retort of this description. Even though the reference to my sister's breasts is tenuously relevant and it strikes me how exasperating it is that a deliciously delivered double-entendre will never be laughed at as heartily as any slight on one's female relatives. "Right, thanks for that Taz. I'll see you then so, and remember, don't molest any children on your way there you sicko. As always we'll be keeping everything strictly legal." Tarzan just says "fuck off you prick!" laughs and hangs up.

So I set off to meet Tarzan on what happens to be a dull but thankfully dry day. This is a typically perfect day for us, as the dullness means that there won't be too many people in the park, which in turn lessens the risk of any injuries to innocent bystanders. Also, crow-hunting can at times be a rather strenuous activity, especially if myself and Tarzan decide on a head to head, which turns out to be the case around fifty per cent of the time. So, a not-too-warm but dry day is usually preferable for our predatory purposes. Naturally we will have to return to the greenhouse by mid-afternoon in order to inspect the condition of our latest crop, and attend to miscellaneous matters of business common to all entrepreneurs; but more of that later. I stop off in the shop to get a bottle of coke. There's nobody at the counter and when I inspect the cash register, I notice that it has yet to be turned on so I just take a bottle out of the fridge, wriggle off the label and leave it on the counter with the correct change weighing it down to ensure it doesn't get blown away. As I leave the premises I take two Disprins out of my jacket pocket and plop them inside the coke bottle and watch them as they dissolve in the dark liquid and begin to foam until they disappear, leaving no visible trace of their chemical presence. I then knock back the mixture in three large gulps. I belch heartily and pop the empty bottle into the bin at the entrance to the park. I walk across the football pitches as some cadaverous old man marks out the white lines, while, what I suppose to be his grandchildren lethargically unravel the folded up nets, which I assume they've been press-ganged into putting up for the day's matches. I lie on the crest of the small hill where I normally meet Tarzan, light up a peanut skin joint and wait.

Tarzan arrives dressed in the most insane clothes imaginable. This is a facet of Tarzan's behaviour which he has been steadfastly pursuing for the last number of years but which really arrived at this most critical stage last summer. It has its genesis in the fact that his grandmother worked as a seamstress all her life and has a sort of cottage industry for herself down the country, where Tarzan still spends most of the time of most of his summers. So last school holidays, it rains for literally a month non-stop and Tarzan's going mad being cooped up in his grandparents' house, with scant entertainment save for the overly vigorous inspection of his genitalia.

So Tarzan gets his grandmother to teach him the basics of using a sewing machine, stitching, knitting and generally how to make your own clothes. But of course, a little knowledge can be a dangerous thing and by the time Tarzan returns to Dublin, he has committed himself to endeavour to make almost every stitch of attire which he wears but lacks any of the artistic, creative or functional nous to make clothes which don't make you look like you've just been dressed by a blind lunatic, who's recently chewed off his own hands.

"Taz, what in the name of god are you wearing? Our behaviour is strange enough without you drawing attention to us. We can at least try and look normal, even if we are going to spend the next few hours shooting crows. Your attire makes me not only doubt the sustainability of our friendship, but implores me to question the very purpose and direction which my own life is taking." Tarzan theatrically affects the face of a scolded child but I can see from his reddened cheeks and glazed eyes that he is slightly taken aback and mildly hurt by my diatribe. He gazes down at his red and blue-hooped cardigan, mauve tee-shirt and brown combat style trousers (all topped off with a Slazenger sports bag), says I'm just jealous of his flair for haute couture and prises the peanut skin joint from between my fingers. We wander up to one of our favourite hunting spots at a small hedgerow near the edge of the park, where a wall and a fence separate us from the motorway. Tarzan unzips the sports bag, takes out the slingshot which he duly hands to me and then produces four tubular pieces of wood, each one wider and longer than the one which preceded it. He then attaches the four sticks together until they have formed a single wooden entity, hollow all the way through and spouted at one end. "Let's fucking do this Dosser" he says. "The bastards won't know what's fucking hit them."

After a rather fruitful day's crow hunting, myself and Tarzan go back to his house to attend to our horticultural duties in the greenhouse in his back garden. Tarzan has a very long but narrow back garden, rather like a passageway I suppose, but to where it leads I'm sure we don't really know. We have erected our greenhouse at the farthest end, but we are separated from the back wall and outside lane by a small, disused garage, that we have employed as a kind of storage depot for materials and supplies. We also have a second greenhouse in school, where we are co-auditors of the St. Leonard's Horticultural Society, but our main base of operations continues to be here. We always enter the garden through the back entrance, so we don't have to walk through the house and exchange platitudes with Tarzan's freaky family or have to explain where we were and what we were doing and what we have in the sports bag and why we look so suspicious and so on. We open the door into the greenhouse and Tarzan stores the sports bag safely in the underground compartment which although may seem a tad over-cautious, is simply an expedient way of minimising clutter. It is also a convenient way to continuously ensure that our Running Away Fund has not been stolen or eaten by rodents. We then inspect the current crop and decide which ones are ready for harvesting and subsequent sale for profit. The Psilocybe Cubensis is not quite ready to be harvested but will require only a further day or two before we can bag and distribute their mushroomy goodness and perhaps even sample a little for ourselves. The Cysticus Scorpius is in full bloom and is ready to be picked and dried, but again will not be ready for sale until next weekend. Therefore all we can really take with us on tonight's foray will be the fully dried Nepeta Catoria which must be portioned and bagged and the Alpha Chlorolose which Tarzan informs me, he has taken the liberty of fully preparing and storing in the underground compartment during one of his insomnia fuelled bouts of acute diligence. Even though I am not completely content with the prospect of Tarzan conducting his own solitary operations, I decide not to say anything as I don't want to aggravate the headcase while we have work to do. Before we get to work, we walk to the rear of the greenhouse to inspect our prize possession which, when we have it fully matured and ready for harvesting could potentially be our biggest money spinner. We uncover the plastic covering which surrounds it to marvel at the beast. It is the Echinopsis (Trichocereus) Pachanoi, or San Pedro Cactus. The affects are allegedly extremely pleasant, although as neither I nor Tarzan has yet to experience them, we will have to test the product ourselves before unleashing it on the market, which of course adds a sense of trepidation to the ongoing excitement and anxiety to harvest it. The problem is that it is taking so long for it to grow to any kind of a size and we are having to put a great deal of care and expertise into its nurturing. But alas that is our calling in life and the eventual rewards will surely make our laborious endeavours all the more worthwhile.

Tarzan sets about watering the remainder of the plants while I prepare a feed for the Trichocereus Pachanoi when Tarzan's mother knocks on the glass pane, holding a tray of tea, sandwiches and biscuits. I rush to slide back the door to allow her a safe entry and to relieve her burden of timely refreshments. This as always, is no cause for alarm. As I have stated previously, myself and Tarzan are co-auditors of St. Leonard's Horticultural Society, so it is not out of the ordinary to anybody's mind that we spend an inordinate amount of time tending plants in greenhouses. I suppose that a lot of people, especially our parents, are extremely supportive of our botanic pursuits as it is a rather quaint way for teenage boys to pass the hours in this new millennium of rising street crime and mindless thuggery. Even if Tarzan's mother was aware of the profitable usages of the plants from which we harvest our produce, the greenhouse is covered in ordinary roses, lilies, Japanese orchids, dahlias and a number of tomato and strawberry plants, (whose fruit serves as the socially acceptable cover for our fledgling cottage industry) which physically camouflage the other plants in the unlikely event of a prescient visitor. "Jaysus, the heat in here would kill a camel!" she says as she steps cautiously through the threshold. "There ya are now; I'll take that from ya." I take the tray from Tarzan's mother and become conscious of the modern social catch twenty two for all teenagers, whereby to call your friend's mother "Mrs. Whatever their second name is" seems antiquated and obsequious, but to call them by their first name seems overly familiar, so in the end you simply call them nothing at all. "Thanks Dosser, you're very good. So how are the two little gardeners getting on? Has the green in the fingers spread to the rest of yis yet? Ha?" "No no, no sign of that yet anyway" I say as a means of conducting myself in ordinary conversation, of which I do occasionally enjoy partaking. Tarzan has not said anything yet and is evidently embarrassed and annoyed by his mother's presence but tries not to come across as being too gruff or ungrateful. "Thanks for the tea ma" he says, "We'll bring the tray back up to the house when we're finished."

"Right so I'll leave yis to it then". I slide the door back a further inch or two to show Tarzan's mother out and close it shut to preserve the heat which is essential for the growth of the Trichocereus Pachanoi.

We both cease our respective tasks of feeding the plants and set about attending to our own nutritional needs. Tarzan dutifully pours out the tea before replacing the tea cosy which seems to depict scenes from the highland games, over the brown enamel pot. The sandwiches are triangular, a mixture of ham salad and cheese, and the biscuits are a selection of chocolate digestives, jersey creams and plain polos. I always feel peculiarly uncomfortable eating sandwiches in Tarzan's house and my stomach's first impulse is to reject the sustenance, but I manage to force down just a few, before hitting the chocolate digestives with the fervour of a fanatical SS officer, exacting revenge on a village suspected of harbouring or aiding local partisans. Tarzan eats the remainder of the sandwiches like a blue whale eating krill, sticks four heaped spoonfuls of sugar into a mug which is shaped like a gorilla's head and lights up a Nepeta Catoria joint. "You know Dosser, I've been thinkin about something recently and I was wonderin if you had any opinions on the matter." Tarzan's tone is extremely sincere, to the extent that it's actually worrying. "Are we still the good guys?" he asks. "I mean, after what happened to that girl, are we still the good guys?" Tarzan looks very perturbed and I know that when he gets like this, I have to reassure him in an almost avuncular fashion. "Of course we are Taz, why wouldn't we be? Listen, what happened to that girl was completely outside of our control. Those lads would have done that to somebody, at some stage, no matter what they were on. We don't kill anybody; we don't shoot anybody or hurt anybody. Those animals would've done that even if they were drunk on alcohol, where half the money goes to the government. Don't worry about it man and let's just keep focus on what we're doing here all right?" I give Tarzan a friendly punch in the arm and take the Nepeta Catoria joint out of his hand. I drain the last of the tea and stand up to continue preparing the feed for the Trichocereus Pachanoi. Tarzan collects up all the tea stuff and brings it back down to the house, leaving me to contemplate on my lonesome while I mix the prepared feed in the watering can and stab out the Nepeta Catoria joint in the ashtray. Tarzan arrives back with the radio and sticks on some utterly awful dance music but I decide to say nothing because I can see he's beginning to get over his earlier perturbations. After a while, I actually start to enjoy the sounds, obviously aided and abetted by the joint we've just smoked. We start to actually dance around as we go from plant to plant, watering and feeding and we're laughing our stoned heads off when there's another knock on the glassy exterior of our translucent abode. I turn around to see the squashed up male genitalia of who I'm hoping (never thought I'd say that before) is Gobber, who has his hood up around his head to obscure the view of his face. He eventually takes it down to reveal his ascetic visage and Tarzan does the dutiful to allow our number one salesman to enter the greenhouse. "Ladies how are we this evening? Is that the alluring aroma of burning Nepeta Catoria which I can smell? You lads look like yous are havin fun anyway. Have yis come out to your parents yet or what?" Gobber sniggers like a hyena achieving orgasm and I simply refuse to acknowledge his not so veiled questioning of the platonic nature of mine and Tarzan's relationship. "And how are you Gobber?" I ask him and I can see from his ruddy expression that he has recently imbibed a considerable quantity of intoxicating beverages. Gobber Gilsenan is a bit older than myself and Tarzan, which allows us entry into a twenty something market that would otherwise be an unreachable land of possible, nay probable selling potential. We give Gobber a certain amount of produce to sell and he gets a handsome wage in return for his troubles. Apart from that, he can also drive, has an actual job so he's not solely reliant on us for income, and also has a far better taste in music than Tarzan. "What is this shite yous are listenin to? Here, stick that on Dosser." Gobber hands me the new Chemical Brothers album *Come With Us,* which I am very thankful for as Tarzan's euphoric trance compilation is beginning to numb my mind and body and consequently diminish my productivity. I stick on the CD and Gobber hands me a roll of cash which I count on the counting cash table before slipping him a nifty for his troubles and sticking the remaining eight ponies in my back pocket (Gobber by the way, is not aware of the underground compartment and so does not know where we keep our running away money, a precaution which is very much necessary as he is still officially an employee of the company and not an actual partner. Also, Gobber has too much of an overt dependence on alcohol which points to an unstable mental capacity and the fact that he is older than us means that he could exert an undue influence over the enterprise if he were to become privy to our inner workings. Essentially, we have to be careful at all times not to allow our powers to become eroded, but I don't wish to sound too serious here or do the man a disservice. He is after all a friend of sorts, I suppose). Now that I can see that Gobber is more than a little jolly, I decide to give us all something to laugh about, or at least accelerate the process. "Anyway Gobber, what's the story? Any exciting tales with which to regale us this evening? I say this while giving Tarzan a wink, while he turns his back to prune a rather vicious rose bush and smothers a laugh into his chest. "Aw do I?" Gobber says; his eyes lighting up like a child at Christmas. "Wait till yis here what happened to me last night".

As we need to arrange our produce from the stores in the garage, the three of us relocate in order to simultaneously listen to Gobber's story and count out our packages for the night's operations. Gobber takes out a box of John Player Blue and clumsily extracts a cigarette with his lips. He rests the cigarette in his mouth while he pats himself down in an effort to locate his lighter. I duly hold out a lit lighter and he inhales the acrid smoke deeply as if it was the source which imparted to him the very power of speech. He leans his head back and blows a cloud of smoke to the felt ceiling, like the inhalation of nicotine has just given him an orgasm.

"Last night yeah, after I'd shipped all that stuff for yous, I get on the bus into town. The bus is takin ages cause there's one of those black drivers drivin it and you know the way they drive really carefully because they're shit scared of crashin it in case they get deported or whatever. It keeps stopping at every single set of lights as well, so eventually, around Camden Street, I just say fuck this and get off and walk. I suck the life out of a cigarette in a minute flat and exhale the last inhaled two-lung full of smoke into the pub as I burst through the door." "What pub was this now?" says Tarzan. "Whelan's" says Gobber, obviously annoyed that his train of thought has been interrupted by Tarzan's untimely, but (in my opinion) quite necessary question.

"So anyway, the place smells of shit and damp clothes and by the time I've downed my thirteenth pint, it begins to smell more of piss and dry lips as I'm tryin desperately to get this fat bird down a nearby lane. "Thirteenth pint? Could you seriously drink that much?" I find myself saying this in more of a thinking out loud way, as I am genuinely interested to know if this is a normal volume of alcohol to consume in such a short space of time. Gobber stops, but actually refuses to recognise the fact that I've just asked him a question and continues on with his story. I also decide to allow him to continue without further interjection as I realise the extent to which it vexes him. Also, he can have quite a temper on him. I remember seeing a fight he had with Stevie Smith when I was a child. It was actually shockingly vicious and I shake my head as if to expel the blood-soaked vision from my mind while I re-focus my attention on my associate's soliloquy. "Yeah so anyway, I keep tellin her that "I love her so very, very much" but she doesn't seem too bothered or like she cares either way and before I can say chubby chasin pay day, we're down the back of the alley as she reefs down my jeans and starts suckin on my cock like it's the last source of breathable air in a nuclear holocaust. After a period of time which I admittedly can't fully recollect, she eventually undoes her jeans and bends over as if to say "gimme some of that good stuff fun boy". I'm still tryin to gather myself as the light from a torch shines into my beleaguered and blood-shot eyes. I cop it's the cops and manage to scramble over the back wall while simultaneously pullin my trousers up into their more orthodox wearing position, leavin Mandy Dingle there with her chubby non-knees in a fuckin muddy puddle." At this stage Gobber's up on his feet and re-enacting his titanic scaling of the wall. He actually stumbles and manages to knock down a stack of old CDs which scatter all over the floor. He looks at them for a second as if he is wondering whether he should tidy them up or not and in the end decides against it before tenderly sitting back down again. "So anyway, the fat bird is still waiting for her 'slice of the action' as it were, when the two coppers rush down the lane after me. I can only imagine that the dirty bitch was happy enough to see the two policemen standin over her (and I'm not goin to lower myself by makin the 'holdin their big truncheons' gag, so I'll continue on without it, thank you very much Mr. Postman) when she eventually peers around her immense physique to inquire as to the reason for the delay of the meat delivery, with a face on her like a struggling butcher a week before Christmas. Maybe the two boys did the work of one me, I don't know, I won't cast any such aspersions on officers of the law."

"But anyway where was I? Oh yeah, so after hoppin over the wall, I run through where the flats are there, just to give meself a bit of distance and I come back on to Aungier Street and just start hittin the pubs, gradually makin my way back in the direction of Rathmines. After a period of time, I couldn't say how long, I'm seriously on my last legs but I decide to hit one more in Cassidy's. So I'm standin at the bar, drinkin a double screwdriver when these two blokes walk up to me. One of them is dark, while the other one has red hair. Although they're dressed in civvies and holdin scoops, they're both fairly tall and have that look about them where you just know they're cops, do you know what I mean? Anyway one of them says to me 'I recognise you from somewhere young sir, have we met on a previous occasion to the best of your recollection?' At this stage they're both lookin dead serious, and the guy who hasn't said a word yet, is lookin at me like he's just walked in on me shaggin his da as his ma takes instant Polaroids while covered in cranberry sauce. At this stage I'm fair near ready to shit myself cause I don't really fancy spendin the night in a cell as it would be a rather sour end to an otherwise wonderful night's drunken revelry. So I'm thinkin in my head that I can either make a run for it or just hand myself over to the relevant authorities. I'm tryin to figure out the most favourable escape plan, scourin the depths of my memory for some killer moves from some James Bond movie or somethin, when I realise that I just don't have the energy or the wherewithal to attempt such an escapade. I resign myself to my fate and I'm just about to put my hands up when I cop that the two boys have big wide eyed grins on their faces and one of them raises his hand in the air and says 'gimme five brother'. I'm a bit lost for words so I just stick up the palm of my hand and the one with the red hair just high fives me, while the dark haired one asks me what I'm drinkin and orders another double screwdriver from the barman."

"So anyway, it turns out that the Mandy Dingle bird is actually a daughter of this Superintendent who works in the station with the two boys and who is apparently a bit of a cunt to work for or whatever. As soon as the two boys went up to her in the lane, she started givin it all the 'Do you know who my father is treatment?!' and all 'He'll have your badges!' and all that kind of shite. Well the two lads were only delighted to learn of her familial connections to their beloved boss, so they slapped the old love bracelets on her and brought her down the station and threw her in a cell. Then one of them, whose name is Tony by the way, (I call him T but I'll just call him Tony for the purposes of tellin the story) has to go up to the Superintendent bloke and tell him the bad news. Of course, he has to say that it was only by the time that they'd already brought her down the station that they'd learned who she was, that originally she was so drunk as to be incomprehensible and that made it impossible to garner any reliable information from her by which they could establish her identity and what have ye. So Tony tells him the whole scenario about him and Slipper (Slipper is the other lad's name by the way), that him and Slipper saw her on her hands and knees in a lane, administering oral sex to what looked to have been a man of African origin, that they were unfortunately unable to apprehend said unidentified man of probable African origin and that when they had attempted to come to the aid of the girl, she had become abusive and violent. That she had spat what appeared to be an immense quantity of semen onto Slipper's uniform and had threatened that she was connected with the Crumlin/Drimnagh organised crime gang and would have us both shot to death in a hail of bullets."

"Of course at this stage the Superintendent bloke is passed any semblance of anger and is just pure embarrassed, shocked and horrified at the behaviour of his not so little girl. He naturally demands to speak to his daughter and they rush down to the cell where the beast is being caged. Tony said that before they opened the door you could get a whiff of somethin nasty, but that nothin prepared them for the sight which met them when they unlocked the cell door. There's the big girl lyin, prostrate on the floor where she'd obviously shit herself before she could reach the bed pan and then the smell of the shit has caused her to retch so that she's vomited that luminous yellow, vodka red bull shit all over the front of herself and naturally, the girls in floods of tears and screamin for her daddy and what have ye. Tony said that he was fightin back the laughter while Slipper had to just run out of the station to get some fresh air cause the sight and the smell of the place was just so foul."

"Obviously, the Superintendent bloke is at this stage, ragin. He can't even bring himself to look at the girl and he orders the place to be cleaned up and for the 'prisoner' to be given a new cell and fresh clothes and whatever. So the place gets cleaned up and the girl is secluded in a new cell and is given one of those plastic smock things to wear while she's in there. So after a while there isn't a murmur out of her and everyone thinks that she's probably sobered up after getting sick and she's probably asleep or at least reflectin on the night's events and how much of a disgrace she must be to her Superintendent daddy. When next of all, there's just this immense crashing boom sound that you can hear all over the station. Tony runs up to the door of the cell and opens it up as quick as he can and there's the poor fat bird lyin on the ground, completely naked, except for the smock which seems to be loosely tied around her massive neck, roarin screams of pure pain and you can see that she's after breakin at least one of her legs, cause the bone's stickin out like when you see a really bad leg break in football. Anyway, the girl's obviously tried to hang herself with the smock thing, but evidently, the material wasn't strong enough to support her ample frame. So there she is, lyin on the floor of a jail cell, totally starkers, with two broken legs and the boys would have simply let her go, only for the fact that she told them she was this Superintendent bloke's daughter. Can you fuckin believe that? And what's worse, is what kind of a way is this to be carryin on when you've got a junior cert to be studyin for? D'y know?"

Gobber then tells us that he carried on drinking with the two officers of the law for the rest of the night and that he reckons they could become useful contacts for the operation if we were ever in a spot of bother over anything. I remind him that we have no illegal substances on our person, currently or ever and that if any of us would ever require the assistance of corrupt police officers, it would more than likely be him to try and weasel his way out of a statutory rape charge. Gobber nearly falls over laughing at this prospect and just says "I am a dirty cunt all the same, I am a dirty cunt" to himself with a knowing and proud grin across his unshaven, drunken face. Myself and Tarzan load up our fully prepared merchandise into our respective sports bags. Tarzan has a separate Slazenger one for this specific purpose while I am currently sporting a World Cup 2002, limited edition adidas carrier bag, as I like to keep up with the times when possible. Myself and Tarzan travel on two rather decrepit but perfectly functional mountain bikes, which are however soon to become defunct due to the imminent but quite alarming prospect of Tarzan's seventeenth birthday and consequential acquisition of his first provisional driving licence.

We sling the bags over our shoulders, lift up the garage door and wheel the bikes into the back lane, leaving Gobber to mind the house so to speak. He usually remains in the garage to sleep off his day time drunkenness on a large bean bag which rests in the corner and he will then continue his weekend festivities when we rouse him upon our return. "Well Taz, which route do you fancy tonight then?" "I think I'll take the Scratchy route tonight if you don't mind," he says. "I'm sick of that Itchy route. There's too many hills for a man of my age." "No problem whatsoever Taz, I rather enjoy the Itchy route myself and if anything, the undulating terrain serves as a convenient way to maintain a healthy level of aerobic fitness, so essential in today's all too sedentary and junk-food orientated lifestyles. I'll meet you down at the corner at 2100 hours. And remember, it's your turn to get the methylated spirits. I'll get the bread."

I set off on my peregrination through the lane, trying to dodge any smashed glass and dog shit before coming onto the main road. A mild wind guides me softly from my back and a pleasant, spring-evening temperature descends on the southern suburbs of our nation's capital. The first stop on my itinerary is country student house number one on Whitehall Road. I arrive at the door and the tall sporty guy, who obviously wouldn't know

Adrenochrome Semicarbazone from Astrophytum Asterias if they ended up in his corn flakes, answers the door and gives me that same disdainful look which says 'I hate you and I hate the fact that everyone who lives here is cooler than me and as soon as I get more money from my father's EU farmers' grant, I'm so getting my own apartment in Rathmines." He calls out "Gerry" like a disapproving father informs their daughter of the arrival of her older and obviously scum bag boyfriend and I wait in the hall for Gerry to emerge from the upstairs bastion of (I'm assuming) chronic masturbation. Gerry eventually arrives down to confirm my suspicions, looking more than a little bit flustered and wearing only a football jersey and what I'm hoping are a pair of shorts that are so short, that they are actually not visible so that his jersey actually looks like a one piece that a girl would wear. The G meister takes a fifty bag of Nepeta Catoria but declines the offer on the Alpha Chlorolose because a few of his housemates are apparently playing hurling in the morning. The next destination is the general Kimmage area, where we have three different regular customers. The first one is Michael "The Terrier" Thompson, so called because he can be regularly seen around the area, walking his rat-like Yorkshire terrier and not because he has any particular combatative qualities. He takes a large amount of the Alpha Chlorolose and says that he's having "a bit of a soiree" tonight if I fancy coming along. I tell him that I've various commercial affairs to attend to and will not be in a position to join the festivities. I then make a speedy exit as I'm pretty sure that he's gay and thinks I'm gay and I don't want him to get the impression that I'm behaving in a demurely coquettish manner by turning down his invitation. The last stop in the Kimmage area is the house of a school friend, Richie Grimes. Richie is one of the few people in school who we sell to, and this policy is in place for obvious reasons. Primarily we don't want to become too well known around the school as purveyors of alternative, mind-altering substances, as it would inevitably lead to an unwanted amount of attention which could raise eyebrows amongst the powers that be. Also, the general cohort of our year strike me as being a tad untrustworthy, in terms of their constitution to withstand the effects of the substances and their ability to conceal the produce from their parents. On top of this, we have been compelled to enforce a vetting process for an undecided length of time due to a rather unseemly incident which occurred, not so long ago and not too far away, but these measures are of course purely precautionary and will be subject to further review in the not so distant future.

Richie is a man however, that we can trust and as usual takes a score bag of Nepeta Catoria. He invites me in for a quick cup of tea and a smoke and I gladly accept as I could do with some refreshment to sustain my energy levels and ameliorate my sense of job satisfaction. Richie leads me into the living room and I sit down on the couch while he puts the kettle on and rolls up the joint. His sister, who's two years older than us, is sitting on an armchair and I'm assuming that she's ill because she has a duvet covering her up to her neck and is surrounded by used tissues. Even though she's currently in an invalid state, she is still extremely attractive and I am traipsing the normally fertile furrows of my mind for some killer one liner, some classic Dosser stuff, when I am resigned to the fact that I cannot conjure anything. I have to admit, that my inter-gender social skills are not what they could be, but in fairness, she's being an absolute cow, and has not given any semblance of recognition to my presence and I really begin to resent her behaviour (or lack of) towards me. She sniffs in irritatingly rhythmical junctures and has her bare feet up on the table in front of her, sticking out from the bottom of the duvet. She's watching pop idol and I find myself unable to stop looking at her feet, when Richie enters the room, holding two cups of tea, with the unlit joint resting behind his ear. "You comin out for this man?" he says and I'm glad to leave as I was beginning to feel slightly uncomfortable in the company of his rudely reticent sibling. We step outside into the garden as the light of the day begins to fade away and that dull, mid-spring greyness settles on the city. "So how's business then?" Richie asks while lighting up the joint and kicking a flat football against the pebble dashed wall of the house. His little Jack Russell is taking a shit in the corner of the small lawn. "Ah you know how it is Richard, it pays the bills and puts food on the table, but I think we have arrived at a stage where we are unable to produce enough supply to keep up with demand. It's a major advantage which our competitors have against us I'm afraid, that there's a seemingly endless supply of dope out there, but still, with good citizens like you who are willing to support our endeavours to offer an alternative, blood-free source of recreational life enhancers, it makes all the effort worthwhile." Richie just breaks out laughing and calls me a weirdo as he doesn't seem to believe that there's any sincerity in what I've just said and I begin to wonder myself. He hands me the joint and proceeds to dribble the football around the garden with the Jack Russell scurrying after him. "Have you done that History essay yet Richard?" I ask him the question in an attempt to halt the overly frivolous activity in front of me, as it's making me a little uneasy and not really in line with the ideal repose which I was hoping for on entering the house initially. He stops and sticks his hand out for the joint which I duly surrender. "Nah, not yet. I'll do it tomorrow sure, what you doin yours on?" "It's an account of operation Barbarossa, failings and successes of. It's hard to find the time to fit it in but I should have the initial draft completed by 2200 hours tomorrow." I'm just about to launch into a summary of the aforementioned successes and failures of the invasion of the Soviet Union, when Richie's sister shouts out to us through the kitchen window that she's bored and wants the dog brought into her to keep her company. Richie shouts back that he has to go to the toilet and that he'll bring the dog in presently. He hands me the joint and rolls his eyes up to heaven as if to say "what an annoying cow" and I slip a bag of Alpha Chlorolose out of the pocket of my combats. As soon as I'm sure that Richie has gone upstairs and is safely ensconced in the bathroom, attending to his excretory needs, I empty the contents of the bag into the dog's bowl and fill it up with water from the outside tap. The dog hurries over straight away and starts drinking the mixture with great fervour, obviously exhausted after his little game of football with Richie.

I'm stroking the dog's back and saying "there's a good fella, there's a good boy" when Richie comes back and slides open the back door and calls "C'mon Charlie, c'mon boy and the little Jack Russell scurries inside and runs into the front room to Richie's sister. Richie sees me out the front door as I can hear his sister shouting "Come on Gareth!" at the television screen. I say my goodbyes to Richie get back on the bike to complete the final leg of my journey. I'm running a little late, so I decide to stop only in country student house number two in Templeogue and swing by my own house to ingest some sustenance and check in with the folks. There's lasagne and salad made for me and my mother's left a note saying that they've gone to visit my auntie Sylvia. I consume the repast with frightening haste and stick a brown sliced pan in my sports bag before remounting the bicycle and setting off to meet Tarzan at the corner of the road.

When I arrive, Tarzan's already there and is on the phone to his mother telling her that she better have sent off the forms for his provisional licence or he'll simply take her car when she's not looking and drive it anyway.

When he hangs up he hands me his takings for the night which I combine with my own in a pink envelope. I give him back a nifty; take the same for me and the two of us cycle around to Tarzan's garage door. I knock on the door and Gobber lifts it open from the inside, looking in the bad humour of someone who's just woken up with a hangover. We wheel the bikes inside and I walk through to the greenhouse to store the night's takings in the underground compartment. When I walk back into the garage, Gobber sticks on *Definitely Maybe*, Tarzan produces the bottle of methylated spirits from his bag while I take out the brown bread. I place the full pan of bread in an upright position in the drinking basin and remove the paper packaging with a theatrical rip. Tarzan proceeds to slowly pour the methylated spirits on top of the mini tower of bread. Gobber's eyes light up. "This is gonna be a great night lads."

Sunday morning awoke in a beauteous haze of sunlight which came sneaking through the gap in my blackout blinds and woke me up like an annoying kid shining a torch in my eyes. Last night's escapades have yet to truly unleash their most heinous effects and for the moment I still feel blissfully under the influence of copious amounts of one hundred percent legal toxicants. I arise from my bed and a heave of exhilaration pulsates through my corporeal frame and I conduct my morning-mirror-bang bang routine with the expertise of a stanislavskian master and kiss my reflection in the mirror as a kind of an ad lib, cherry on top of my fully baked performance. The one thing which begins to perturb me is the thoughts of going downstairs to my awaiting family, which I face with the dread of a condemned man awaiting the hang man's noose. It's not that I don't love them or anything; it's that my ability to conduct platitudinal everyday conversation is diminishing at a rate of knots similar to the speed attained by a Boeing 747 crashing into the Pacific Ocean. Note to self; focus on being able to facilitate normal behaviour in everyday situations; reasons hitherto fore assembled: Number One, it's what everyone else does, Number Two, it'll keep people off your back, Number Three, it will stop people from thinking you're up to something and Number Four, you might actually get a ride out of it eventually.

After my considerationary deliberations, I run downstairs to find an empty house and a note from my parents to say that they've gone to Dun Laoighre and that they'll be back for dinner. There's a breakfast left on the table for me which I can't even think about eating so I just force down some milk in an attempt to quell the unruly natives which are ambushing the peaceful settlements in my stomach. I head out the door and I spot my sister just as she's being dropped home by her current boyfriend whose actual name is Dwayne. I call her a slut as she passes me on the drive and give Dwayne a ceremonial wanking gesture which he disappointingly seems to take in good spirits and just laughs and gives me a beep as he drives off in his ridiculously souped up Fiat Punto. I begin my perambulation towards the church and observe the blue sky overhead and immediately realise that I am over dressed for the current ambient temperature and I am forced to take off my jacket and carry it across my arm like a countryman up in Dublin for the day. As I walk across the field, I notice that nearly every single one of the newly planted trees has been broken and feel disgusted at the mindless, directionless and soulless creatures which we have the misfortune of calling our modern youth. I then realise that it was probably Gobber and Tarzan who wreaked this havoc last night on a meth-induced rampage and the thought causes me to laugh out loud and I have to catch myself before I begin to look like a crazy person. Note; remind the two of them that the vandalism of public shrubbery is against the law and therefore outside the remit of our operations, also buy more Disprins and cigarette papers on the way home from mass; Sub Note; ensure that the tone of voice employed when speaking to Tarzan is not overly dictatorial and acerbic as I do not wish to alienate him or make him feel as though he is not an equal partner in our enterprise. Sub Note to the Sub Note yo, change underpants after returning home from my ecclesiastical excursion.

There's also a burnt out car lying like a sacrifice to the scum-bag god, encircled by the empty remains of strewn Dutch Gold cans and I begin to quicken my step as I can see from the corner of my eye, as an old drunk makes a stumbling attempt to walk in my direction, presumably to ask for a cigarette. I exit the field by the swinging gates and observe the tall spire of the church and I can feel the effects of last night's escapades beginning to get progressively worse. I walk into the church and stand at the back, leaning against the wall only after I've procured a misalette from the table at the entrance which I will bring home to serve as proof of my attendance at the Sunday morning service. I survey the sea of grey and balding heads which comprise the majority of the congregation and it occurs to me how alien human beings can actually look if you really intensely focus on any one particular aspect of their anatomy. Especially when it's an aging man's bald head as he kneels forward on a church pew or the incongruously black hair on a woman whose face has become withered by the greyness of a long life. The young talent visible in the church is diminishing by the week and there is scant eye candy to perv on, aside from a few overdressed pieces of skirt seated at the top of the church near the altar, who have evidently come to the church to baptise their latest offspring and who probably haven't set foot in the place since the priest dipped their last bastard's head in the supposedly holy water. One of them is actually a piece of pure filth and possesses more than a passing resemblance to Anna Kournikova, and is even wearing a white sporty-type one piece, similar in style to those preferred by the golden-haired, tennis racket-wielding Slavic goddess. The congregation rises to their feet as Fr. Carey walks superciliously onto the altar as the last of the great altar boys, Michael Malone, carries the bells and cruets to the little table beside the sacristy. Just as the priest begins, I see Peter and Paul walk into the church and stand at the back wall across from me. I cast my gaze in the brothers' direction but it takes a while for the dozy bastards to see me before Peter or Paul, I'm not sure which one, catches my eye and grins a smile of recognition. He taps his brother on the shoulder and cups his hand around his mouth while whispering in his brother's ear. They both then proceed to give me a simultaneous nod, which because they're identical twins is a little bit disconcerting in a horror movie kind of way. I walk out the door of the church and shiver at the re-exposure to the elements even though it's positively mild out. I scrunch up my eyes to demonstrate my distress at facing the sunlight, as the effects of last night begin to pulse through my head as though I'm being shaken like a pair of maracas at Mardi Gras. Peter or Paul then slaps me on my left buttock with the force of a tiger tank bursting through lines of bedraggled Russian infantry and I try to hide my evident displeasure and attempt to accept the egregious assault in the spirit of ribaldry.

"Great Fuckin' arse ye have there Dosser, I'm tellin ye. If only I was a few years younger I'd be ridin that like Tony McCoy on Gold Cup day." The two brothers start cackling like they're already under the influence of Adrenochrome Semicarbazone and I feel myself struggling to endure their giddiness which I feel to be a little unnecessary and inappropriate at this time of the morning. Due to my acute lack of energy and diminished lucidity, the best I can muster in response is "Yeah you'd like that wouldn't you, you gay bastard" which causes both of them to practically collapse in convulsions of laughter. "Dosser, you are a knob end, seriously man" Peter or Paul manages to eventually get this sentence out amidst his conniption, although it actually takes about a minute for him to formulate the entire sentence, as each word is punctuated by bursts of laughter, similar in sound to the firing of an MG34 machine gun. It's striking really that although I'm fairly sure neither of them, barely have a Junior Cert, when it comes to slagging contests of this nature, it's virtually impossible to match their quick-wittedness. We're talking Stukas against Polish cavalry here. We eventually make our way over to the bell tower and stand in the hollow at ground level, where I suppose that originally, the bell-ringer would have began his ascent to the top of the bell tower, before they introduced the automatic tape playing bell, which serves as Ireland's answer to the Adhan, hailed from the minarets of Islamic countries. It's only when we arrive in the bell tower that I realise I have no Nepeta Catoria on my person and inwardly curse my carelessness and stupidity. But the anger which I feel for myself is subverted by the ire which consumes me when I see the abomination which unfolds in front of my very eyes as Peter and Paul proceed to spit in the face (metaphorically speaking) of everything I stand for and am trying to accomplish in my life. "Is that cannabis resin?" I ask, in a slightly incredulous tone, in an attempt to convey the hurt which I feel without becoming overly aggressive, as let's face it, Peter and Paul would kick ten types of shit out of me without breaking a sweat. They both, in fairness to them actually look a little guilty, as if I'm their father or mother and they've just realised what a disappointment that they must be to me. Peter or Paul adopts an explanatory tone but one which is laced with sympathy, like he is a doctor, informing me that I only have months to live. "Man I just can't get into that shit. It gives me a sore throat an all, d'y know what I mean?" His brother stands in to elaborate on further complications, like he's the consultant oncologist, explaining the exact nature and potential course of my villainous affliction. "It's not just that man; it just doesn't do that much really. Fuck all effect like. An it can be difficult to get hold of ye a lot of the time. We can get a bit hash anywhere, anytime. Ye know?"

"No I don't fucking know. Do you realise the amount of blood, pain and suffering that is caused to god knows how many people in order to bring that vile substance into this country? The people you are ultimately, financially supporting by purchasing that particular product are not exactly, "choice" characters, I can assure you of that. And ok, fair enough if you feel the Nepeta Catoria is not to your taste, but will you still consider the Cystisus Scoparius or the Alpha Chlorolose for example, or the many other substances which I can offer you as a guilt-free alternative to the conventional life-enhancing products available on the streets of our fair city?" "Guilt-free my bollocks Dosser. I wouldn't touch that Alpha what's it called, ever again, and you know fuckin know why I wouldn't." Peter or Paul has acquired a venomously serious look in his eyes and I can feel the tension between myself and the brothers growing to August 1939 levels. After a few seconds of uncomfortable silence, the other Peter or Paul comes over to me and puts an avuncular arm around my shoulder and says "it's cool man, don't worry about it. You've well enough goin on for yourself as it is" and it's only than that I realise that I am genuinely upset, especially by the previous comment relating to the Alpha Chlorolose. Eventually the mood settles down a little, as the brothers sit on the ground to smoke their joint. I obviously, point-blank refuse to indulge in the imbibing of the noxious smelling stuff and crouch down and stare out of the bell tower with what I hope is a wistful and thought-tormented expression, resting on my face. I am disturbed from my reverie when Peter or Paul says, "did you hear what happened to Richie Grimes' dog?! Wait till yis hear this. This is fuckin mad shit."

As soon as Peter or Paul utter these words I begin to feel much better about myself, Vis a Vis my current surroundings and general personal situation after our minor disagreement. Of course, as Peter or Paul launches into the story, I am not completely free of any sentiments of guilt with regards to Richie, but mostly I feel a certain sense of fulfilment, comfortable in the knowledge that I have unquestionably achieved something with my weekend. Naturally, there is a certain amount of unease in my mind as I do not want Richie to think that his dog's erratic behaviour was in any way a consequence of any actions of mine, so I will have to ensure that I behave in an innocent and positively sympathetic manner when I see him in school. He is a great customer after all. Anyway, it turns out that the twins' older brother, Stevie, is actually conducting a sexual relationship with Richie's sister, which makes sense on so many levels. 1: She's extremely attractive but possibly suffers from self-esteem issues and certainly lacks any sense of street wisdom culminating in her instigation of a relationship with a well-known reprobate. 2. Her evident reluctance to conduct any form of conversation with me, however rudimentary and inconsequential can only be explained by the fact that the crime of talking to another man is probably punishable by emotional, psychological or even physical abuse at the hands of aforementioned reprobate boyfriend. While I turn my head to give my full and unadulterated attention to my reliable narrator (a little obsequiousness is unfortunately a necessary requirement when in the company of any of the Smith brothers), I have to make sure that I don't show any signs of guilt or prescience with regard to the circumstances described. Also having been unaware of Richie's sister's attachment to the eldest Smith brother (or is there another one inside?) I am hoping that he did not become an unintended victim of my chemically catalysed practical joke, as this would inevitably present its own very serious and not to mention unsolicited consequences.

As Peter or Paul continues with his story, I can't quite believe the words that are emanating from his crooked little, barely-perceptible-moustachioed-mouth. After I had left Richie's house to continue on my Saturday night rounds, Stephen Smith arrived to check on his latest concubine, ostensibly to lend a sympathetic ear to his suffering girlfriend but really he was more than likely ascertaining her ride-ability and/or ensuring that she was not pretending to be ill because she had realised that he was a psychopath and was attempting to escape his recidivist clutches. Whatever his reasons, what he bore witness to could leave me in a potential spot of the proverbial bother and I will really have to play all my trump cards of diplomacy, in order to smooth this situation over and score a "fooling Neville Chamberlain" style scenario to escape unblemished. Anyway from the events that Peter and Paul describe to me, the scenario seems to have happened as follows: As they sit watching the television, the lovely couple and our beloved Charlie that is, they're waiting for the winner of the competition to be announced and it's been done in that manner which hasn't at all become staid, tiresome and downright fucking irritating, where the whole studio descends into darkness and the light shines only on the potential victors, leaving we, the viewers in a near paralytic state of tension (not). Richie's sister is obviously totally engrossed in the entire charade and she's shouting "COME ON GARETH!" and "Oh my God I can't look!" at the television screen when eventually the viewing public is put out of its misery as the presenter of the farce says "it's Will!"

So apparently Stevie Smith being the consummate gentleman that he is, begins to console Richie's sister as she's at this stage, openly crying and he then proceeds to go to the kitchen to search the fridge for any beers which would evidently serve as the best way to handle this uncomfortable situation. He has his head half way into the fridge (as I'd imagine that Richie had safely stowed his cans in his bedroom, aware of the probable presence of a Smith in his domicile that evening), searching for some liquid analgesia with which to numb the pain of the moment, when he hears loud barking noises and screams coming from the front room. He rushes in thinking that the dog is attacking Richie's sister when he sees the little Jack Russell gyrating furiously on his girlfriend's leg, with an erect penis apparently at least half the length of the little mutt himself. The poor girl is screaming, still in a state of intense emotional trauma after the Pop Idol result and Stevie Smith starts trying to pull the dog off her, but it's proving to be akin to wrenching a Leitrim man off his cousin and before he can manage to free his girlfriend from her canine assailant, the diminutive beast ejaculates a quantity of semen which Peter or Paul humorously, if somewhat dubiously describes as being "Atlantic." At this stage the girl is finding the whole situation to be extremely traumatic, exacerbated by the fact that her handsome and daring beau, has apparently keeled over laughing at what he's just witnessed. On hearing this I begin to feel a great deal more comfortable with regards to my personal safety because it's obvious that Stevie is a man who has an excellent sense of humour and as long as he manages to remain free from any major mishaps, it means a lot less for me to worry about. But it gets much worse unfortunately and as the tale continues, I begin to feel slightly nauseous and the bell tower seems as though it's closing in around us. After the little Jack Russell climaxed all over Richie's sister's pyjama bottoms, she hurriedly takes them off in a fit of disgust and the post coital canine starts wrestling with her as he tries to drag the pyjama bottoms away with his ravenous jaws. As the dog steadfastly refuses to relinquish the by now, ragged bottoms, blood starts dripping out from the rat-catcher's anus, oozing onto the carpet, in an inexorable deluge of bloody diarrhoea. The dog has without question lost control of both its mental and physical capacities and its very last action is to jump onto the admittedly sizable chest of Richie's sister and discharge a volume of vomit which apparently would have done credit to a Great Dane, all over her Tee shirt. By now Stevie realises that all peaceful means of resolving this conflict have been exhausted and the only remaining course of action open to him, is the swift and total annihilation of his enemy. He manages to haul the beast off the ample bosom of Richie's sister, who manically tears the vomit-encrusted Tee shirt from her person. He bashes the head of the dog off the marble fireplace and succeeds in stunning the Jack Russell with this first blow. He then proceeds to repeatedly smash the little mutt's head on the sharp edge of the marble, to ensure that there is no semblance of life remaining before administering the coup de grace, by twisting his neck in order to sever the spinal cord from the brain. Breathless and covered in an assorted conglomeration of blood, flesh, vomit and faeces, he again can't help but see the funny side of things and more to do with the pure release and subsidence of adrenaline and the dawning realisation that the ordeal is finally over, he collapses to his knees and begins laughing hysterically which naturally does not go down too well with Richie's sister. She's lying back on the armchair, completely naked, with her legs pulled up to her chest with her arms wrapped around them, telling him to "Stop laughing you bastard! Stop laughing!"

When next of all, the door bursts open behind Stevie's back. It's all too sudden for him to even stop laughing and he turns around with what I'm guessing was a both gormless and frightening grin straddling his ruddy complexion, to see two completely shocked looking policemen and behind them, the crying face of Richie's mother and the stony, murderous eyes of Richie's father. Stevie begins to proclaim his innocence and is shouting "It's not what it looks like!" amidst the hysterical screams of the Grimes women. Richie's father by now loses control and bursts past the two Guards to land a karate-style kick to the side of Stevie's head. Stevie hits the ground and Mr. Grimes (who once had trials with Leeds United apparently) manages to make a few more connections with his feet as the Guards allow him to soften Stevie up before hauling him back and slapping the handcuffs around Stevie's bloody wrists. Stevie is still protesting his innocence and is shouting at Richie's sister to corroborate his appraisal of the circumstances which would explain the creation of the macabre vista witnessed by the Guards and Richie's parents as they entered the house. But she's too hysterical to articulate any contribution to the argument and before you can say "a practical joke that's gone a little too far", Stevie's hauled off on a charge of sexual assault, animal cruelty, possession of cocaine (had it in his pockets, nothing to do with me) and disturbing the peace. While Stevie's being led out of the front door, Richie emerges from his room and stridently descends the staircase. It turns out that Richie had been upstairs during the entire sordid affair and had been able to hear the terrible screams and general commotion which had occurred in the front room. So while he was up there, he called his parents and the Guards, as he was too petrified and probably too incapacitated from smoking so much Nepeta Catoria to see what on earth was happening for himself.

I ask Peter and Paul if they're going to exact any kind of retribution on Richie for notifying the police of the disturbance and they seem unsure. They're willing to accept the fact that he had no idea what was happening in his house. For all he knew, a rampaging serial killer had gained access to the building and was savagely murdering his female sibling, only as a precursor to the eventual mauling and possible buggery of Richie himself. And in fairness, if one could survey for oneself the actual scene in the room, that's probably exactly the appearance which it gave. I am a little worried about this aspect of the scenario as I really don't wish to see young Richard come to any physical or indeed social harm over this. The Smith twins appear to believe that he didn't act outside of what they would feel to be the generally accepted rules of the street and Peter or Paul decides that they will simply "give him a bit of a talking to." I'm not quite sure in what way to understand this statement but I decide in the interests of maintaining an un-harassed conscience to take it literally, as it's the only possible way that I can live with myself. The twins furthermore go onto explain that their mother had been able to speak to their older brother, who filled her in on the details of the case and that they were quite confident that he would walk away from all the charges bar the possession charge, which even then would more than likely amount to a metaphorical slap on the wrists. Their mother had explained the details to them over the breakfast table this morning so they stated that they were only really now digesting all of the information available to them and were collaboratively deciding on the best course of action in all areas.

It evidently turns one o' clock as we can see the congregation filing out of the church and opening out their umbrellas as a light rain begins to precipitate gently onto them. I say my goodbyes to the twins and as I walk home back across the field, I struggle to hide the smirk which invades my face as the images of Stevie Smith covered in canine faeces and blood, dance around my brain. It strikes me that the most shocking part of it all, is the fact that he told his own mother all of this, who in turn passed these details onto her younger sons over the breakfast table. I mean, mon dieu. That family really are scum.

Tarzan's Story (Number One)

I really have to say that I don't think this weekend could have gone any better. Yesterday's crow hunting was definitely one of the best, if not *the* best day's hunting I think we've ever had. By the time I'd got the bag out from the top secret underground compartment and checked on the running away money, I just got this really good feeling you know, not only about our chances for that day, but just about my life in general I suppose. For instance, I've got my seventeenth birthday coming up which means I'm finally going to get my provisional driving licence so I won't have to cycle that poxy bike around the place all the time. Dosser's being a bit of prick about it though. Every time I mention the fact that I'll be getting a car soon, he kind of just goes real quiet, like he doesn't trust me to be able to drive a car without crashing it all the time. I reckon it's just because he's jealous and really he'd shit himself if he had to try and drive a car. I'd say he knows this himself in a way and that secretly, it makes him feel like he's not got the set of balls that I have. I drive my ma's car all the time anyway. Whenever she's out in town or whatever and she's taken the bus in, I get the keys and take the beast for a spin. It was Gobber that first gave me the idea. One day when I was on the hop from school, he called around while I was out in the greenhouse, watering the plants. He said that he was bored and that we should take the car out for a spin. I told him that I had too much work to do with the plants and he said that I was always the one doing the work and that Dosser never did fuck all. Eventually he convinced me to get the keys from the kitchen and we took the car up to the mountains. Gobber drove it up first and then I got in the driver's seat and Gobber showed me what to do. He told me how the clutch worked and taught me how to change gears and I was bombing around in no time at all. I don't think I was ever as good at anything in my life. Gobber said that if I crashed it or anything, he'd just hop in the driver's seat and pretend that he was the one that'd crashed it. He said that he was fully comped, whatever that means, but I just took his word for it because he seemed to know what he was talking about.

It was sound of Gobber to show me how to drive, but I didn't really like the way he talked about Dosser, saying that he never did any work and he was always making me do everything and all. Even though Dosser can piss me off sometimes, he's still my best mate and has been for years and for some reason I just don't like people slagging him off, even though I could be thinking exactly the same thing at the time. It's just the way it is I suppose. Weird though. Like, I can't tell Dosser about me and Gobber taking the car out because he'd go mad because he has this thing where he doesn't want us to do anything illegal. Even when we were kids he used to talk about all the mad things you could do without breaking the law. That you could cause all kinds of havoc around the place and the Guards couldn't touch you for it. Like that's how we started off shooting the crows. That was the first thing we always used to do. Dosser was saying one day that you could go to prison if you even touched a swan. That swans were like a protected species even though they could break your arm if you went near their young. When I was really small I used to love going down to the canal or over to the lake in the park to get chases off the swans. If you went up near their big nests, the mother would run out and stretch herself up really tall and spread her wings so it looked like a dinosaur out of Jurassic Park or something. Then it would start hissing just like one of those raptors. One time over in the park, one of the swans swung its wings and hit me across my back when I was trying to wreck its head. I was lucky that I'd turned away or I would've got it in the face. Anyway, I was shitting it when it happened and I picked up a stick and fucked it at the beast. The parkie saw me and gave out shit to me. He brought me back to my gaff and told my ma everything that I'd been doing, tormenting the swans all the time and it was obvious that he'd been watching me for ages. It was only when I told Dosser about this story a few years later that he explained to me about the swans and about how they were like, untouchable. But then he said that you could do whatever you wanted to crows. That they were just like rats, that they ate crops and that there were so many of them that you could kill as many as you like and there'd still be loads of them left. But he said they were really clever as well, much cleverer than most birds. He said that if you killed a crow and left it in your back garden that no other crows would come into your garden because they understood that it was dangerous because they could see that they're mate was dead. That's why when you're hunting them, you have to be quick because if you shoot one and all the other ones see its body, they'll all fly away and you won't kill anymore. But that just adds to the fun I suppose. Really it's almost like a real sport. Better than most shit that's on telly anyway.

But yeah, crow hunting was the first thing we started doing anyway. We started that when we were kids and it was a great way to spend the summers. I even started doing it when I was down in my granny's on my own but it wasn't the same really. I suppose I'd miss Dosser talking about our "villainous corvine nemeses" or whatever it is he says sometimes. But it was a good way to get some extra practice in. It gave me a chance to make a better dart gun as well. The one I still use today, I made when I was thirteen down in my granny's. I even treated the wood with varnish so it'll never go rotten and it's definitely more accurate than Dosser and his sling shot. He is good with it though in fairness. I tried to use it once and broke my finger. When I pulled the elastic back, I didn't let go of it properly or something and I ended up snapping it on my left index finger. It was serious agony and Dosser just fell around the place laughing when it happened. I got sick the pain was that bad and this only made him laugh even more.

After a while Dosser started coming up with other things we could do apart from crow hunting. First we started blowing deodorant through a sock. You put a sock up to your mouth and get a can of lynx or whatever and you spray the deodorant into your mouth, but through the sock so it's just the gas or whatever that goes through and your mouth won't get all wet. It was all right for a while, until one time Dosser gave me a sock to use when we were up in his bedroom and I put it to my mouth. It was only then that I noticed the sock was all wet and had this weird smell and Dosser started laughing again. He said he hadn't realised but that the sock was covered in his "ejaculatory seminal fluid" and he "apologised profusely". That was the one time in my life that I actually lost it with him. My lips were covered in this gooey liquid and I spat it in his face. Then I grabbed him by the scruff and pushed him to the floor and I was on top of him, ready to start punching him in the face and he was screaming "Desist! Desist from this beastly assault!" when his ma came in and screamed at me to get out. Ever since then she's always been a bit weird around me. I don't think she likes me very much or his da either. He deffo doesn't like me, but then again neither does my own da.

After that we kind of forgot about the deodorant or we just decided not to do it anymore, without even talking about it like. It's like we just didn't have to I suppose. So then we started looking for other things to do. We used to do this thing called the American Dream. It's when you bend over and touch your toes and start breathing real heavily for about a minute or something. Then after the minute, you stand up real quickly and someone pushes you, kind of between your stomach and your chest and you kind of faint for a minute. It was deadly actually, much better than the deodorant which was shit anyway to be honest. We used to do it up in my room all the time. Nearly every night of the week, just up there fainting. Ten times a night and all. Great crack though. Then one day I was having my breakfast with my ma before going to school and she was like "So you and Dosser really are great friends aren't yis? Thick as thieves yis are altogether. You know if you were really good friends with him, I mean in a special kind of way, you would tell me, wouldn't ye?" I didn't really know what she was getting at, at first so I just kind of shrugged it off like I wasn't arsed having a conversation or whatever. It was only when she started saying things like "What do yous be doin up there like? Like, I can always here this kind of pantin out of yis all the time. Are you positive you've nothin you want to talk about?" It was only then that I copped that she thought me and Dosser were bum bashers and I had to think of something really quickly as an excuse. I told her that we were doing press ups and sit ups because we were thinking of joining the school rugby team. She was only delighted to hear this and you could see that she was relieved on one hand, but she was proud of me too for wanting to play with the team or whatever as well. So then she came back from the shops one day with a pair of boots and a gum-shield and everything because she wanted to like support me or whatever. So everyday then I had to bring the gear with me to school, but there was no way I was going out there to play with all those bum-bashers, so I'd head over to the park on my own or with Dosser and I'd have to take out the jersey and shorts and everything and dip it into these muddy puddles and rub it off the grass and all. Then I'd come home and have to give the gear in for washing so it looked like I'd been out training. Then it started to get a bit out of hand. I noticed that the fellas who play sports in school were always walking around the place with black eyes, or sometimes they'd have their arms in a sling or be going around the corridors on crutches and all. So I started having to punch myself in the face while I was over in the park dirtying the gear up. I found that it was too difficult trying to give yourself a proper punch in the face, so I started using this stick to just give myself a couple of whacks so I'd come home with a few scrapes or maybe a bit of a bruise on my face. I'd be sitting down at night then, watching television, holding a pack of frozen peas or whatever up to my black eyes and my ma would be bringing me in cups of tea and I'd be getting extra large portions of dinner and everything, so it seemed like it was really worth it most of the time. But then everything just started getting too mad. My ma came home one day while I was sitting at the kitchen table, dabbing all these cuts on my face with a bit of cotton wool and Dettol, when she said she had a surprise for me. It turned out that the Irish rugby team were going to be in town, launching their new jersey or something and that she had entered a competition on my behalf or whatever and that we'd won and that now I was going to get to meet all these famous players and all and that we'd be going into town for it the next day. I just didn't even know what to say but I knew straight away that I'd have to put a stop to this as soon as I could. Well she was so delighted that we'd won that I thought I'd better give her the day out before I put an end to it all, so I went along the next day and I even got off school for it and everything. But it was much, much worse than I seriously could have imagined. My ma made me wear my full school kit: shorts, socks, jersey, everything, and I got my photograph taken with some bum basher called O' Driscoll or some shit. So there I am standing in the middle of this sports shop and this bum basher has his arm around me and there's my ma taking a photo and all these other like, professional photographers I suppose as well. And there's all these kids walking around the place wearing the new Ireland jersey or whatever and all these other bum basher rugby players that were around the same age as me. It was a seriously embarrassing day and I realised that I'd have to do something to make sure it wasn't going to be a complete waste of my time so I decided to prank it up. Pranking it up was something that me and Dosser started doing as well. I suppose we'd always pranked it up, but it was only really around then that we had a name for it. All it means is just doing some mad shit to someone or something to get a bit of a laugh. Never anything too dangerous or anything, just something to stop us from getting bored and

I suppose like Dosser always says, it can't be anything illegal; well nothing that would see you end up in prison or whatever.

Anyway, when this O' Driscoll bloke had his arm around me, I noticed that his mobile phone was almost falling out of the pocket of his tracksuit bottoms, so as the photographs were being taken, I put my own arm around his waist and I was holding my jacket in the same hand. I managed to take the phone out of his pocket, without being seen, using the jacket I was holding to block everyone's view of what I was doing. Anyway, when my turn was over he was all "take it easy dude" and I just walked off smiling like I was really happy that I'd just had my photograph taken with him, when really I'd never even heard of the bloke and couldn't have cared less that I'd met him. There was a queue behind me anyway, of all these bum bashers that wanted to get their photograph taken with this O' Driscoll bloke, as in they really wanted a photo like. As I walking back along the queue I managed to slip the phone into this kid's pocket as his ma was combing his hair and wiping his cheeks with a snot rag or whatever. Then me and my ma just stood to the side and watched all the other photographs being taken and me obviously keeping my attention mostly on the little kid with the phone in his pocket. Eventually it gets to the little kid's turn and him and O' Driscoll have their arms around each other and the little kid has this really proud look on his face and his ma is actually fighting back the tears she's that proud or whatever. But then of course, it all goes horribly wrong for them. Just when he's finished having his photograph taken and he turns around to walk back to the side of the shop or whatever, the phone falls out of the kid's pocket and smashes onto the floor and it all comes apart as it hits the ground and the different bits fly all over the place. At first, the O' Driscoll bloke's being all helpful and he bends down to pick up the different bits of the phone and everyone around is getting out of the way and all, trying to make space and looking to see if there's any more bits lying around the place. Then after a few minutes, I could see that O' Driscoll's starting to get a bit red in the face and look kind of dead serious and all. The kid's ma starts to get the same expression on her face as the two of them look at the phone as O' Driscoll puts it back together and holds it in his hands. Then he just kind of stares down at the kid who just kind of stood there during it all, like he didn't know what to say or do and he just says, "That's my phone for god's sake." The kid's ma just looks at her son like she's going to kill him and the kid

36

just starts bawling his eyes out and he's like "I didn't take it! I swear to god I didn't take it" and everyone around is really like shocked and all and the atmosphere turns really sour. The O' Driscoll bloke just says "right that's it!" and just storms off leaving everyone in the shop just staring at the little kid as he's bawling his eyes out and his mother just drags him out of the shop with a pure look of embarrassment on her face and it's obvious that she's like, fighting back the tears as well. But yeah anyway, that was what we meant by pranking it up. Sometimes I felt like I always did my best pranks when I was on my own and Dosser wasn't there to see. I think I was always sort of afraid to suggest ideas for pranks when he was around because sometimes he'd just laugh at them or whatever and say they were "infantile nonsense." But that has to have been one of my favourites and sometimes I still wonder what happened to the little kid and his ma and all.

But even though I'd really enjoyed the prank that day, I knew that the whole rugby thing had just gone too far and that I'd have to put an end to it once and for all. It was just too much effort, dirtying the gear all the time and hitting myself over the head with sticks was something that even I realised I couldn't keep doing forever. I decided that I just needed one big injury and that then I'd be able to forget about the whole thing forever. So this one Saturday morning, I told my ma I was going out to play a match and I left the house with my gear and everything and cycled over to the park. I met Dosser over by the lake. He was sitting on a bench talking on the phone to Gobber, who we'd only really started to hang around with around then. Dosser was telling him that we'd "require his transportational assistance at ten past midday" and then he hung the phone and looked at me. "Are you sure you want to do this? He said to me. I just nodded and said "let's go" and we walked into the trees where we had this little hut that we used to use sometimes for hunting crows or just messing around in general. It was around this time that we'd started on the urinal air fresheners. I know it mind sound disgusting but it's actually really good crack and we didn't give a shit anyway. We used to go into the toilets in shopping centres and in McDonald's and all and take all those little yellow and blue air fresheners out of the urinals. Then we'd head over the park and smoke them up. All you need's an empty coke can and a lighter. You cut off the bottom of a coke can and then you've got this little kind of bowl that you put the urinal air freshener on. Then you light it up with a lighter or a match or whatever you have, put the little bowl thing back at the bottom of the can and you inhale the smoke off it through the part you'd normally just drink the coke out of. We used to do it all the time anyway and this day Dosser had all the works with him. He got out the can cutting knife and everything and started getting the can ready and taking out the urinal air fresheners and all, while I got changed into my full rugby gear. After I'd put on my jersey and socks and all, I found a puddle that was just a bit away from us and rolled around in it a couple of times. By the time I got back to Dosser, he was laughing his head off and it was obvious that he'd already been smoking it up. I sat down next to him on this tree that we'd kind of bent over so it was like a little bench while he lit up one of the air fresheners and put the can together and told me to take a deep breath. I put the can to my mouth and breathed in the smoke for as long as I could, until I could feel my head start spinning and my eyes go all blurry. Then I smoked up another one, and another, and at that stage even Dosser wouldn't let me do anymore. I was beginning to feel properly out of it after smoking up those three urinal air fresheners, so I guessed I was in just about the right frame of mind to put my plan into action. I went over to a tree and started to climb up it. At first it was really difficult because my head was all over the place, but then I suppose it got easier until I really started to enjoy it. I got as far up as I could go and just sat up there between two branches for a while and I started looking around the tops of the trees to see if there were any crows anywhere. Then Dosser started shouting at me to "execute the final stage of the plan" and I stopped looking for the crows. I looked down to make sure there was a nice clean patch of ground under me. Then I started shaking this branch that kind of jutted out to make sure that it was sturdy. Then I grabbed the branch with my two hands and swung out so that I was just hanging there on the branch like a gorilla. Then I just swung back and forward on the branch a couple of times and let go. I remember it was just like jumping into the sea off a pier, except that instead of landing in water, I landed straight onto the ground. All I really remember is this loud cracking noise and it must've been around then that I passed out. It was like the best American dream I'd ever done.

The life and Times of
Gobber Gilsenan

There's nothing like a bit of Sunday drinking to clear the head. I'm sitting on the 15A, staring out the window and all I can think of is those first few large bottles that'll knock the fairly sharp edge of the headache which is causing me to squint my eyes against the sun coming through the window. Methylated fucking spirits. What the fuck was I thinking? I need to knock that practice on the head fairly sharpish and get myself back on the straight and narrow fairly pronto. The two boys are starting to lose the run of themselves completely. Dosser, the uppity little bastard seriously gets on my tits sometimes, but I suppose I have to be thankful for the income I'm getting from their little business venture. You have to hand it to them all the same. Dosser the little shite certainly has brains to burn and fair play to them for having the energy to do what they're doing. I personally wouldn't have the patience or the time, waiting on all those plants to grow, nurturing them and spending all that time in that sweat box of a greenhouse. They've too much reliance on one another as well I suppose. Even though Dosser is without a shadow of a doubt, the brains behind the operation, he still has the greenhouse in Taz's garden, plus the fact that Taz is such a big bastard, has probably prevented Dosser from having his annoying, shite-talking little head flattened for him. That's why I could never operate the way they do. I need to just go about my business by myself because even the notion of collaborative decision making makes me feel physically nauseous. That's why as soon as I got my trade, I went straight out on my own doing the flooring. I hated sitting in that joinery shop, listening to all those aulfellas, rabbiting on about the price of bread and butter. Fuck that and get a life. We're only here on this earth for one reason and one reason only; sex. And how do you get sex? By going out, and drinking as much as is physically, emotionally and psychologically possible. And how do you procure the means to bank roll such a labour intensive strategy? By doing whatever you can to make the necessary funds available, provided you don't absolutely hate whatever method of money procurement you decide to pursue. And you see that's the difference between me and everyone else you see in the boozer. Most people think that it's ok to do a job you hate as long as you go out and get hammered at the weekend, as if by getting locked on Friday and Saturday nights, you're somehow negating the misery of your nine to five existence. This of course is the philosophy of the amateur drinker, and should be avoided at all costs. Then of course there are people who actually enjoy their jobs and may not feel the need to spend every available minute of free time on the batter. This is also a blatantly flawed philosophy on life, as they have neglected to pursue our fundamental purpose which is to ride as many of the opposite sex as possible, which in turn can only be achieved by drinking as much as possible. The simplicity of it all makes it even harder to understand why everyone in the world doesn't realise it. Basically it seems clear to me that you find something to do which neither drives you mad with desperation, nor something which will become your main focus in life. You do something which simply is. Work should really be as unemotional as withdrawing money from an ATM because all work really is, is putting cash in the ATM in the first place.

I decide to get off the bus just as it goes over Portobello Bridge. Even though the pubs around here will be pretty empty at this hour on a Sunday afternoon, I spend so much time drinking in the vicinity that I find it almost impossible to pass through the area without stopping for a scoop somewhere. Also, it's not a bad idea to drink my way into town from here in fairness and by the time I get down to Dame Street, the place should be fairly lively and you can be as sure as an Irish publican of an income, that I'll be fairly lively too. I get off the bus just as two pieces of Serie A talent strut by me on the footpath in the direction of Rathmines. They're facially stunning and done up to the nines but as I turn around to take a good look at their arses I realise that they must be fairly young. The only fool proof way of telling a woman's age is to assess the size and shape of their arse. As soon as a girl has the war paint on, they could be absolutely any age, but they can never truly alter the size of their arse. Even tits fail to serve as a reliable barometer, as some girls can have pretty much the same size tits all their lives. The arse however can experience incredible fluctuations between the ages of sixteen and twenty one, so it's essential to always check the size, shape and texture of a bird's posterior before putting her in the starting line up for her home ground debut, just to ensure that you're keeping within the rules of the Federazione Italiana del Gioco Calcio. I decide to head into the Portobello pub just to get the cure in, as I suddenly get the unwelcome sensation of a hot flush and I begin to doubt my ability to walk any further without the help of some alcoholic refreshment. I stroll in through the front doors of the pub, cigarette lit as is my usual manner of entering a premises and take a stool at the front bar where there's just a few old timers, pure Franco Baresi type players, sitting reading the paper and solidly sinking pints of Beamish and Guinness. I order a large bottle of cider and ice from this young spotty-faced-student-type barman who seems to be looking at me like he's a little bit wary of my presence in the place, like I've disturbed the convivial, piss-smelling atmosphere which existed before my arrival. I check the clock above the bottles of spirits on optics, as the spotty-faced barman puts the bottle and the glass full of ice in front of me. It's half past two and I hand over the cash while simultaneously pouring the cider over the ice and watch it fizz up and settle as, my change lands before me on the bar. I practically inhale the cold cider and quickly order another one which makes the barman look as if he's going to press the panic button. I maintain a sickly sweet smile on my face while giving him a wink, just to antagonise him in a way that's so subtle that he can't actually say for definite that I'm winding him up, even though we both know that I am. I decide to take the second drink a little slower and sip on it meditatively while watching a football match on the television in the corner. It's some English Premier League shite, but it'll do to pass the time while I steadily take my medicine and I begin to sense a feeling almost close to normality. Two tossers walk through the door, one wearing a Manchester United strip and the other an Arsenal one and they both order Lucozades and sit at a table half way down the pub. As I watch them make their way to their table, I'm suddenly hit with the realisation that I despise these two fuckers that I've never even met before. It's not a problem for me if people don't drink. If you don't want to challenge for the scudetto, that's your business and I certainly won't hold it against you. But I hate when fuckers walk into a boozer and don't sit at the bar when there's empty seats there. It's like, what's your problem? Is our company not good enough for you over here my good sirs? Why do you have to sit so far away from everyone else, thus dirtying another part of the place and doubling the workload of the barman? But above all, I hate people wearing English football jerseys into the boozer, especially like these two pricks, who although they're obviously friends, have this real antagonistic discussion going on, constantly during the game, like that's the only way they can interact with each other. After a few minutes of listening to their mind-numbingly clichéd comments on the game, Arsenal score and the bloke in the Arsenal jersey starts going "In your face! In your face!" to his mate in the Manchester United top who looks like a little kid who's just lost an egg and spoon race. I decide against having another as the two idiots are making me a little tense with annoyance and I walk out of the pub, turning around to give an air-kiss to the spotty-faced barman as I walk through the doors.

I stop off in another few boozers, making the switch to pints of Heineken as I do so, as my stomach couldn't sustain a full day drinking cider without erupting in open revolt against my beverage selection policy. I'm beginning to feel almost in peak condition as I head into The Swan for further hydration. The place is actually pretty full and there seems to be some kind of family-type celebration going on over in one of the corners. They've got a full spread of party food laid on the tables which makes me feel a little bit hungry, as I realise I haven't eaten since about lunch time yesterday. There's also a quality little chinky bird taking drinks orders from the party and the fuckers are making absolutely no attempt to tone down their Dublin accents as they tell her what they want and you can see that the chinky bird is getting flustered as the punters look at her, incredulous that the girl is having problems understanding them. I sit down at the bar and it turns out I went to primary school with the barman, who's still living around the corner from me. "Gobber, what's the story man? Long time since I've seen you around. How's tricks?" He extends his hand across the bar and I'm kind of half glad to see him, but in a way it's a bit of a strain in the manner it sometimes can be when you meet someone you've known all your life without ever actually been proper mates with them. "I'm in flying form here Roberto. When did ye sign for these cunts then? You were still workin down The Millers when I saw ye last." "Yeah, had enough of the place. That Jimmy fucker was wreckin me head. Bit more chilled out down here man. What about yourself? You out of your time now and all?" "I am yeah. World's me oyster now Roberto." I take a business card from my wallet. I'd five hundred of the fucking things made up. But instead of saying "Expert Carpenter" which it's supposed to, all five hundred of the cunting yokes say "Expert Crapenter", so I've decided against distributing them as liberally as I initially would have planned to. Needless to say, I haven't paid the dyslexic bastards who made them up for me but there's no point throwing them all out either. I hand the card to Roberto, as I'm guessing he probably won't even notice and I know he wouldn't have the balls to say anything to me even if he did. Well not to my face anyway. "Mobile number's on the bottom there Roberto. Whenever you or any of yours require an honest chippie, give us a shout and get us a pint of Heineken there when ye get a chance man, I've a mouth on me like a nun's fanny." Roberto proceeds to do my bidding and the mention of his family makes me remember something. "How's your sister actually Roberto? Is she still living with the folks?" I say this with an innocently cherubic face. One time, years ago she actually gave me a blow job behind the church and after I'd blown my load into her gob, she got sick all over herself. It wouldn't have been so bad, only I told every single person I knew about it, until it became almost an urban legend around the area. She became famous for it in a way. It'd be like "Do you know Maggie Joyce?" "No, which one's she again?" "You know the one, Gobber made sick because of the amount of jip he spunked into her mouth." "Aw yeah her? Yeah I know her now." I'm not sure if Roberto knows about it, I'm assuming he does but really I couldn't care either way, but I'm still interested to judge his reaction. He goes a little bit red in the cheeks and pauses slightly so I perceive that he probably does remember the incident and I have to say I'm getting just a little bit of entertainment by putting him into this awkward situation. "She's grand yeah. Has a kid an all now. A little fella." "Go way. What's his name? What age is he?" "Scott it is. Cheeky little bastard and all. And he's only two he is. Real intelligent like." "Ah well at least he's healthy. That's all that fuckin matters. And are you the godfather or anything?" "Yeah I am" he says with a proud smile. "Doesn't like me though. He's afraid of me for some reason." "Ah so he is intelligent" I say, with an air of what I hope is mostly good humour, but with just enough edge so he can feel a little prick. "Ha Ha", he laughs kind of nervously. "I walked into that one right enough." He says this while walking over to the other side of the bar to serve another patron and I can tell that he's glad to get away from me for a minute. Mission accomplished. Before leaving, I manage to persuade Roberto to procure me some sandwiches from the party beside us and I scoff them while I start walking through the threshold. "Ciao Roberto. Remember to hang onto that business card and say hello to Maggie for me." He just gives me this wave and says "See ya Gobber" and I can tell that he's only delighted to be rid of me.

I continue on in the direction of Dame Street, stopping off in a number of hostelries along the way including The Mean Fiddler, Ryan's and The Corner Stone until I find myself in some pub on George's Street and at this stage I'm beginning to feel admittedly, a little bit twisted. I order a pint of Heineken from what looks like some kind of Latino barman and as I take a fiver out of my wallet, I realise that I'm running seriously low on beer vouchers. I sip away on the pint which actually has this serious tang off it, but I'm not bothered sending it back because the place is getting fairly busy and I don't feel like causing the barman anymore hassle than he's currently negotiating because I'm not that much of a prick all the time. I spot this small group of young indie-looking players over the other side of the bar and I can see that one of the crafty little shites is rolling a joint underneath the table. The Latino barman has been joined by a Chinese bloke and the two of them don't have a chance of spotting it, as an English stag party walk through the door and invade the bar like it was a small defenceless country. I feel in my inside pocket and count the bags with my fingers. One, two, three, four and five. I've got this new stuff that Dosser and that teacher of his put together in school. Apparently it's an ephedrine based concoction that the two boffins fabricated in the lab that they're using in there. The stuff is still only on sort of a trial basis, so I'm taking it for a little bit of a test run at the moment. It's supposed to basically have the same effects as coke which is exactly what I'm going to tell people it is. Dosser has this ridiculous notion in his head (or up his arse, I'm not sure which but I suppose it's basically the same thing) that he's somehow occupying a moral high ground in the world by selling all these alternatives to the mainstream drugs on the market. He sees this as more than just a money-making scheme but also as some kind of crusade, but basically he's just a fucking knob end who needs to get a life. He wants me to make sure that customers understand what it is that they're buying, but the fact is you just wouldn't sell as much if each sale was accompanied by a fucking question and answer session on the source of the product. It's easier to just tell people that what they're getting is whatever drug it's supposed to be mimicking the effects of. Of course it's all right if you're just hanging around in Whitefield, or anywhere else in the general South west Dublin area and you've got regular clients who know the whole score, but out here on the mean streets of the big bad city, you've got to do what's easiest, and after all I do sell more than those other two shite bags combined. Ah but no, I'm being too harsh on the boys. They're good lads all the same, good lads.

I stroll over across the pub to a table next to the young fish to see if I can get a bite. There are four blokes and two birds, one of whom is all right, the other one is a little bit masculine looking and in a weird way reminds me of Michel Platini. I sit down at the table and check my phone to make it look as though I'm waiting on someone while taking out a cigarette and putting it into my mouth. I pat down the pockets of my jacket and then turn to the kid who's still rolling the spliff under the table and ask him for a light. He looks at me nervously first of all, as he's just beginning to burn into the unrolled joint that he has resting on a beer mat perched precariously between his two knees. "It's cool man, get the shit into ye" I say, while raising my hands to communicate that I don't have a problem with what he's doing. He kind of laughs and says "cheers man" while lifting the flaming lighter to my unlit smoke. I sit there in silence for a few minutes, while the kid finishes rolling what is an unquestionably dodgy looking joint and sticks it into a Silk Cut purple box. They continue their conversation which seems to be mainly about people they know and crazy events which happened to them but they obviously don't seem that interesting or crazy to me and I'm struggling to see the funny side to any of their stories, as the girls in particular become nearly incapable with laughter. I'm looking over at one of the girls, the good looking one obviously, and I can catch her glancing over in my direction a couple of times and eventually, she clearly goes a little bit red as I just refuse to look away when our eyes meet or show any sign of embarrassment myself. Eventually I strike up a bit of a conversation with the bloke beside me whose name is David. I tell him by a bizarre coincidence that my name's David too and that I'm a sales advisor for a leading computer software manufacturer. It turns out the boys are all in college doing sound engineering and I'm obviously thinking, chi-ching. After a while I've fully ingratiated myself into the group and I offer to get a round in for everyone, thankful that there are a couple of light weights among them who actually refuse a drink. The night goes on and I'm all sweetness and light, sitting almost coyly in the corner and chuckling along with the mostly inane chatter which is spilling from my companions' mouths. I'm still having a good stare at the good looking bird when I can and then I notice when one of the boys leans across and kisses her as he goes up to the bar. The dickhead doesn't even offer to get a round in even though I forked out for his last pint. I fight my natural temptation to take the cunt up on his evidently amateur credentials. Instead, I rub my foot off the good looking bird's leg, in a way so that it seems like an accident but I don't bother making any kind of an apology, just to fuck with her head a bit. The lads are getting fairly sozzled and the Michel Platini bird is near paralytic and keeps pointing over at me and my supposed namesake and keeps saying, "I can't believe you're both called David! It's sooo funny!" I just laugh along in a good humoured fashion until David invites me to head outside with this other bloke, Connor, to smoke the joint he was rolling earlier. I duly oblige and we head around the corner just out of the doorway of the pub. The Connor bloke asks me about my job and I tell him that it's just a kind of a stopgap thing? And that really I'm an artist? And that I really want to be able to sell my paintings for a living sometime? And that hopefully it'll happen pretty soon? The boys are pretty impressed by this and when the joint is handed to me I realise that I'm actually starting to feel pretty twisted myself. The joint is badly rolled, but it's so loose it's like inhaling a smoke bomb. We smoke the weapon down to the roach and I'm actually light headed after it. Just as we're about to head back into the pub I say to the lads "I've got a bit of coke here if you fancy a line? Just to repay the favour like." The two boys look at each other like they're a little unsure but you can see that they've got a street credibility thing going on and neither of them wants to be the un-cool cunt to refuse a free line off an obviously cooler, older player who's trying to do them a favour. We go back into the pub and head straight for the jacks. The English stag party are in full voice and I wonder why large groups of young English men find it impossible to be in each other's company without launching into a collective chanting of some supposedly humorous song. I reckon it must be a part of their cultural inheritance as an imperialistic, warlike people that demands conformity to a pack-like social structure. My head's beginning to spin and my deep thinking's making it worse as I practically stumble into the jacks. The two boys are doing that stoned teenager thing of laughing in each other's faces with their eyes and mouths wide open and I tell them to wait outside as I head into the cubicle. I do out four lines onto the cistern and snuffle up two for myself. I wipe the remnants of the two lines from the cistern with my index finger and dab the powder onto my tongue. The stuff feels and tastes exactly like coke, to me anyway, and I'm not too bothered about trying to pass it off as some of senor Escobar's finest, as I know for certain that the two boys aren't going to notice anything unusual about it. Plus, I'm actually doing them a big time favour here as I never had time to mix the shit with anything. I only have the few sample bags that Dosser gave me and because I need to report back on its effects and potency, it's probably best that I've left it in its driven snow state anyway.

Before I leave, I decide to dump a quick load in the jacks. The cubicle's actually fairly enclosed so I'm pretty sure I should get away with this without the two boys hearing anything. I sit down on the jacks pot and all that comes out is a vile smelling liquid, pure beer and whatever bacterial culture was growing on those ham sandwiches I got off Robert Joyce earlier on. I give my arse a quick wipe and button myself up. I open the cubicle door and walk out. "There's a line each in there for yis lads. Some dirty cunt had a shit in there earlier obviously. Place is rank, just so you know." To my amazement, the two clowns actually head in together and close the door behind them and I can't be bothered to tell them that the only reasons two blokes would go into a cubicle of a pub jacks together, are if they were either bum bashers or doing some kind of drug. Just as they close the door behind them, a black bloke comes into the jacks, carrying two small rucksacks. He puts the two bags up beside the sinks and starts taking out a load of deodorants and soaps and what have you. I head up to him and I'm like "There you are my man. I'm fuckin stinkin here homey. Hook me up with some of that lynx and shit." I walk over to the sink and he turns on the tap and squirts some soap onto my hands. Then he hands me some paper tissues and I ask if I can take some of the deodorant. I give myself a good spraying as I probably am fairly stinking at this stage and put my arm around the guy. "So where are you from an all man?" He starts telling me he's from Lagos and he's been here for eight months and I notice thankfully, that David comes out of the cubicle and walks straight into the pub and Connor walks out a minute later. The black bloke is too engrossed in our conversation to notice that they've just come out of the same cubicle and I'm just like "Yeah, fuckin hell man. I hope it all works out for ye an all. Aw shit. I've actually got no change on me here. I'll get ye next time yeah?" I give him a pat on the back as I head back into the pub and he doesn't look too pleased, but I'm fucked if I'm paying for the privilege of washing my hands in a fucking toilet. I mean have we lost the run of ourselves in this country or what?

I head back over to the table and the two boys are sitting there, looking very pleased with themselves and I decide it's time to go for the jugular. They end up making life very easy for me when David tells me that they're heading back to a party in some gaff in Inchicore and asks me if I want to join them. I tell them I have to wait for a group of workmates who are joining me soon but I offer to give them a bag or two of the gear if they've an interest. David and Connor debate it between themselves for a second and the bloke who seems to be doing, but clearly not satisfying the good looking bird gets involved as well. Eventually, David tells me that Connor will head to the bank machine, which he duly does and I manage to offload two bags for a ton. The boys say their goodbyes and take my number which I give as a digit incorrect because I'm a great believer in passing trade in this business, especially when the stuff is still in an experimental stage of development. As they're walking out the door, the ride of a bird turns back around for one last look at what she's missing and I realise that I'd murder a bit of T-Rex right now. I take out my phone and scroll through the phone book and decide, fuck it, I'll text *her*. I go to Write Message and for once in my life I'm struggling to think of what to say. I decide I don't want to come on too strong and to keep it nice and casual so I just write; "Hey, what's the story . . . haven't spoken to u in a ages! How's things . . . any news?" I press Send and conclude that I'm content enough with the wording of the message. I stick my phone in my pocket and try to just relax and put it out of mind, so that I'm not just sitting there waiting on her reply. I drain the last mouthful from my pint and make a decision to give the English blokes a try. They're getting fairly messy at this stage and they must have smashed at least four glasses between them by now. They're not doing it deliberately or anything, they're just messy drinkers. Every time one of the glasses hits the ground, the sound of it breaking is accompanied by a massive cheer and the Chinese barman has a real intimidated look on his face as he manoeuvres through the Saxon horde to clean up the spillage. The boys are mostly old enough, the majority of them have skin heads and they're all fairly big bastards as well, dressed in short sleeve shirts to a man, except for one, who I'm assuming is the stag, who's wearing nothing but a kind of adult nappy, a pair of flippers and a snorkel and diving goggles. I move up the bar and nestle in between them to try and get served from the barman. I'm waiting patiently, exuding an air of nonchalance although surrounded by five or six of the well-on English blokes and I know it's only a matter of time before one of them tries to engage me in conversation. Eventually, just as I manage to finally get the attention of the Latino barman one of the stag-party turns around to talk to me. "You all right there mate? You from around here then are ya? We're 'avin some fookin laugh over 'ere mate I tell ya." The bloke's in his late thirties and judging from his accent, he seems to be from somewhere in the north of England. "Yeah local man here so I am. Yous seem to be enjoyin yourselves true enough. How long are yis on it?" I ask with a nod towards my pint, as I bring it towards my lips to moisten my mouth which is feeling a little dry after those couple of lines. "We 'avent bloody stopped mate, I'm tellin ya, an we aint bloody stopping neither! We've a fookin plane to catch at seven in the mornin' so I says to Gary 'ere, I says Gary", the English bloke pokes one of friends with his thumb who up until now has had his back turned to us. The friend, who I'm assuming is Gary, turns around to join in the conversation while my new acquaintance continues on. "I says to Gary, I says. What's the fookin point in goin' to bed when we've a fookin plane to catch at seven in the mornin? We'll only be back and we'll be gettin up so what's the point in tryin to sleep at all? Fookin all nighter mate. Only bloody way. Separate the men from the bloody wankers!" "Men from the bloody wankers!" Gary shouts this out while lifting his glass into the air and it's obvious that this has been some kind of recurring catch cry all weekend. I start laughing and raise my pint and shout "Men from the bloody wankers!" and Gary and the other bloke start cheering and we all take lengthy sups from our drinks. After this little exchange, it's all best buddies' time and I become an honorary member of the stag party. It turns out that the not-Gary bloke's name is Simon and that he's a chippie too. I tell them my name's Edward and I don't bother inventing an occupation because carpentry gives myself and Simon some common ground to walk on, so to speak. The rest of the boys are really getting rowdy and I end up becoming involved in some suicidal rounds of shots while acquiring the nickname "Steady Eddie", due to the ease I down the shots with. After a while, myself and Simon are discussing the pros and cons of laminate versus hardwood flooring, when Gary reaches across to speak in my ear. "Do you know anywhere we could get some coke or summat?" he says with a conspiratorial air. Too fucking easy. I tell him that by a bizarre stroke of fortune, I've actually got some on me now.

Simon gets in on the conversation and the two boys are only delighted and start rubbing their thighs with excitement. I tell them that I'll sort them out with a few lines because in fairness, I've been involved in about five rounds of Sambucas and I haven't paid for a single one. The boys won't hear of it and they're all "no fookin way mate, come on, you're doin us a favour 'ere, we won't leave ye short" and they're actually pulling fifties out of their pockets and practically forcing the notes into my hand. I tell them I've got two bags on me for fifty each but I'll let them have both of them for eighty. Simon still won't accept the offer and he takes fifty out of Gary's hand who seemed ready to snap up the discount price and fifty out of his own and hands the cash to me up front. I take the money with a kind of "oh all right then" sigh and manage to slip the two bags to Simon without anybody noticing. The two boys head off to the jacks and I'm left on my own again as some of the stag party seem to have moved on somewhere else, while a couple of stragglers are having drunken heart to heart conversations over some stale looking pints of Guinness and Bacardi and coke chasers. I take out my phone to see if *she's* replied yet. Nothing. I say fuck it and put the phone back in my pocket and put it out of my mind immediately. The two boys come back from the jacks and they're looking a bit jumpy and keep sniffing and looking around themselves. Gary just gives me a big pat on the shoulder and smiles, while Simon says "Let's move on then shall we?"

We head into Temple Bar and hit a couple of pubs before we eventually find the rest of the stag party. The two boys are hitting that gear pretty heavily and even I'm beginning to worry about the pace they're using it up at. We're standing at the bar in some pub that's wall to wall tourists and the two boys head off to the toilets again. They ask me if I want to join them but I tell them I've had enough of the stuff already. There's two guitarists playing ballad kind of music and the rest of the stag party are making a comical attempt at Irish dancing, so I'm left on my own again. I check my phone again and I've got a message. It's from some bird called Jessica and this really isn't bravado or anything but I've genuinely got no idea who she is, or have any memory of putting the number in my phonebook. It says "hey, hows u? How'd d wkend go? Do u still wanna meet up dis wk? Wb." I erase the message straight away and delete the contact from my phonebook. I decide I'll text *her* just one more time and I write: "Howya. Sorry don't know if u got my message there but I was just seein how u were?

We should meet up this wk maybe to catch up?" I press Send and just think fuck it. I put my phone back in my pocket just as Gary and Simon arrive back at the bar. "Here he fookin is. Steady Eddie. The man with the plan. The man with the big, big plan. How are you? Let's get some fookin ale in, I'm fookin dryin up 'ere mate." Simon's looking absolutely fucked and Gary's not exactly the picture of health, but I'm that gone myself at this stage that I'm past caring. A pint drinking contest develops at the bar and I actually have to hand it to the Saxons, their stamina is pretty impressive. Simon's up against one of his mates and he downs a pint of Carlsberg in absolute record time. Of course, it's only a matter of seconds before the entire stag party is chanting: "STEADY-EDDIE! STEADY-EDDIE!" so I duly stand up to do my country proud. I'm against Gary and even before battle commences, I get this feeling that everything's not right with him. I knock back a Heineken with the ease of Paolo Maldini defending an attack from a struggling Udinese side at the San Siro and I put down my empty glass. I turn to look at Gary who's miles behind me but refuses to stop drinking his pint of Guinness until it's finished. It takes him what feels like an eternity to drain the pint and when he eventually does, he just stands there for a moment, trying to maintain his balance while all his mates start cheering and rubbing the top of his head. Eventually all the colour drains from his face until he looks like a corpse and collapses onto the floor. Most of the lads start laughing and one of them even takes out a camera and takes pictures as Gary's lying on the ground. I can see he's still conscious and he's obviously just in a bad way from the accumulative effects of an action packed weekend. A few of the boys, including Simon carry him outside for some air and I head into the toilet as I fancy doing just one or two lines from the remaining bag, just to get my energy levels back up to match pace. After I hoover up the two lines, I do another two and another brace before rubbing a nice pinch around the inside of my mouth. I check my phone again and there's still no reply. Bitch. Fuck it. I put my phone back in my pocket and promise myself not to check it for at least another hour. I walk back to the bar and I can see that Gary's still outside and he seems to be propped up against the wall beside the entrance of the pub while a couple of the English lads are putting a bottle of water to his lips like they're feeding a baby. I order a double screwdriver at the bar and head outside to check on Gary. He's still conscious anyway but he seems to have gotten sick all over himself and the two boys beside him are looking a little bit over concerned if you ask me. Simon walks out behind me and he stares at me while looking like a worried little kid. I ask him quietly if he's ok. He says he's fine but I can tell he's paranoid and that he's lost his nerve, just as we're getting into the vital stages of the game. One of the blokes who are crouched down beside Gary, turns his body around and looks at me with what I would call an aggressive expression on his face. I try not to make eye contact with him and I light up a cigarette, but I can see out of the corner of my eye that he's pulled the bag of shit from Gary's pocket. "Did you fookin give that to him ye stupid cunt?" he says to me and I turn around to face my opponent. "What?" I say, with the cigarette just hanging out of the corner of my mouth, before I take it out with a sharp pull of my wrist and take a nice refreshing taste of my screwdriver. "I said did you fookin give that him ye fookin Irish cunt? Ma brother's epileptic ye daft bastard." I just look at Simon as if to say, nice one for telling me you prick and look straight into Gary's brother's eyes. "Listen your brother's a big boy man. It's not my fault if you English can't handle a session. Why don't yous fuck off home and stick to drinking half pints of lager with your boyfriends and don't be complainin to me about your brother being a fuckin eppo." As I finish saying this, I'm preparing myself to defend a frontal assault from Gary's brother when I just feel the crack of knuckles across my right eye. It takes me totally by surprise and I just about manage to stop my head from smashing against the brick wall beside me. I realise to my astonishment that it's Simon who's after hitting me with the solid, and I almost feel like congratulating the cunt on the punch, it was that well delivered. But before I know it, there are legs and arms flailing at me from every direction, as Gary's brother and the other bloke join Simon in the attack. All I can do is cover my head and parry a few shots away. Then I manage to swing the glass and smash it over Simon's head but I feel a sharp sting in the palm of my left hand and I realise that I've cut myself. I decide to play this one clever and run out of there as fast as I can. I run out onto the road and nearly lose my footing on the damp cobbles and curse the reasoning for persisting with cobble stones in one of the city's main drinking centres. I get back onto the path as soon as I can, avoiding a group of Spaniards or Italians (I admittedly can't definitively say which) as they look at me like I'm the epitome of everything that's wrong with northern European culture. I emerge at the central bank and I'm certain the English lads haven't bothered following me. I look at my hand and the palm is nicely sliced up, but the blood is probably making it look worse than it is. I can feel my right eye beginning to close over and I practically see the swelling around it by looking at it out of my left eye. But what I'm really feeling is the pure adrenaline of the moment and as I breathe, every breath sends this rush through my body, up through the veins in my legs and into my abdomen, flushing out in saccharine streams of air through my lungs. I can feel it pulsing through my shoulders and down my arms and I can feel my step quicken as I cross Dame Street and head towards the corner of George's Street. I take out my phone and there's still no reply but I couldn't give a fuck. The one message I need to take from tonight's festivities is very simple. Yes Mister Dosser Doyle, that shit fucking works.

Slowly, like a newspaper page descending to the ground in a warm breeze, she breathed. And for the first time in many days or weeks, she couldn't for certain say which, she began to feel as though she could see a lightness in the world, a lightness that had once seemed to fill every moment of her existence but that had evaporated swiftly, like water that would splash on the concrete steps of her house as she held a watering can over the daisies and sweet peas which guarded her doorstep. This lightness had first vanished when she felt the cold pain of a deathly human fire, chasing her through the weather-beaten pathways of her native streets, and she realised for the first time in her life, that not all life in this world had the same warmth of love that she carried with her, walking the same cracked pathways and wearied roadsides up and down all the seasons of the year. She knew for certain now, that the scope of human life was far larger than she previously could have imagined. The capabilities of the human mind were so boundless, that people could actually stretch their instincts, far beyond the realms of civilisation, so that ultimately they in fact, achieved a sense of mindlessness, and it occurred to her that mindlessness was an idea which had so many alternative and contrasting forms. For instance, mindlessness could be the inner peace achieved by the rhythmic incantations of Buddhist monks, who after many moments or days or years or even decades, can remove themselves from their surroundings, and exist in a separate realm of life, whereby their minds have transcended the thought-tormented nature of the human experience and they instead occupy a tranquil and enviable state of mindlessness. As she considered this cognition, she imagined surveying a Himalayan hilltop, rushing through the heavenly air and looking down on a solitary figure, sitting with legs akimbo on a rug of cushiony astrakhan. She could see this bald and peaceful creature, with eyes closed to the warming yet un-intrusive sun, embodying a healthily brown complexion, glowing midst the blue of the sky. And as she observed the scene, she felt the sensation of rushing through the air, soaring above the snow-laden peaks, and moving with the graceful ease of an albatross, ever closer to god.

This vista appeared to her as the archetypal definition of one side of mindlessness, what she considered to be the largely positive and life-affirming side and the one which she aspired to arrive at herself. There was however, that other side of mindlessness, that side which had beaten down human love for millennia and would continue to do so until the end of our epoch as guardians of the earth. This end of the spectrum of mindlessness, anathema to the picturesque portrait of serenity that she envisaged for hours on end, still managed to battle its way into her visions and held her in a gripping terror as she fought to dispel it from her frighteningly conscious thoughts. On these occasions, she could feel the sweat begin to stream from the pores of her burning skin and once more, that coldness of human fire, blew its pernicious flames at the safety of the Himalayan hilltop.

Demonic figures, flashed into her consciousness, harrying her into a corner of a room without a door or window to provide her with at least a chance of escape, baying to see her blood and tears as she vainly tried to stop them from wrestling her to the ground. And the more she struggled to kick and punch and scrape and scream; she became suddenly aware of an indefatigable inertia, consuming every pulse of her bloodstream, like fire through a decaying life. And as the time continued to pass, she came to understand the interminable and inexorable nature of the struggle between the two opposing sides of mindlessness. At times, the realisation of this certainty of continuation breathed an acceptance into her eyes, as the revolving world neared our hemisphere ever closer to the sun. And she felt a closeness to the humming holy man, so that it almost seemed as though her albatross wings were descending slowly from the highest gushes of the warm air, with the inanimate indifference of paper, floating in the suburban sky. But then, as clear as these sensations thrilled through her resting frame, the damning mindlessness of cold human fire, again assailed her dreamful wanderings. The philosophical acceptance of the cyclical nature of her situation, dissipated over the snow laden peaks and what remained, was the hopeless realisation of a horrifying and hurtful predicament. The only respite from the tormenting tug of war, which pulled the fraying rope of her sanity like the sun and moon beckon the embattled waters of the sea; was when pictures of her juvenility came like soul-saving seraphs, to replenish the diminishing energies of hope, which refused to allow her lungs to cease their unconscious labours. She saw visions of lying on green grass, making necklaces with the wild daisies she picked from the meadow that refused to vanish in the shadow of the factory wall. She heard the whispering trickle of the stream that ran the length of the verdant fields beside where she lived and felt the warming love of friendship, as hopscotch cries sounded beneath the twilight of an August evening. She recalled the tiredness and hunger she would feel as she returned to her mother's embrace, with the delights of a soda stream and Television game shows and the eventual somniferous, sinking into a dreamlike and easy sleep.

Sleep, was now all she knew. Sleep had become a way of life for her. Her body had seemed to take control of her mind and decided that sleep was the only path to safety in this world. For now, sleep was an escape. It had become a way of departing from a time and place that no longer seemed able to facilitate her existence in its space. Her body had come to the conclusion, that it was only by surrendering her freedom to move, that her mind could seek to achieve a redemptive state of mindlessness. And so it appeared that she had. She was almost certain that she was finding her way through the labyrinthine mire that barred her entry into the world of liberating unconsciousness, although it was proving to be a long and difficult process. But often, at times, she believed she could hear a voice calling to her from somewhere beside her; from a world she felt she knew existed, even though she could not see it. At first she thought the voice was coming from her mother, calling to her to join her in heaven, with the same mellifluous voice, that would soar from the back door of her house, to bring her back home from skipping games on the road. But soon the voice separated into disparate tones, as each syllable that she heard distinguished itself in a syncopated rhythm of difference. Then the sounds of multiple voices were accompanied by numerous odours which she imagined were circulating in this unseen world and wandered aimlessly into the universe she had created for herself. They were strange smells, not like the imagined aromas of the daisies and sweet peas which she nurtured on her doorstep, but smells that seemed somehow connected to distant memories, that were unimaginably lost under layers of dust-covered years. Then images began to come to her, not from beneath her soaring albatross wings, but out of a once darkening void, from where she wondered if the lightness she yearned to touch had crept. Normally the images passed as phantoms, veiled in glowing whites and blues of motherly light, sometimes silent but often accompanied by the sounds of ascending voices. One day, she heard the patter of footsteps and felt the bristle of hair on her forehead as pursed lips planted a solitary kiss on her unmoving skin and she dared to wonder that she knew who it was. But as soon as these vestiges of a living world came to awaken her, she could feel herself descending once more into the breeze, blowing softly and rhythmically into her emptying mind.

The Thoughts of Dosser Doyle
(Volume Two)

The week in school trudges on in the way that only school can. I find increasingly these days, that my ability to maintain concentration during most of my classes is undoubtedly diminishing, although I don't think I've quite reached Tarzan's stage of academic ineptitude. It is quite incredible how little information he actually acquires during a day's lessons and if it wasn't for his assiduity in his role as co-auditor of St. Leonard's Horticultural Society, I have no doubt that he would have been asked to leave this fine educational establishment a long time ago. In any case, I haven't really been in any of his classes since we were streamed after third year, so for all I know Tarzan could be performing idiot-savant like feats in his ordinary level subjects, but for some reason I remain sceptical about this possibility. I'm sitting in French class on a Tuesday after lunch and I'm still sweating after an epic performance during the football match in the yard. I'm also sitting right behind Blobby Nolan, whose malignant body odour and ceaseless flatulence are making the lesson doubly unpleasant. I have zero interest in playing sport and even less interest (if that's mathematically possible) in watching it, but I find my participation in the lunch-time ritual of pubescent jousting to be a kind of necessary evil. Although I both, naturally and intentionally gravitate towards existing outside of the mainstream, teenage, new millennium society, I am socially aware enough to realise that total ostracism from said contemporary society would serve little or indeed, no purpose at all. What would be the point in me coming into school every day and sitting on my own in the corner of the classroom and speaking to no one, trying to communicate some form of intellectual disdain for my peers, when it would take more energy to pursue this policy, than to simply conduct myself in a semi-normal fashion and generally blend in with the uniformed masses parading the corridors? Therefore, my relationship with school, in terms of the institution itself, my teachers and my classmates, really becomes a series of quiet and seemingly unremarkable compromises, between my natural inclination and moral affirmation to recognise the deeply flawed and often reprehensible nature of mainstream society and my common-sense acceptance, of the need to occasionally exist, not necessarily as a direct participant in said mainstream society, but certainly as a neutral and accepting neighbour, unwilling or at least disinclined to cause any unnecessary or unwarranted clashes. For example, my participation in the lunch-time football match is on condition of two major stipulations: Number one, I play in goal and Number Two, if any schoolyard Galacticos decide to comment on my dubious goalkeeping ability, Tarzan will ensure that their ebbing ambitions of playing professional football in England will be put beyond any possibility of being realised. This to my mind, seems a healthier and altogether more sensible way for me to interact with people who could otherwise be my sworn enemies, than let's say, watching the lunch-time football match, while sitting on the step behind the swimming pool with a gang of Goths, sharing one John Player Blue between six people. My natural lack of sporting prowess means that goalkeeper is the only position on the pitch that I could even conceivably attempt to fill. Now, I do realise that it is not necessarily an easy position and I don't wish to degrade it in anyway, but after years of playing there, I suppose I actually have got up to a certain standard of performance, whereby I am at least, credibly acceptable as a custodian of the space between two jumpers. Also, the standard of the games wouldn't exactly set the world alight anyway, so I manage to avoid having my shortcomings exposed in any hysterically embarrassing kind of way. So my sacred goalkeeping position is one example of the compromises I make in my scholastic life in order to stave off the potential pariah status which could have befallen me had I so wished. Another and the most obvious example, (not to mention most important) would be my role as co-auditor of the school horticultural society and this is more an example of a compromise between me and the educational institution itself, rather than between me and my fellow students. My role as co-auditor of the society has allowed me to appear as a fully functioning member of the school, in the eyes of the powers that be, whereas my total subversion and corruption of the position has enabled me to satiate the anarchical beast inside me, urging me to destroy everything in the world which has become moribund beyond hope. And if I may say so, my manipulation of the society and subsequent rise to power was nothing short of a stroke of Machiavellian, conspiratorial genius.

When Tarzan and I were in third year, the horticultural society was quite literally on its knees. It was being organised and controlled by a decrepit old priest named Father McEvoy, whose sole acolytes were these two unbelievable geeks in sixth year who were nicknamed "The Proclaimers", and who I believe have subsequently come out as being bum bashers and are currently bum bashing each other in some den of bum bashery in Harold's Cross. Anyway, it was around this time that I realised I wanted to do something special with my life, and having tired of childish solvent abuse and American dreams, I longed to find a way of enhancing my day to day existence without resorting to the mindless purchasing of illicit narcotics. So, initially we began to try different avenues of possibility. First, there was the disastrous attempt at smoking banana skins, which resulted in nothing more than an alarming amount of projectile vomiting, brought about after we smoked the skins of around 56 bananas, refusing to believe that the whole thing was a myth and adhering firmly to the hope that eventually it would yield dividends. Mellow yellow my arse. Next there was the attempt at inhaling petrol fumes out of jerry cans, which ended in Tarzan's hair going on fire, although the post-fire damaged hairstyle actually turned out to be an improvement on his normal "Hi I'm a crazy person Afro". But the worst and needless to say, near cataclysmic folly, was when we went in search of Psilocybe Cubensis over in the park on one ill-fated yet fateful day. For the one and only time in my life, I put faith in Tarzan's ability to be a fully contributing member of our non-society and believed his on-sight identification of Psilocybe Cubensis, whose recognisable characteristics he had allegedly researched on the internet. We ended up eating some form of highly toxic mushroom and the two of us collapsed in an absolute attack of nausea and unimaginable sickness. Luckily for us, Gobber Gilsenan, who up until that point, was nothing more than a figure you would cross the road to avoid, was over by the river with Stevie Smith and company, drinking flagons of cider and witnessed our obvious difficulties. He managed to put both of us in the recovery position, ring an ambulance and bring samples of the poisonous fungus to the hospital. He really did save our lives that day; he even pretended to be my older brother and waited while we had our stomachs pumped.

But despite this near fatal foray into the world of legal life-enhancers, my determination to realise my ambition remained as resilient as ever. It was then that kismet really began to play its part in directing the future course of my life. One day while walking the corridor, I heard the vice-principal, Mister Sweeney and Father McEvoy talking about the aging priest's imminent retirement from his educational duties at the end of the year and it all began to click. It occurred to me that as soon as the year was over, the priest would be held up in some museum for members of a defunct profession while his two, acne-scarred, subordinate horticulturalists will have left the school anyway, without there being exactly a multitude of hopefuls queuing up to occupy either of the vacant positions. I immediately realised that this was the chance that I had been waiting for and went straight to Mister Sweeney to pitch my idea. I told him that I was aware of the potential collapse of the horticultural society at the end of the year and that I would be extremely interested in taking the torch from The Proclaimers if it would be at all possible. Luckily for me, Mister Sweeney is a total pushover, the kind of teacher that you could convince you had been talking to the previous day when you'd actually been absent without official leave for two weeks, and he duly consented. I realised the potential of this coup from the outset, and I was aware that I was doubly lucky, as I knew no lay teacher would have any interest in giving up their free time to become involved and take over the position previously held by Father McEvoy, and, consequently our operations would more than likely be practically unmonitored, except for the occasional pop of the head in the door from Mister Sweeney. As soon as the whole plan was cleared with Father McEvoy and the Principal, Mister Murray whose eccentric behaviour had arrived at a juncture where it had actually ceased to be funny and was instead, completely embarrassing and downright perturbing, I set about preparing myself for my eventual succession to the horticultural throne. One day, before the end of term, Father McEvoy showed me around my new empire after school. The amenities present were more than ample and I was as excited as an alcoholic on payday as he took me to see the large greenhouse, sizable shed, vegetable patches and bedding areas at the rear of the school which would become our base of operations. Father McEvoy was a very peculiar man, who spoke with a half-African accent and had apparently contracted malaria on eight separate occasions, although I'm admittedly not sure if that's even possible. He just walked around the shed and the gardens, picking up tools and saying things like "Ya use dees for putting da plants in da ground der, so you do" and "dose plants drink a lotta water, but dose ones do only be needin da water, every now an den." After walking around in what seemed an interminable agony of him rambling incomprehensibly and me listening in a baffled and sometimes alarmed silence, Father McEvoy eventually stopped at one seemingly inconspicuous shrub in the corner of the greenhouse. He caressed a leaf off the plant and rubbed it between his two hands, before bringing them to his nose and smelling the massaged leaf in a long and deep inhalation. Then he brought his two hands over to my nose, encouraging me to experience the clearly evocative aroma. "Dis one be called da dagga plant. In Africa, da people do be usin dis plant as a smokin plant. Sometimes in Africa, it be so warm at night ya couldn't sleep for da heat, but if ya smoke some of da dagga, ya can sleep all night if ya wants." I actually couldn't believe what I was hearing until Father McEvoy opened up the drawer of a table that's propped up against the side of the greenhouse and took out a perfectly rolled cigarette. "Dis be da dagga here now, I needs to smoke it from time to time now I'm in me old age." Father McEvoy then proceeded to light up the cigarette and smoke it in short, sharp, drags before offering it to me for a taster. "Ere, take a bit of dis, it won't be doin you no arm in anyways." I obviously couldn't say no and he continued to walk me around the greenhouse, demonstrating how to connect the hose to the faucet, just outside the back door and how to lock the cabinet where he kept the weed killer and such, while I polished off the dagga cigarette, before he offered me a lift home.

I got him to drop me back to Tarzan's house; Number One because I didn't want him to know where I live, lest febrile, African herb smoking priests should come knocking at my front door over the summer and Number Two, because I wanted to recruit Tarzan into the operation and generally fill him in on the important details of what we were about to dedicate the foreseeable future of our lives towards. So for the entire summer holidays, Tarzan and I researched everything we could about all things horticultural on the one hand, and all things alternative life-enhancing substances on the other, greatly aided by my family's purchase of our first home computer and my personal discovery of the limitless powers of the internet. But it wasn't all comfortable intellectual research and there was a great deal of back breaking manual labour to be done as well. It was around mid-July that we cleared out the old garage in Tarzan's back garden and we also came to the conclusion that we would need some kind of greenhouse outside of school as well, as we would not be able to gain access to the school greenhouse during mid-term breaks and miscellaneous school holidays. Eventually the two of us had to get summer jobs in order to accumulate the requisite financial resources to allow us to buy the various items of accoutrement which any aspiring subversive horticulturalist would need, and so the two of us started on a paper round for this old guy named Mister Delaney, who conveniently lived in the same locality as ourselves. He even provided bikes for those employees who didn't possess one, so we unsurprisingly told him that we didn't have bikes and took his communal ones as we felt an opportunity might present itself whereby we could somehow profit from the situation. The work itself was extremely tiresome, although the laborious tedium of it did strengthen my resolve to find an alternative way of bank-rolling my future life than engaging myself in some form of standardised occupation and I longed for the summer to come to an end. It did however provide a great deal of opportunity for me and Tarzan to prank it up, but we only managed mostly infantile nonsense, like knick-knacks, or ushering dogs into front gardens to defecate on doorsteps, anything just to try and alleviate the incredibly soul-sucking monotony of it all. I suppose the best prank we pulled was the pornographic magazine caper of around late July. During our delivery rounds we only dealt with the Evening Herald and nothing else, lest our hands turn to stone and our eyes lose their sight for reading the print from a rival rag. But after a while, we noticed that there was this knob end who was maybe a year or two older than us, delivering The Star to houses around the area, mostly to different houses than we were delivering to, but there was some overlap, there being a few particularly studious people, who evidently felt the need the read the same crap written in two different ways every day. Anyway, we could just tell that The Star delivery boy was a complete bum basher and we began to take a really strong dislike to him. He had this really expensive mountain bike and he always wore those sun sunglasses that kind of strap around your head, and he even occasionally wore a star spangled banner bandana. You could see he was really popular with the people of the area and it was like he had become a local character, an immovable fixture that the old men and women whose houses he called to, couldn't live without. Sometimes he would try and make small talk with us as if to create some type of communal paper-boy bond between us, so we would have to fight against our natural urge to shoot him in the face with our crow-hunting equipment and laugh along with him as if we were fully supportive of and enthusiastic participants in, the common-profession banter he had instigated. He would make these inane attempts at humour by saying things like "Hey dudes, fancy seeing you 'round' here!" and "Hey guys, what's 'news' with you?!" and we just had to continue to play along with his ridiculous conversation, without pointing out the fact that he had to be the world's oldest paper delivery boy and was about as agreeable as a swarm of wasps at a picnic, while simultaneously suppressing our desire to shove his spanking new mountain bike up his Jap's eye. We knew we just had to bide our time and wait for the right opportunity to bring the bandana wearing, cheerfully pleasant bastard down to his knees.

The plan was so easy really, that it was simply impossible for it to fail and we initiated it on a fine summer's morning as children played rounders and hopscotch, while the smell of freshly cut grass permeated into the very fibre of one's soul. First of all, we began our paper round, just ten minutes later than normal, to ensure that he delivered his copies of The Star to our common recipients before we arrived with The Herald, but we still weren't far enough behind him that we had completely disappeared, lest we began to look obviously suspicious. He could still see us going about our heraldic duties and we still engaged in the regular mindless small talk whenever our paths crossed. So, as soon as we arrived at the houses we both delivered to, we would pick up the copy of The Star which he had recently deposited on the doorstep and place a copy of The Herald beside it, while simultaneously, inserting a brand new jazz mag, in between the pages of The Star. We were able to procure the erotic literature from a seemingly bottomless store of filth that we uncovered from a box in Tarzan's garage. We assumed that the box belonged to one of Tarzan's older brothers, who I've never actually spoken to because he's been living in London for the last number of years. Most of the magazines were fairly hardcore European smut and a sizable number of them concentrated on that kind of body builder, muscle women, for which Tarzan's brother seemed to have a little penchant, judging by the adhesive properties of the pages. Anyway, we had plenty of material to work with, so we were prepared to deliver our supplementary cargo for as long as was necessary. We did this to maybe eight or ten houses and the hard work was over. After the first day, nobody appeared to have noticed or more importantly, said anything about the unusual deliveries but after a week or so, the full repercussions of the prank were beginning to come to fruition. One day as we were free-wheeling down St. Michael's Avenue, we saw a septuagenarian man being restrained by his distraught wife as he endeavoured to charge at the sun glass wearing wank bag and duly unleashed a litany of profanities that I wouldn't even lower myself to repeat. The bandana-headed irritant, just stood there motionless, with a gormless expression across his face, looking like his entire world was collapsing around him. As he turned and wheeled his precious, unnecessarily sophisticated push bike out the front gate and continued to his next port of call, we pedalled further along the avenue, just close enough to see what might happen, but at a safe enough distance so as to remain unseen ourselves. As he balanced his bike on the front wall of the next house and walked gingerly towards the front door, a bucket appeared from the top window and a stream of its emptied contents rained down on his be-bandanad head. He stood as still as a statue in total shock and I'm pretty sure I could see him, just begin to break out in a convulsion of sobbing when the sirens of justice began to sound and a squad car flashed by us down the avenue. The last we saw or heard of him, was when his handcuffed and crestfallen figure was bundled unceremoniously into the back of the squad car, as middle-aged men comforted their sobbing wives who watched the scene defiantly from their doorsteps. Well the entertainment value of this particular prank quickly dissipated and the rest of the summer continued in the dreary vain it had assumed up until then. We had both become extremely fed up of the job at this stage and wanted the ordeal to be over as if we were on a forced march to a Russian prisoner of war camp in Siberia. Eventually, Mister Delaney made our escape from this wretched existence very easy. One afternoon, at the end of the summer, the police came knocking on his door to ask him a few questions about some accusations which had been made against him. It turned out that he had been overcharging customers who had their newspapers delivered to their houses and who paid for the entire year's quota in one large some at the start of the year by around £100. With around 120 customers on the books that was a tidy little profit. Also, in a slightly seedier and less admirable turn, he'd been involved in a sexual relationship with a minor for some time and to top it all his "victim" was a local girl who actually lived on Tarzan's road. He claimed that she had lied to him about her age but combined with the great newspaper fraud of the year 2000, the man had an eastern European republic's chance of withstanding a blitzkrieg and he was incarcerated for a year or two anyway.

Well this was probably a little more than the serendipitous opportunity we had hoped for, but we sold our own bikes for a nice half a monkey each and kept the disgraced Mister Delaney's two-wheelers, the same ones we still use to this day. I suppose even non-unionised, non-tax paying, part-time paper boys are still morally, if not necessarily legally, entitled to some form of redundancy so it's probably only fair enough. So anyway, by the end of the summer we had saved up enough money to purchase basic equipment, various different packets of seeds and brand new gardening tools, and it was around then that we first set up the running-away fund. Most importantly, we convinced Tarzan's mother, who spoils him in a ridiculously overbearing manner, to provide us with the remaining capital to buy a greenhouse and assemble it in his back garden. As soon as we had the base of operations established, there was no turning back and by the end of fourth year, we had firmly taken hold of a sizable market share in the life-enhancing substance market, as well as becoming quite the connoisseurs of the range of products ourselves. Of course, once we'd established the greenhouse in Tarzan's back garden and returned to school in September, we were only really beginning the process of becoming what we are today and it involved a great deal of imagination, auto-didacticism and even the forming of secretive international relationships, but I'll have to deal with that later, as I have been most untimely called upon by my French teacher, Miss O' Neill, to answer homework question number nine.

"Elle tient a son cheval comme a la prunelle de ses yeux." I read out the phrase quickly as I successfully predicted that it was the one that was destined for me, and have been quietly skimming the phrase in my textbook for the last few minutes. I pronounce each word correctly, without drifting into the realms of a theatrically over the top, Jacques Cousteau like accent, as I don't want people to think that I'm putting too much effort into my schoolwork. As I've stated previously, the key to my relationship with school is not to draw attention to myself in anyway, although my exceptional proficiency in history is clearly unavoidable. Miss O' Neill is unable to stop a little smile of relief from invading her complexion and duly continues her quest for correctly completed comprehension questions. "Tres bien, merci beaucoup. And number ten, did anybody get that one?" Luckily enough, I managed to do the French homework while walking to class at the end of lunch. It's a little bit annoying really, but

I always have to ensure that I have completed my homework for French class because Miss O'Neill never fails to ask me to read out one of my answers. She's a timid, little country girl, who only arrived at the school this September and if anything, she seems to be more nervous now than she was at the start of the year. She's still quite young, twenty two at most and seems to become embarrassed the minute the class walks through the door. Her face is permanently red during a lesson and even when she's correcting the homework, she doesn't actually ask anybody directly to read out their answers, as she doesn't have the confidence or the assertiveness to make such a demand on one of her charges. Even when she asks me, she merely looks down in the general direction of where I'm sitting and kind of moves her eyes around the vicinity, but it's obvious that she's waiting in hope for me to respond to her request. That's why it's so annoying. She only ever asks people who she knows will have the homework done and never asks the less conscientious students who everyone knows definitely won't have it done, because she doesn't want to face the possibility of conflict with said indolent students. So now it's resulted in a situation where I've become one of her most reliable and diligent pupils, and in a weird way I've found myself bound by almost a sense of duty to this role. I suppose it's because I've developed a bit of a soft spot for her in a way, and I've used her personally constructed sexual persona as a masturbatory aid on six separate occasions, although two of these ejaculations occurred consecutively during a particularly boring Saturday morning, when the inclement weather precipitated the cancellation of our weekly crow-hunting expedition. Just observing her now, it occurs to me that she's probably not really that exceptionally good-looking, but it's undoubtedly an immutable facet of all-boys' schools, that perfectly average looking female teachers can achieve almost mythical goddess-like status by virtue of being simply young and not fat. I'd imagine that if you walked by Miss O'Neill on the street, she might not even warrant a second look but in an institution, populated by callow teenage boys, middle-aged women, crest fallen men and the one or two beleaguered stragglers of a vanquished theocracy who are still wandering the corridors, she becomes an oasis in a wilderness of desperation. I suppose, that's probably why her classes are relatively incident-free despite her suspect teaching abilities. Nobody really has the inclination to cause hassle to someone that we're all probably wanking over, so she manages to avoid being the target of any adolescent mischief, but I suppose she's still only here a very short period of time and that situation could change very quickly indeed.

My answering of homework question number nine has at least got my contribution to the class out of the way and I can now relax, safe in the knowledge that I should have no further role in today's lesson. I surreptitiously slide my phone out of my trouser pocket to check the time and there's ten minutes left of this incredibly uneventful French class. I've also got two messages, one from my father, who only took possession of his first mobile phone last week, and seems to be using me as a kind of a crash test dummy for his initial, tentative text messages and the other one is from Gobber. I read my father's one first, while holding my phone underneath my desk and holding my French book vertically on the table, to serve as a kind of a visual barricade. The text is written in all block capitals and it says "IN THE BACK GARDEN WHAT A BEAUTIFUL DAY WE ARE HAVING CHICKEN FOR DINNER." I immediately delete the message for reasons which are evidently without need of explanation. Although I do appreciate that my father's inability to be fully employed due to a work-place accident many years ago, has probably affected his chances of climbing Mount Everest, I do have to wonder with some perplexity as to why I have to become a confidante to his journalistic expressions of everyday banalities. I then scroll down to Gobber's digital epistle in the hope of encountering something a little more worthwhile or at best entertaining. Instead it reads "Just saw ur sis hooverin her car in d petrol station. Hav creamed my cacks cos i cud see her thong as she bent over d backseat." It never ceases to amaze me, how often the initial pique of interest which stimulates one's mind on first observing that one has received a text message, is instantly quelled by the inconsequential and unnecessary nature of their content. By the time I've finished reading these pointless interruptions to my peregrinating cognitions, there's only six minutes left to the bell. Miss O' Neill has turned her back to the class and is writing some sentences in English on the board and I gather that she wants us to take them down into our copy books and translate them for homework. The phrases aren't difficult in anyway, so I manage to translate them instantaneously and write them immediately in French in my copy book, thus halving the entire workload and leaving myself plenty of time to attend to my horticultural and chemical manipulation duties for this evening. She's wearing these ludicrously tight jeans that have become notorious around the school due to their immeasurable inappropriateness, as you can practically see the skin of her arse, such is the closeness of the denim to her posterior. Sean Malone, who's sitting at the front of the room, starts gyrating in his chair in a romping motion and looks around with an idiotic smile on his face in search of some sycophantic laughter, which he duly receives. Anto O' Sullivan, then accidentally on purpose, throws a pen to the top of the classroom so that it lands right beside Miss O' Neill's leg. She turns around, mildly startled while Anto jumps out of his seat and walks up the blackboard to retrieve his ink-based writing implement. "Aw sorry Miss, I was just giving Sean a lend of the pen there, sorry." Incredibly, Miss O' Neill bends over to pick up the pen and return it to its original proprietor and as she bends over, her arse is actually quite near to Anto's genitalia, so it conceivably looks like he's about to do her from behind. "Thanks Miss" Anto says, while turning around without even giving it to Sean Malone in order to credibly substantiate his concocted story. The rest of the class smother giggles into their chests while Miss O' Neill either fails to notice, or chooses to ignore the entire childish charade. The entire scene is depressingly pathetic, and it is certainly one of the problems with being in mostly top-stream classes, that the level of devilment is nothing short of abysmal. My musings on the inverse nature of the relationship between academic ability and classroom Tom Foolery are interrupted by a knock on the door and the appearance of the unwelcome face of our year head, Mister White. "Excuse the interruption to class Miss O'Neill but I just need to speak to one of your students please. Mister Doyle, are you behaving yourself today? Is he behaving himself for you Miss O' Neill?" he says, as he strolls into the classroom with the demeanour of a hot shot lawyer in a courtroom drama and the atmosphere amongst my cohorts instantly alters. Miss O' Neill nervously mumbles in the affirmative while Mister White walks towards me with a casual menace and he's moving more into the bad cop in the interrogation room territory as he nears my desk. "Oh he is then is he Miss O' Neill? Well that's good to hear because he's not behaving himself for everybody, isn't that right Mister Doyle? Being a right feckin nuisance is what he's being for some people, isn't that the truth Mister Doyle? Mister Johnson in particular I believe, Mister Doyle. Well I'll tell ye what you can do for me Mister Doyle, seems you're in such a fine mood today, you can come to my office at four O' Clock and I'll see if I can find a bit of work for you to do then. Is that clear?" "Of course sir." I say, in my opinion, perfectly audibly and without any hint of sarcasm. "What's that Mister Doyle?" Mister White asks me, evidently contradicting my own appraisal of the volume and intonation of my previous statement, and while spitting half the contents of his liquid lunch over my desk. "Yes sir" I repeat, with admittedly a little more gusto. "Yes sir. I will be down straight after the bell." He seems a little more satisfied with this response and backs away slowly and calmly from my desk with an air of self-righteous fulfilment. "Right then Mister Doyle. I'll see you then so and then I'll be leaving you in the hands of Mister Johnson seems he's the fella you think you can mess with. And let it be known to everyone," he once again elevates the volume of his voice for this last part and does a quick visual sweep of the classroom in order to convey the importance and generality of the address, "that if you want to mess with any teacher in this school, you're not just messing with that one teacher, but you're messing with all of us, and what's worse for yis lads is, you'll be messing with me. And you don't want to be messing with me." The last line is delivered with the pseudo-sentimentality of a clip form an Oscar winning performance. It's true that the theatricality of the man is pompously ridiculous but he is a little bit intimidating, especially when he shouts at you in such close proximity to your face. As soon as he closes the door behind him, the class breathes a collective sigh of relief as everybody looks at me with perplexed, gasping faces. Miss O' Neill gives me, what I'm pretty sure is a slightly disappointed glance, but I wonder if I'm reading a little too much into her expression and being just a tad unrealistic about how important it is for her to have students like me whom she can hold in high-esteem and look towards, as a refuge from the merciless tide of apathetic indolence which assails her on a daily basis. Then I really am sure that she's been adversely affected by this revelation of my supposed bad behaviour when she shakes her head and sighs. I begin to feel a sensation that's almost as near to guilt as I think I'm capable of feeling, when Blobby Nolan turns around to me and asks incredulously "what the fuck did you do?" and all I can think to say is "I'm going to kill Mister Johnson."

The next two classes are English and Irish respectively and thankfully, both pass without any major incident or any unwarranted assailing of my character by menacing, hyperbolic year heads. As it's four o'clock, I walk admittedly a little sheepishly towards Mister White's office passing the principal, Mister Murray at the front door as he shakes hands with the exiting students while saying "thanks for coming to school now, see you tomorrow please god", wearing that manic expression which seems to be permanently fixed on his face these days. I arrive at Mister White's office and the door is slightly ajar, just enough so that I can see and hear him as he's talking on the phone. I quickly gather that the phone call is not work-related as I can hear him say "beef, I want beef. I'm not havin' feckin' fish again, I'm not a bloody Eskimo." He appears to raise his head abruptly while finishing his culinary demand and I perceive that he has evidently seen me waiting at the door as he roughly clears his throat, says his goodbyes to his dutiful spouse and slams the phone down in an absurdly purposeful manner. He rushes out of his seat like a greyhound out of a trap and opens the door with a pugnacious swing of his arm. "Right you, ye clown. Come down and we get ye sorted so." He fires this command at me from his skinny-lipped mouth and he powers down the corridor with the proprietorial air of a victorious wehrmacht general, of aristocratic, Prussian military stock, inspecting the remnants of a recently captured Ukrainian village. I gather that he wishes for me to accompany him and I follow behind with the grace of a hungry puppy chasing after its owner, while sensing a surge of resentment against the conceited bastard for making me feel and look like a naughty child. As we frogmarch down the corridors, I begin to feel slightly self-conscious as the uniformed hordes turn to stare at me like I'm a condemned man on death row. I can even see Tarzan emerging from the senior toilet, holding some first year in a headlock, but Mister White either doesn't notice this bout of horseplay or else simply chooses to turn a blind eye to it. I realise that I haven't seen Richie Grimes yet this week and I wonder if his absence is in anyway related to that little incident which occurred in his living room on Saturday night. I truly hope it isn't and if he hasn't been able to see the funny side of the entire scenario yet, he really should question the integrity of his sense of humour. I mean it's not like anybody died or anything, well no human life was lost anyway. I might even buy him a new dog if I absolutely have to, although total denial and affectation of complete ignorance of the situation is definitely the policy that I will be pursuing in order to deal with the matter for the time being at least, purely as it is the only logical course to follow, as me losing a customer or making an enemy of the Smith brothers would serve absolutely no purpose whatsoever. Mister White picks up the pace as we near the science lab where I will have to atone for my alleged transgressions against Mister Johnson. Mister White remains completely quiet during the entire ordeal, which makes me feel even more ridiculous and even a little nervous, even though I am fully aware that any sense of trepidation is completely unnecessary. We pass by Miss O' Neill as she bends down to put some paper into a photocopier, while Mister Murray stands uncomfortably close to her, holding a freshly pealed banana and staring unashamedly at the same arse which caused so much hilarity in my French class. It occurs to me that I might actually send her a letter, or some form of written correspondence as an anonymous tip-off, just to suggest some alterations to her normal attire and proffer some ideas of what are generally regarded as appropriate, professional and yet seductively sophisticated ensembles, when we arrive at the science room that Mister Johnson appears to be permanently situated in this term. Mister White deigns to administer a perfunctory knock on the door, before opening it with his customary aggressive jolt and I toddle in after him, grateful at least to have reached some sanctuary away from the prying eyes in the corridor. Mister Johnson is standing on the elevated platform where the teacher's desk is situated at the top of the laboratory. He's wearing a full white coat and goggles, while holding a wriggling earthworm in a forceps with one hand, and one of those surgical type blades in the other. I can tell immediately that it's all just for show and as he raises his eyes to look at his recent arrivals, he affects that blank expression of ignorance on his face, like he's totally unaware of the reason for our presence in his classroom, but when you actually know him, it's easy to see that his eyes are laughing and that he's taking the complete piss. I mean, why does he need to wear goggles if he's dissecting an earthworm? I mean, is it in case the perfidious Lumbricus Terrestris breathes fire at his face, thus employing its legendary defensive mechanism, responsible for the pitifully avoidable deaths of so many overly curious toddlers and careless fishermen alike? "Now Mister Johnson", Mister White begins, "I have this little scallywag here for ye now. Put your baggage down at that table there Mister Doyle." I compliantly follow my year head's directions and take my schoolbag off my shoulders, placing it on the ground underneath a desk while putting my jacket that I had been carrying over my arm on the back of a chair. I immediately

71

become self-conscious about my hands and I'm not sure whether to hold them at my sides, which always make me feel a bit Frankensteinesque, or in my pockets, which would certainly seem a tad casual, so I eventually find a compromise for my vacillating mind by employing one hand to each postural position. "Hands out of your pockets now Mister Doyle, you're not standin on the corner wit your mates now boy." I actually have to bite my tongue at this latest reprimand and outrageously inaccurate appraisal of my personality and decide to just hold my hands behind my back, it being the only remaining option, and I immediately realise that it actually is the optimal stance, as it gives an air of being suitably respectful while at the same time feeling quite comfortable and indeed relaxing. "Now Mister Doyle", the culchie swine continues, and I make a mental note to discuss plans with Tarzan to initiate a pranking-it-up operation, the likes of which we have yet to embark upon, in order to bring this meddling fool down to size. "Do you want to talk about what you did during Mister Johnson's class or are you goin to just stand there and gawk at us like a bloody imbecile, ha?" He just stands there and stares at me expectantly, waiting for me to begin a confessional testimony and I'm suddenly very aware that I can't think of anything to say. I glance at Mister Johnson who has affected this "how very disappointing" expression and is shaking his head like he is incredulous at my brazen obstreperousness. "Well, what have ye got to say for yourself then?" Mister White raises his voice with this latest accusatory question and his tone is becoming even more noticeably agitated. I realise that I'm compelled to think of something as Mister Johnson, who at this stage I feel like slicing open with his ridiculous surgical knife which he is still incidentally and quite unnecessarily holding in his hand, is refusing for whatever reason to come to my assistance in any way. I'm about to launch into some concocted story, trying to decide between saying that I was uncharacteristically talkative during yesterday's science lesson and not having my homework done when Mister Johnson eventually yields to his own good conscience and delivers a timely interjection in order to put me out of my misery.

"It's okay Mister White, I don't need to hear anything out of this fella's mouth. I'll go and get the evidence and show it to him, and then we'll see what he has to say." Mister Johnson manages to wink in my direction as he's saying this and Mister White seems completely oblivious to the satirical tone of voice the rookie science teacher affects during moments such as these. Normally, Mister Johnson pulls these kinds of capers on Tarzan, who isn't bothered by them in any case, plus Tarzan has a habit of landing himself in hot water anyway so it doesn't really make much of a difference to his scholastic life. I admittedly do find these moments a little more taxing and just a smidgen more humiliating, but I haven't managed to raise my embarrassment threshold quite to the level of Tarzan's, despite both of our consumptions of legal life enhancing substances being pretty much identical. Mister Johnson puts down the surgical blade on the desk beside us and kind of toddles around in circles with the earthworm still prised between the large tweezers in his left hand, wondering where to place the squirming invertebrate and I'm trying to guess what piece of contrived evidence the mad man is going to produce in order to convict me on this trumped up charge. Eventually Mister White grabs the earthworm with a thrust of his arm and squeezes it in his hand, like he thinks he's some kind of strongman that a James Bond villain would have for doing his dirty muscle work for him. Even Mister Johnson can't hide his incredulity at the unsightly spectacle and it becomes evident when Mister White realises that he hasn't really thought this one through as he tries to conceal an expression of mild disgust from enveloping his red face. He then reclaims his hand with a violent motion, like he was pulling a bloody calf out of a cow in labour and throws the remnants of the squashed worm at a bin that resides next to the white wall of the laboratory. Unfortunately, his accuracy has obviously been affected by his years of heavy drinking and the worm lands a little high of the bin, sticking to the white wall in a tangled and unseemly mess. Neither myself nor Mister Johnson says anything as Mister White takes a generically monikered handkerchief out of his trouser pocket, wipes his hands of the offending puss and congealed intestine while muttering "bastard yokes" to himself, quite audibly but under his breath, before replacing the handkerchief into his pocket with an awkward, stuffing motion. "Now Mister Johnson", he says, while composing himself after his recent bizarre conduct. "Where's this evidence ye have for me anyway?" "Oh yes Mister White", Mister Johnson says. "I have the very thing you're looking for right here." Mister Johnson places the tweezers which once imprisoned the earthworm in its metallic grasp on the desk beside him, before strolling proudly over to another desk and slowly drawing out a stool which was pushed carefully underneath it, taken from the exact position occupied by my good self during my biology classes. Mister Johnson then carries the stool over as if he's about to present me with a gun which has been forensically proven to have been used in a recent murder case and is covered in my finger prints and forcefully places it at my feet, like he's both literally and metaphorically laying the charge before me. I look down at the wooden part of the stool and I'm more confused and perplexed at what I see than anything else, as I try to decipher the childish squiggles on its amber coloured surface. It takes me a few seconds to realise what the mass of black marker hieroglyphics signify, as it suddenly becomes very clear indeed. On the stool there is a childish drawing of a female with superhumanly large breasts and accompanying gigantic nipples. Underneath the somewhat surrealist depiction of the womanly form lies a caption which reads "Miss O' Loughlin is a ride and has massive tits! DD". I immediately recognise that the initials are meant to equate to my own and along with the fact that the stool was found where I normally sit, serves as a clear indictment of my guilt in this transgression. I understand that the wanton defacement of school property is normally treated with nothing more than a slap on the wrists and I'm willing to accept whatever meagre punishment may be dealt my way. The portrait of a voluptuous female figure is really primary school stuff and in all honesty, I'm more annoyed about the fact that Mister Johnson has fabricated such a juvenile and low brow prank for me to have committed and the manner in which this may affect my intellectual standing and reputation amongst the school's elder statesmen, then I am about the actual punishment. I am however, still a tad in the dark as to the identity of the dedication on the picture. I have no idea who Miss O' Loughlin is and I'm repeating the name over and over in my head, trying to assign a corresponding visage to the appellation when it finally hits me. At first I'm a little disturbed and at most a little upset at the realisation, before becoming curious and more than a little suspicious, as I make eye contact with the impish Mister Johnson, and I know there has to be something more to this.

Miss O' Loughlin is this ghostly septuagenarian woman, who sporadically manifests in Mister Johnson's biology classes to inspect him on his educational abilities. I only know her name because Mister Johnson introduced her to us in September and cunningly informed us that she would be visiting our class from time to time in order to keep track of our behavioural and intellectual progress. Of course, this kind of mendacity doesn't really work with fifth years and we are perhaps unfortunately for Mister Johnson, well aware that it is he who is being scrutinised and not our good selves as he may wish us to believe. We've all had our fair share of student teachers at this stage of our scholarly journey, and witnessed some extremely memorable and quite laughable psychological collapses during their inspections. It is incredibly amusing to watch formerly idealistic neophytes, literally melt in front of your eyes, it's truly the essence of good entertainment and if you really want me to watch reality television, you could do worse than installing cameras in student teachers' classrooms and making a programme out of the shambolic and often disturbing events that unfold. I think my personal favourite meltdown was when we were in first year and for two or three months we had this fat, cross-eyed religion teacher for the last period on Friday afternoons and who we imaginatively enough used to call "Fat Cross-Eyed Religion Teacher." His classes were complete chaos and resembled what I imagine a small Lithuanian village would look like, while being looted by advancing red army conscripts who had just discovered the location of a local girls' boarding school, after recently finding the keys to the town's vodka distillery. There would just be this absolute frenzy of mayhem, as pens, pencil cases, chairs and desks flew through the air while twelve and thirteen year old boys, some of whom were actually shaving at this stage, wrestled each other around the classroom and screamed nonsensical statements like they had regressed to some infantile mental state, just for these forty minutes every week. The actual format of the classes became paradoxically formulaic, as the lessons gradually degenerated into a predictable routine of destruction. Normally, Fat Cross-Eyed Religion Teacher would make some pitiful attempt at beginning a lesson which would quickly descend into anarchy and he would spend the next twenty minutes running around the classroom, shouting at people to sit down and ordering them to the principal's office as they laughed in his face at the absurd impossibility of his command. He had this really bizarre high-pitched northern accent as well and really in retrospect, the guy had absolutely nothing going for him from the start;

really he should never have been let near a classroom in the first place, as it was clear to see for any semi-sane human being that he was simply a time bomb waiting to explode in a fiery morass of adolescent aggression. Everyone would then start mimicking his accent and shouting at each other to "sit dine, sit dine" and "go way ti the principawls office yie." Tarzan used to love impersonating the shrill northern intonation of Fat Cross-Eyed Religion Teacher and would shout it out louder than anyone else while laughing hysterically. He thought his affectation was the most accurate portrayal among the entire group, even though it sounded nothing like Fat Cross-Eyed Religion Teacher and sounded more like a mentally retarded Pakistani on speed. But of course there wasn't exactly a queue of people waiting to enlighten Tarzan on his lack of impersonating skills as even then he was at least twice the size of the smallest of our classmates.

Anyway, Fat Cross-Eyed Religion Teacher's classes continued on in this vain for a number of weeks until one day when we marched merrily to our final period of the week and saw this decrepit old man dressed in a dodgy suit and carrying an ancient briefcase, positioning himself in a seat at the back of the classroom. Even at that stage, I think we'd worked out that the old guy was there to evaluate the ineptitude of our reluctant educationalist and the tension in the air was so palpable you could practically ride it, as we prepared to take our seats. The lesson took on its usual format with Fat Cross-Eyed Religion Teacher telling us to open up our books on page forty nine and there was some piece about Helen Kellor which he obviously intended to be the main focus of the class. As I said, the guy was a danger to himself and to society. I mean, out of all the topics and all the people we could have studied that day, why did he have to pick a story about a deaf, dumb and blind woman, who was the subject of so many tasteless yet hilarious schoolyard jokes. A newspaper report on paedophile priests probably would have had more chance of succeeding, but as I said, the man was a complete idiot; he was truly living on planet cross-eyed land. I suppose at first, things were actually much quieter for much longer than would normally have been the case, as we were all conscious of the inspector in the room and as I said, we were only first years, he probably wasn't really expecting too much hassle out of us, especially as St. Leonard's would have been considered a decent enough educational establishment in the first place. But soon enough everything began to go badly awry. As my classmates were taking turns reading aloud the article on Helen Kellor, the murmuring sniggers gradually rose in volume until there was open and voluble laughter among the entire cohort. Then came the classic one liners. Kieran McDermott shouted across to, I think Adam Lynch, "Jaysus, she'd be a handy victim for you Lynchie ye sicko. She wouldn't know what was happnin an ye'd already have blown your muck inside her!" Jimbo Walsh interposed and said "Not as easy as your ma was for me last night macker. Except I was the victim in that case. Your ma's a sick beast man!" All this was taken in the amiable spirit of ribaldry but it initiated the general slide of the class into all out war. Kieran McDermott took out a full A4 pad and started ripping out pages and scrunching them up into spheroid paper projectiles which he then proceed to fire indiscriminately around the room. Eventually he made the mistake of hitting Tarzan, who now that I think about it, was more than likely producing an inordinate amount of testosterone at that time and had a fuse on him like a badly constructed, improvised hand grenade, that's just been made by a drunken Albanian partisan. It wasn't so much that the spheroid paper projectile made contact with Tarzan that really set him off, it was more to do with the fact that it actually stuck in his hair without him noticing, until everyone started pointing and laughing at him and he went red in the cheeks and shook his hands through his hair, thus dislodging the offending object in the process. He looked at the spheroid paper projectile with a countenance of disgust and I, having become well accustomed to this expression, realised immediately that my associate's inherent anger at the world would once more manifest itself in a revenge-driven tornado of rage. Tarzan looked across the room at Kieran McDermott who was laughing idiotically but in such an affected way that it was obvious, at least to me anyway, that he was attempting to mask the sense of unease which must have been rising through his body, as he saw Tarzan's towering presence move its hulking mass towards him. For what must have been no more than a second but which felt like an hour, there was actually complete silence in Fat Cross-Eyed Religion Teacher's class as we all waited for Tarzan's next move. Eventually, in typical showbiz fashion, he delivered a fitting climax to the suspense he'd created by grabbing his desk and hurling it across the room at Kieran McDermott, in a single motion of animalistic fury. The feat is actually doubly impressive on reflection, as it was one of those desk and chair in one combinations that we all used in that classroom, and the awkwardness and weight involved in launching one of those across the room with both the accuracy and ferocity of a V2 missile on an English city, is truly a demonstration of strength to a near herculean proportion. Anyway, the chair and desk combination scored a direct hit on its intended victim, inflicting superficial damage, namely a broken nose which proceeded to gush blood all over the classroom floor and the unceremonious extraction of two front teeth, which were a little over-protruding in any case and the consequential repair job was in fact an unequivocal improvement. In reality, Tarzan probably did Kieran McDermott a massive favour in a multitude of different ways. I'm fairly sure he received compensation from the school as a result of his injuries as a thirteen-year old Tarzan could hardly have been expected to be held culpable alongside an inept student teacher who was also at the time being assessed by a fully qualified inspector. I also remember there being a marked alteration in the temperament and conduct of Kieran McDermott which has lasted to this day. He's a thoroughly more affable and agreeable young man these days and he has certainly never dared to be anything other than the absolute gentleman to both myself and Tarzan. But of course the injuries sustained to Kieran McDermott's person on that occasion were only half the story, which is why my musing's on Mister Johnson's Miss O' Loughlin-related prank brought me to this in the first place.

Fat Cross-Eyed Religion Teacher's inspector who I think at this stage, the majority of the class had completely forgotten was even there, was I began to notice, extremely still in his seat at the back at the class. I turned around to observe him as the majority of my classmates gathered around Kieran McDermott, arguing over whether he should lean his head backwards or forwards in order to stem the tide of blood and mucus that was oozing from his fractured nasal related facial feature. Robbie Turner stormed into the melee of erroneous medical information shouting; "Stand back! I'm in the Order of Malta!" while pushing people out of his highly-qualified, self-important path, barking at people to get him some tissues as if it took a genius to think of doing that. Fat Cross-Eyed Religion Teacher had finally broken down and sat at the top of the class sobbing with his brainless head in his chubby hands. Tarzan had simply ordered the boy who was placed behind him, to relinquish his seat and had positioned himself in his freshly commandeered chair and desk combination, leaning back with an air of satisfaction, evidently content at the mayhem and disorder he had brought to our Religion class. I remember turning my gaze once again to the inspector at the back of the room and I noticed that aside from being perfectly still, his eyes were shut tight and he was slouched in his chair and desk combination, almost like he had fallen asleep while watching an episode of Miss Marple or whatever people of his vintage get their kicks from on the television. I think I realised fairly soon that it would be pretty near impossible for anyone, no matter how decrepit they were, to have fallen asleep in such a small space of absolute chaos and I was just about to point out to anyone willing to listen that there appeared to be a deceased old man at the back of the classroom when I heard Robbie Turner yelling; "Man down! Man Down!" and rushing towards the slouching figure. He quickly grabbed the man's wrist to check his pulse and then started slapping him repeatedly on the face shouting; "Don't die on me, damn you! Don't die on me!" He managed to wrestle the increasingly whitening figure of the inspector out of the chair and desk combination and lie him down on the ground, flinging other desk and chair combinations around the room in order to establish himself in an adequately spaced resuscitating area, to administer CPR to his by now, clearly dead patient. Turner ripped open the inspector's shirt and drew a small pen knife from his own school trouser and cut the man's tie from around his neck. He then began pressing down heavily on the inspector's chest with his two hands, pounding his patient's heart with his clasped hands, while stooping down to close his mouth around the old man's, breathing air into his inert lungs in an action which even then caused ripples of laughter and cries of "bum basher!" from the assembled student body, that looked on with an increasingly knowing sense that the man had met his maker. Adam Lynch took a ten box of John Player Blue and a book of hotel matches from his pocket and lit up a cigarette for himself. He then walked over to Fat Cross-Eyed Religion Teacher, who remained sobbing on his chair behind the teacher's desk, and in perhaps the first gesture of kindness or understanding that any of had ever shown our budding professor, offered him one of his cigarettes. At first, the crying figure appeared slightly stunned and unsure of what to do before accepting with a look that showed that he had resigned himself to the inevitable and had realised that perhaps teaching was not for him. Adam lit Fat Cross-Eyed Religion Teacher's cigarette from the burning ash of his own and the two of them sat at the top of the class, surveying the wreckage before them. Robbie Turner refused to admit defeat and continued to breathe air into the dead man's lungs and pump his still heart, but by now with a slowing and tiring cadence. I half expected him to reach once more for his penknife and attempt open heart surgery right there and then when a knock sounded on the door and we all turned to see Mister Murray, who was at that time only a mere teacher and had yet to rise to the rank of Principal, poking his head into the classroom. He seemed to briefly scan the entire room before turning his gaze on a petrified-looking Fat Cross-Eyed Religion Teacher and said; "Can I borrow your overhead projector by any chance? The bulb seems to have gone in mine."

As my inner-recollecting of that eventful and indeed legendary class period comes to an end, I quickly realise that my reminiscing has actually caused me to emit a slight chuckle which I masterfully manage to mutate into a short, sharp and chesty cough and judging by the face of Mister White, who is manically staring at me with a hateful and vindictive glint in his eyes, my ruse appears to have been successfully executed, and he doesn't seem to have noticed my laughing at this rather inopportune moment. I'm also reminded of the precarious nature of my immediate situation, after almost forgetting about my current predicament while daydreaming about the halcyon days of my youth, as Mister White elevates the stool to my eye level, so that I have a clear and unobstructed view of my supposed handy work. The legs of the stool are in such close proximity to my face that I'm actually flinching as my grating year head launches into another tirade. At this stage I've grown rather weary of this entire charade, but of course I'm compelled to listen as Number One: He's shouting at me at a volume, similar to that achieved by a mating warthog at the moment of ejaculation, so that it's physically impossible for me not to listen and Number Two: Because I am naturally curious to get to the bottom of Mister Johnson's prank, as it is only gentlemanly to recognise a fellow prankster's work and possibly if it's a well-worked and majestically conceived piece of Tom foolery, it will unquestionably serve to relieve the tedium and boredom of everyday life, which is the number one motivating factor behind every single action which myself and my associates perform in our daily lives. Mister Johnson is at this stage standing slightly behind Mister White and is actually making wanking gestures behind his superior's back, before adopting an overly sincere and concerned countenance whenever my year head turns to meet his gaze. I really have to hand it to Mister Johnson all the same. His subversion of the educational establishment has reached a level that even I can only aspire towards at this stage of my life and I will deign to admit that I have to admire the man's work on so many levels. Mister White continues his diatribe but lowers his voice a little and I'm guessing he's doing this for a theatrical effect, in order to highlight the important and life-defining nature of his words. If he doesn't practice this stuff in front of a mirror at home, then I'm not a leading purveyor of alternative and legal life-enhancing products, sold in order to subvert the subversive and provide me with the necessary financial clout for eventual world domination. "To think that someone could do this, in my school, honestly Mister Johnson, I don't think I've ever seen anything as insensitive in all my years of teaching. I really can't understand how you can live with yourself Mister Doyle. It makes me doubt my very vocation to think that a St. Leonard's boy would carry out such a monstrous act of wanton vandalism. Do you know what Miss O' Loughlin did when she saw this Mister Doyle?" Even I'm beginning to feel guilty by now, such is the sincerity of Mister White's tone. I suppose he really is a decent actor. Maybe that's why he's such a disagreeable old sort, because he's the classic failed artist turned teacher, who's venting the anger caused by his unrealised ambitions on his scholastic charges. "I don't know sir, but I suppose maybe she was hurt by the drawing?" This response seems to almost please my verbal assailant before he once more becomes a little heated. "You're damn right she was upset, you're damn bloody right. But apart from that she's quit her job, working as a school inspector and she didn't even miss more than a day or two while she was battling her cancer." Mister White's tone reaches a level so high that it sounds almost like he's on the brink of an emotional collapse. I'm merely a tad surprised at the revelation of Miss O' Loughlin's illness and it's only when I see Mister Johnson sniggering behind Mister White's back that I manage to fill in the blanks for myself. Mister White continues; "Do you know what Mister Doyle? I'm not even going to waste any more of my breath on you. Mister Johnson has assured me that he has a serious punishment lined up for you so you'll atone for the transgressions you've made on a sick and elderly woman through the power of hard work and toil. And listen to me Doyle." The lack of a "Mister" evidently conveys my descent in respectability in a linguistic manner. The guy truly is some performer. "If you ever step over the line again." While speaking, Mister Johnson spits ceremonially on the floor between us and then wipes it across with his foot in a sharp sweeping motion, slightly losing his balance while doing so and very nearly falling over. He quickly regains his balance and composure, although blushing a modicum in the cheeks. Mister Johnson completely turns his back to the whole scene and pretends to arrange some sheets of paper on his desk, but I can tell from his almost imperceptibly gyrating shoulders that he's in tears laughing. Mister White finishes his monologue by saying. "You step over this line again Doyle." He gestures towards the trail of saliva he's just constructed at the base of my feet and I look reverentially down to marvel at his dramatic prop, while noticing for the first time, droplets of spittle that have been deposited on my good school shoes over the course of the entire charade. "I'll have your ass Doyle, and I mean it. I WILL HAVE YOUR ASS."

Mister White finally exits the room with his usual contrived swagger and Mister Johnson finally turns around as soon as Mister White shuts the door behind him. "Ha ha Dosser, the look on your fuckin face man. I thought you were gonna mess yourself there for a minute. You need to lighten up a bit. Tarzan woulda just lapped that shit up. You need to lay off the Alpha Chlorolose. It's evidently havin a detrimental effect on your nervous system. I've told you that stuff's not safe in the long term. That's why we've got to finish producing this substitute pronto. I've a lavish lifestyle to bank roll here man, ye know what I mean?" Mister Johnson grabs his balls while uttering this rhetorical question and kind of gyrates a little, while adopting an expression of animalistic lasciviousness on his face. He's a lot like Gobber in that respect, in that he seems to be constantly informing me of the vastness of his sexual experiences, although in fairness to Mister Johnson, he doesn't really go on about it as much as Gobber and what's more I'm almost positive he's nearly always telling the truth, whereas the veracity of Gobber's testimonies of sexual conquests is certainly up for debate. "Well with all due respect sir, it was merely the equivocation surrounding the events of the last twenty minutes that caused me to feel understandably a tad nervous, I mean, I had absolutely no idea what was going to happen from one second to the next, and I must admit I was slightly aggrieved upon learning of Miss O' Loughlin's illness. If what I'm suspecting is true, vis a vis the connection between her cancer and the infantile scribbles that you appropriated to my good self, I have to say that even I feel that's in bad taste and I once urinated in a baptismal font."

"Yeah, ha ha. You suspect correctly my good man. Double mastectomy two weeks ago and you, you sick and deranged little bastard thought it would be funny to draw a picture of her with oversized tits on the underside of a laboratory stool! You're fuckin lucky by the way. Aul Whiteser wanted to fuck you out of the school. I managed to persuade him to let me deal with it, citing your immaculate conduct record and academic potential as reasons to back me up. I suppose he probably wasn't really bothered with the hassle of it all himself. He blows out of steam surprisingly quickly sometimes."

"Well I suppose I'll have to thank you for that, even if you did land me in the excrement, unnecessarily if I may add, in the first place. Do we really have to go through these overly complicated theatricalities all the time, just to enable me to stay behind in the science lab? I mean, could we not just say we're working on some kind of project, The Young Scientist competition for example?"

"Ah well, of course we could, but where would the fun in that be Dosser? You're too long in the tooth for that award anyway; it's purely a Transition Year thing now. Ah but come on Dosser, don't look so down. Mister White will forget about this in a few weeks, guaranteed. There'll be no need for any more excuses from now on. I have to be careful man, I can't have anybody thinking that I'm molesting you in here, even though I suppose at your age it'd almost just be straight up homosexual activity. That'd be even worse, well maybe not worse but you know what I mean. Imagine I got accused of tappin your pretty white ass in here? My carreer would be over before it had even begun. Take one for the team Dosser, take one for the team."

"But what about the emotional damage inflicted on Miss O' Loughlin? Did she really deserve to have a student mock the fact that she was suffering cancer, and had just had the most tangible corporeal vestige of her womanhood surgically removed?" Of course I can see the hilarity in Mister Johnson's actions but you know, I must endeavour to try and make him feel at least a tidbit of remorse after the humiliation I have just endured.

"Ah, she was a bitch man. She was givin me such an average mark for my teaching practice, she had to go. She told me my lessons needed more "spunk", no word of a lie. I told her I'd give her all the spunk she wanted but I don't think she got it. Or maybe she did actually, maybe that's why she was such a bitch to me?" Mister Johnson puts his index finger to his cheek in a ponderous fashion and looks up to the ceiling as if searching for an answer to his consideration. I notice for the first time that his eyes are a little blurry, and I'm certain he's been smoking something, I suspect Cystisus Scoparius, judging by the sickly sweet aroma, that is just now beginning to assail my senses as Mister Johson leans over me to grab a bunch of keys off the desk behind me. "Right come on then Dosser, we better get to work. We don't want to be here all day. I've a date with a serious piece of pussy later and I know she's got a busy evening cos she has to put your dinner in front of ye when ye get home! Ha ha, ah no I'm only messin man. I wouldn't touch your ma with Tarzan's."

Mister Johnson grabs the bunch of keys off the desk and walks leisurely up onto the platform at the front of the classroom and behind the teacher's desk to the cabinet of dodgy-ness. He crouches down to rummage in the cabinet and I can no longer see him behind the teacher's desk, except for when his arm periodically appears to place the various items of all our necessary equipment on the desktop. I walk over to the coat stand in the corner of the room, where I take my personal white laboratory coat off one of the hooks, and procure a pair of surgical gloves from the box on top of a chest of drawers, that contains items diverse as desiccated daffodils, showing the various sections of the flower's reproductive organs, to the cadavers of dissected rabbits. As I proceed to clothe myself in the requisite vestments of laboratorial science, I notice on the back, that the word "Tosser" has been written in large black pen, the same implement which I suspect Mister Johnson utilised in his recent diagrammatical escapade. I turn around to my associate, who has managed to peak his head just above the edge of the desk so he can witness my reaction to this most unimaginative of practical jokes. He's grinning widely and the goggles on his black-haired head are perched in such a position, that they give him the look of a giant insect from an archaic science fiction film. "Very mature and indeed professional of you sir, I'm glad much needed school funds are being so conscientiously and economically employed by our ever diligent teaching staff. I suppose you didn't manage to learn a sense of humour during your time at university then?" Mister Johnson pounces to his feet while slamming the door shut of the cabinet of dodgy-ness. "It's you who doesn't have the sense of humour Dosser. Lighten up homey and throw me over the box of gloves." I duly consent to my colleague's request and fling the vessel of latex-based hand garments as close to his face as I can manage, without appearing overly-truculent or as though I'm actually bothered by his inane and infantile decoration of my coat. The only reason it bothers me in the slightest, is that a great number of the student cohort in my year, seem to have adopted "Tosser" as an acceptable moniker for me, playing on my actual name by ingeniously replacing the first letter with another. It's surprising really, that this insidious trend didn't start until a number of years ago, but I literally have only begun to notice its endemic usage in the last few months. Mister Johnson is of course well aware of this recent development which is why he has committed this vile act upon my person. My normal reaction to any adverse conditions such as these, which could affect my standing amongst the student body and therefore, mainstream society at large, is to feign total insouciance towards the situation as I believe that if I allowed anybody to perceive that it upset me in anyway, it would only serve to encourage an escalation of the problematic development. Obviously, much to my surprise and annoyance, I must be conveying visual cues of discomfort to the people in my immediate environs, otherwise Mister Johnson would not have picked up on it, and I must endeavour to ameliorate my powers of emotional dissembling in order to prevent and discourage further transgressions centring on the usage of my novel nickname.

Mister Johnson snaps the gloves on while stretching them to the utmost of their elasticity. "You should really refrain from doing that" I advise, "you'll only cause apertures to appear in the fabric, methanol can be a serious irritant you know." "Oooh, sorry mister know-it-all" he retorts, "who's the science teacher here eh? WHO'S THE FAHKING SCIENCE TEACHAAH?" He screams this last sentence in a kind of bad cockney accent, while pressing his face right up to my own and laughs in his customary high pitched alto. "Did ye never see the film "Scum" no? Fuckin savage film. Nice anal rape scene in it. Man on man shit, right up your street Dosser." I simply choose to ignore him and take the CD player and the CD bag from the dusty, smelly cabinet below the wash hand basin on the teacher's desk. I turn on the CD player and search through the CD collection before settling on *"The Best of Punk and New Wave"* compilation and duly withdraw the musical accompaniment for today's proceedings from its plastic abode. When I open the case, a pang of frustration surges through my cerebral cortex. "Has Tarzan been at these CDs again? The *Trance Nation* CD is in *The Best of Punk and New Wave* compilation case. Does he really expect me to listen to that soundtrack to the lives of the culturally bereft? I mean, do I wear Ben Sherman shirts with tracksuit bottoms?" "Relax Dosser, Tarzan's entitled to his taste in music. There's no right and wrong when it comes to taste is there?" Mister Johnson deliberately says this in order to goad me into exploding into a rant on the artistic credibility of the various categories of popular music throughout the generations, but I manage to summon up a Christ-like demonstration of restraint and refuse to rise to the bait, bearing in mind we have a serious amount of work to get through over the next two hours. "Ah I'm only playin witcha Dosser. Go down to the back of the room there and get the hair dryer and a couple of coffee jars from the back press. I'll sort the music out. You know you can trust me." He gives me a wink in an almost avuncular fashion and I feel like smashing him across the face with the CD player for his utterly offensive condescension when I realise how important Mister Johnson has become to our operations, and instantaneously, feel strangely thankful for the improved use of facilities and astronomically increased profit levels that his arrival to St. Leonard's has brought us. I begin walking down the classroom and Mister Johnson shouts "the hairdryer's in the Shamrock Rovers bag, coffee jars are where you left them" while I can hear the dulcet tones of Jello Biafra beginning to ascend through the dusty air.

I carry the Shamrock Rovers bag and two large, empty Nescafe jars back to the teacher's desk. Mister Johnson arranges bottles of methanol and toluene on the table, placing a large fan on the very edge, right next to the wash hand basin. He then reaches underneath the desk and after a few moments, resurfaces with a wide and rather deep metal tray, filled with the aromatic leaves of the Ma Huang plant, one of the newest editions to our horticultural family. We've managed to cultivate quite a sizable crop in the greenhouse here in school, but as we are still very much in the development stage of our latest life-enhancing product, the level of Ma Huang growth has yet to be justified. I harvested three large plants yesterday morning and managed to drop them into the science lab, just before the start of Mister Johnson's first class. Mister Johnson hands me the large metal tray and for the next two hours, everything is strictly business. "Here you are Mister Doyle. If you'll forgive me, I took the liberty of pre-grinding the Ephedra Sinica leaves for you as I understand how bothersome you find that particular process to be. Now be a dear and take the tray over to your usual operating table and don't forget to put on your breathing mask." I duly carry the tray over to my operating table and withdraw a face mask from the deep, right pocket of my lab coat. The mask appears just a tad dusty, but it will still surely suffice for this particular purpose. The ground up leaves of the Ma Huang tend to invade one's facial orifices when manipulating them, so the face mask has become an essential item of accoutrement. The fumes from the methanol also tend to cause one to become nauseous, so the face mask serves to offer at least some protection from that particular occupational hazard. I set the metal tray down on the table and fetch a large cream-coloured bowl, a square piece of cloth and a colander from another storage cabinet that we use, located around half way down the room. I bring my recently acquired pieces of equipment back to the table and I start whistling along to *Sound of the Suburbs* beneath my dusty face mask, as Mister Johnson appropriately adjusts the volume on the CD player to equate with the quality of the song. I can see that he is by now, measuring large amounts of Sudafed tablets on a weighing scales. Mister Johnson claims he is having an illicit affair with a pharmacy lecturer in college, who is able to supply him with certain useful prescription and non-prescription drugs. Whether it's true or not is quite irrelevant, as the man unquestionably has access to a greater amount of laboratorial materials then his position as a student science teacher warrants. As I've stated previously, he has been an invaluable addition to our operations, but I do wonder occasionally if there's a possibility we have become too reliant on him. I set the bowl down on the table and place the colander within its ceramic embrace, before lining the colander with the sheet of thin, bandage-like material. I take my personal weighing scales from the shelf above my personal operating table, along with my personal weighing vessel, which is a lunch box size metal container. I set the weighing scales on the table and measure out 850 grams of the ground up Ma Huang leaves. I then proceed to scoop up four loads of the ground-up Ma Huang with my two hands cupped together and allow the powdery substance to fall within the clothed colander. Once I've completed this stage of the process, I walk over to the teacher's desk and retrieve a bottle of methanol from beside the wash hand basin, along with its accompanying measuring cup. Mister Johnson is currently sliding the Sudafed tablets into the empty coffee jars, using a scoop that I'm almost positive he must have pilfered from the "pick 'n' mix" in the local newsagent. I return to my own base of operations, pour 400 millilitres of methanol into the measuring cup, before emptying the odorous liquid on top of the Ma Huang powder. I shake the colander slightly and mix the powdered leaves with my gloved hands as if I'm in the process of making the base of a cake. I lift up the colander and observe the liquid, which has the appearance of dirty water, draining into the bowl beneath it. Once all the liquid has run through the colander, I measure out another 400 millilitres of methanol and repeat this washing of the powdered leaves process, a further two occasions. Once all of the liquid has drained through the colander after the third rinsing, I very carefully carry the bowl and its precious liquid, over to a small desk in the very top corner of the classroom. I can feel my hands beginning to shake and I start to feel rather self-conscious for some reason, and the more I think about the precariousness of the situation, the worse my nerves become. I glance over in the direction of Mister Johnson. He looks briefly over at me and smiles, but very much in an empathetic and non-derisory manner. We really are quite professional once the hard work begins, after all, there is a great deal of financial potential in the end product of our present endeavours, so it pays not to annoy your colleagues when your both working towards the same end. "A tricky one that" he says, as he begins to pour methanol straight from the bottle, on top of the Sudafed tablets in one of the coffee jars. I manage to deliver my precious cargo to its intended destination, without landing face first in its contents or smashing the bowl on the laboratory floor. The Ma Huang and methanol mixture will be left on the table for around two weeks and allowed to evaporate until all that is left is a powdery, off-white substance. This will then be added to the pseudo-ephedrine powder, which we will extract from the Sudafed tablets. I walk over to Mister Johnson and find myself standing behind the teacher's desk and looking down the length of the classroom. It strikes me how strange it feels to survey a room I've sat in for the last five years from this novel perspective and for a brief moment I imagine how daunting it must be to actually stand up here in front of a class of 30 teenage boys, more Neanderthal than Homo Sapien and set about explaining to them, the biological properties and inner workings of the female reproductive system. I'm disturbed from my momentary reverie as Mister Johnson jolts me in the arm with his elbow and hands me one of the coffee jars which is now three quarters full of Sudafed tablets mixed with methanol. "Here you go Dosser, I know you've a fine pair of wrists on ye, well one good one anyway, what?" He then proceeds to pick up the second coffee jar from the desk and starts shaking it violently, before breaking into a kind of gyrating dance and working the coffee jar like it's some kind of percussion instrument while singing "Shake your money maker, shake your money maker!" He starts laughing and looks at me to see if I find his performance similarly humorous. I merely observe him with an incredulous stare. I don't find it funny; I just feel embarrassed.

After shaking the coffee jars for around ten minutes, we leave them to stand and will return to them tomorrow. By then, most of the Sudafed tablets will have semi-dissolved, forming a cloudy mixture which will eventually separate into two layers, with a kind of semi-solid substance resting on top of the methanol. The top layer will be the precious pseudo-ephedrine that we need to extract to create a wonder life-enhancing product that will undoubtedly take the streets by storm and hopefully replace the vile and pretentious substance of cocaine in the long run. I'm currently trying to decide on a brand name for the product, in order to aid the potential of word of mouth advertising and have found myself vacillating between the possibilities of "White Gold" and "Faux-caine", but I worry that the latter may be a tad too clever to really catch on among the general public, but I suppose these concerns can be dealt with in the coming weeks and the hard work of mass production must be attended to first. Once the pseudo-ephedrine has made its way to the top of the coffee jars, we can siphon off the substance and distribute it in shallow plastic trays. These trays will then be placed in the freezer which Mister Johnson somehow managed to liberate from the science building in University College Dublin and only once the pseudo-ephedrine becomes frozen, can we really begin the final stage of the quite laborious process. Mister Johnson walks into the storage room of the lab, right behind the teacher's desk to where he has ergonomically located our recently acquired chest freezer. While he roots around in the storage room, I set about changing the CD and eventually settle on Joy Division's *Unknown Pleasures*. Mister Johnson re-emerges with his usual "Here's one I made earlier" comment, carrying two trays of frozen pseudo-ephedrine, two sizable cooking pots and a large roll of filter paper. He hands me the two trays and the roll of filter paper and says "Get to work there Dosser" and I duly relocate back to my own personal operating table. I have to say, that Mister Johnson's constant commanding is beginning to irk me somewhat, however aware I am of how indebted our business and societal-ameliorating venture is to him, and I compel myself to accept his instructions in the interests of expediency and the maintenance of a healthy working environment. I place the two trays and the filter paper on my personal operating table, and retrieve another large white bowl, in addition to the hair drier which I take from the Shamrock Rovers bag. As I attend to my current labours, Mister Johnson is filling the two large cooking pots with water from the wash hand basin. He then sets about assembling the two-hob, makeshift cooker, which he has ingeniously fashioned via the manipulation of the Bunsen burner on the teacher's desk. His resourcefulness and ingenuity truly are admirable and the look of concentration on his face, spurs me to return to my task with a renewed vigour and sense of purpose. I cover one of the trays in a sheet of filter paper, before placing it upside down, on top of my large white bowl. I plug the hair drier into the nearby socket where the table meets the wall and proceed to hold the hair drier over the tray, and watch the viscous drips begin to fall slowly at first and then steadily into the awaiting white bowl, as the frozen pseudo-ephedrine begins to melt away from the tray. Once the entire contents of the tray have melted, I set about repeating the entire process with the second tray, before setting the entire mixture aside, and storing it in the storage cabinet, to the right of the teacher's desk. From this cabinet, I retrieve a bowl of the same mixture which Mister Johnson apparently prepared by himself yesterday and carry it over to where water is furiously boiling on Mister Johnson's makeshift cooker. I give Mister Johnson a signalling nod and he then proceeds to empty the boiling water from the two pots into the wash hand basin, both now being suitably sterilised. I decant the viscous pseudo-ephedrine equally between the two pots which Mister Johnson then replaces onto the two hobs of the makeshift cooker. After a few minutes, the mixture starts to reduce and becomes even thicker and Mister Johnson removes both pots from the heat. He assembles a new, gleaming white fan on his desk and faces it in the direction of the two pots before turning it on. He then once more disappears into the storage room before returning with a large Pyrex container. At this stage, the mixture in the two pots is beginning to form small crystals which we proceed to decant into the Pyrex container, using Mister Johnson's pilfered "pick 'n' mix" scoop. Mister Johnson reaches for the bottle of toluene and empties the contents on top of the white crystals. He mixes the two substances with his gloved hands before emptying the mixture back into one of the cooking pots, adding a small amount of water and replacing the pot on one of the makeshift hobs, while positioning the fan, so it blows over the pot as it simmers. We boil this mixture for a further five minutes and then filter it through some filtering paper. What comes through the filter paper should be superfluous waste products and what's left on top of the filter paper is an even more refined pseudo-ephedrine. We then put this refined pseudo-ephedrine and some acetone into another empty coffee jar which Mister Johnson duly agitates, before once more filtering through filter paper. Mister Johnson repositions the fan so it blows its electrically powered air over the pseudo-ephedrine in order to dry the substance. At this stage I look at my watch and hold it up for Mister Johnson to see; it's 1720 hours. He nods his head and I make my way to the door in order to retrieve my bicycle from its locked position beside the gymnasium. I stop to take my keys from the zip pocket at the front of my schoolbag as Mister Johnson prepares a sodium hydroxide solution and obtains a small plastic, wallet-like container, full of litmus paper from the storage room. I rush out the door, taking a quick visual sweep down both directions of the corridor and see nobody except for the mentally deranged cleaner who tells everyone he's a trained airline pilot, as he replaces replete rubbish bags with those of the vacuous nature. I quickly make my way down the corridor to the school's side entrance which leads me to the gym across the tarmac where my bicycle is parked. I remark the briskness of the early evening, noticing the visibility of my breath as it escapes from my lungs and mingles with the unseasonably cool April air. I unchain my pedalled transportation device from its open air incarceration and cycle it over to the main entrance of the school which is situated right beside the science lab and will therefore facilitate an easier exit for me on completion of my duties for this evening. I relock my two wheeled vehicle to a drain pipe beside the front door of the school and quickly make my way back to the science lab. As I re-enter the room, Mister Johnson has both the fan and the hair drier blowing over the by now, pure ephedrine, in order to expedite the drying of the valuable substance. Once fully dry, it will be first combined with the residue from the evaporated Ma Huang and methanol mixture, before other agents such as caffeine, glucose and vitamin C powder are added in order to increase the volume of our harvest, and also to decrease its potency for various and obvious reasons. "There's the man" he says while switching off the hair drier and removing his goggles and face mask from his ocular and oral areas respectively. The fan will have to be left blowing over the ephedrine for a further hour or so, just to ensure that any liquid residue is fully evaporated. "We'll just get tidied up here then you better shoot off. Don't want Mister White gettin suspicious. I'll have Tarzan in with me tomorrow to bag the goods, then you can come and collect them whenever you like. Will I get Tarzan to bring any back with him?" "You actually may as well sir. I've been working myself rather hard of late. Just tell Tarzan to bring the bags back to the greenhouse and to stash them 'you know where', he'll understand what I mean." I'm actually quite looking forward to having a couple of days off as a bit of rest and relaxation is well overdue. Plus, I have a whole series of World War Two in Colour recorded on tape, comprising of four hour-long episodes, as well as a feature length documentary entitled The Nazi War Machine, that I'm extremely keen on viewing post haste. I join Mister Johnson at the teacher's desk and take a couple of the bowls and metal trays which we have made use of during this evening's fabrications and begin rinsing them in the wash hand basin. Once the items are fully clean, I hand them to Mister Johnson who subsequently dries them with blue tissue paper and returns them either to the back storage room or to the cabinet of dodgy-ness. We leave the bowl of ephedrine and the fan where they are and Mister Johnson explains that he will remain behind for a further half hour, upon which time he will store away these last two remaining items. "Right, that's us so. Fancy a wee dabble before ye shoot off then?" Mister Johnson asks this while producing a small foil wrap of our previous attempt at this product, the samples of which we gave to Gobber who I really must catch up with before we decide to produce anymore, in order to ascertain the level of success or lack thereof which he may have experienced in the realm of on-the-street sales. "I see no reason why not sir, after all, I can't really expect others to do what I wouldn't do myself now can I?" I have of course, tested the product on several previous occasions and have found it to be overwhelmingly pleasant, with a side-effect of minor nasal irritation. Mister Johnson carefully unfurls the foil wrap and rests it safely in the upturned palm of his left hand, before scooping a sizable pinch onto an old 20 pence coin and sucking the white powder up his right nostril. He duly hands me the 20 pence coin and I cautiously procure a pinch for myself and inhale it through my own right nostril. "One more for the road sure" Mister Johnson says with a wink and a glint in his eye, and I naturally accept his offer, this time inhaling the snow white powder up my left nostril. "Plans for this evening sir?" I ask, sniffing sharply, three times in quick succession, feeling my eyes begin to water, slightly. "Have to meet that old lecturer bird I was tellin ye about. She's fuckin needy man. Husband left her for a younger woman, secretary or some clichéd bullshit like that. She's emotionally damaged man, but what can I do? She's become seriously vital to our whole venture here. I think she'd literally gimme her house if I asked her. Far from ideal set up but what can ye do?" I nod as a physical, communicative gesture of acquiescence and decide to refrain from any verbal response, limited as my knowledge of inter-gender relationships is to small number of tentative kisses behind a chip shop while on holidays in Wexford. I gather up my belongings, zipping up my adidas jacket to my chin and curse myself inwardly for neglecting to keep my gloves in my jacket pocket. I put on my bag and even now I can feel my energy levels increasing, along with the rate of my breathing. "I'm extremely unenthusiastic about the prospect of this cycle home sir. The temperature is ridiculously un-spring-like and I fear that it is certain to rain, as I've become convinced that precipitation awaits my departure from school before initiating its inclement and unwelcome descent upon the Earth, such is the regularity of this occurrence. What do you reckon sir? Is it possible that the celestial deities could be waging a meteorological guerrilla war against me for their sadistic pleasure?" "I reckon you should get a fuckin move on Dosser before your paranoia lands us both in trouble. Take it easy on the road out there and remember, keep everything strictly legal." Mister Johnson raises his hand in the air as a signal for me to high five him, a practice I normally have certain reservations about but at this moment I slap his palm with mine with such gusto that it causes him to grimace and I can feel a healthy stinging sensation on my hand as I march through the science lab door and once more into the corridor. I head towards the main exit and I can see down the corridor, Mister White struggling to lock his office door, clumsily negotiating the key with his right hand while simultaneously holding an old leather briefcase under his left arm with a large bundle of sheets prised precariously between his fingers. As I watch my old tormentor, I momentarily sense a melancholy surrounding his aura and almost pity him before the chill of the evening breeze assails my skin and causes me to emit a sudden, sharp shiver which brings me rapidly back to my senses. I quickly unlock my bike and wrap the chain around the cross bar as fast as I can as I don't wish to meet Mister White as he exits the building. I jump onto the saddle and pedal away with great ferocity, as a surge of energy pulses through my limbs and half way down the road, I can feel my body temperature rising as a result of my high-paced aerobic activity. I pick up quite a bit of speed on the long road leading up to the small roundabout and decide to freewheel for a little bit, most graciously aided by the downhill gradient of the road and a moderate breeze blowing at my back. I inhale the pleasant air deeply into my lungs and briefly lean my head back to turn my eyes to the sky, before the blast of a car horn enlightens me to the fact that I've drifted out somewhat into the middle of the busy main road, so I am forced to readjust my positioning lest I end up at the wrong end of a six car pile-up. I turn left at the small roundabout, glancing to the right in order to check for oncoming traffic before doing so and once more exert myself when I get back onto the straight, standing up in the saddle and sprinting as fast as I possibly can in order to make the green right turning arrow at the junction up ahead, which duly turns amber as I skilfully lean the bike to the right, taking me onto to the final stretch of my journey home. I sit back on my saddle, pedalling at a leisurely pace and I can feel the surge of energy with which I was so recently infused, begin to dissipate and I am aware that the effects of my recent dalliance are rapidly fading. For the next few minutes, I know that I will be caught between the no man's land of almost high and almost sober and at a time like this you can only wish for two things: that you either had more, or that you'd never done any in the first place. As I approach the bus terminus, I can see an unruly and most uncouth looking collection of four young men from Whitefield Community College, assembled on the footpath. One of them is throwing chips at three girls who are gathered around the bus stop, and are coquettishly half-running away as a means of evading the fried potato missiles. Two of the other young men appear to be engaged in some form of wrestling match while the fourth is kicking a flat, plastic football against the exterior of a bus shelter. A few minutes ago, I would have simply charged by this hooded throng, but the fact that I am currently experiencing an energy slump, coupled with the ending of Peter and Paul Smith's educational journey make the entire scene up ahead appear a little disquieting. Normally when Peter and Paul were still attending school, this wouldn't have been such a problem, but the fact that they are no longer among the groups of boys who form a virtual gauntlet by the roadside, means that I no longer have any personal connection with any of the group, and so there is no one there to grant me safe passage by the bus stop. I continue on down the road, exuding (or at least feigning) an air of calm as I pass by the small group of vacuous minded adolescents. I look straight ahead of me, pretending almost not to notice the group and just when I'm certain that I've made it by without any unwelcome incident, I perceive an incoming projectile out of the corner of my right eye, unwaveringly bearing down on me. Next, I hear a loud thud and I suddenly lose control of my bicycle, and I can see that the flat plastic football the fourth member of the gang had so recently been kicking against the bus shelter, is somehow lodged between the spokes of my front wheel. The ball emits a violently strange whizzing sound as it wrestles with its metal entanglement as I battle to regain dominion over my vehicle. I quickly realise that I have an Abyssinian infantry unit's chance of withstanding a mustard gas attack of steering back on course, as I veer straight across the road, narrowly avoiding an oncoming 15A and I'm spectacularly catapulted over the cross bar and land on my left hand side, skidding uncontrollably for around five metres before coming to an abrupt halt at the foot of the three, by now screaming girls. I can feel a stinging pain pulse down the length of my left perambulating limb, along with a dull heaviness in my left shoulder as cries of "Aw scarlet for ye youngfella!" and "The state of ye!" emerge from the cackling mouths of the females above me. Their male companions are laughing uncontrollably, but even I, in this moment of great personal trauma, can sense that they are overplaying it, in order not to lose face in front of their associates, as they fight against their natural human instinct to come to the aid of a fellow human being in distress. One of them starts shouting "The fuckin state of ye, ye fuckin posh cunt ye!" and I'm just about to point out that I more than likely have stronger Working Class credentials than him, when I hear the sudden roar of a diesel engine and the eardrum piercing squeak of a familiar set of dodgy brakes. I sit up momentarily to facilitate my ability to move my head and as I turn my torso around, I can see Gobber's white van, with both himself and Tarzan sitting in the cab, and for the second time in as many hours I consider the genuine possibility of the presence of an omnipotent and omniscient being, exerting some kind of control over the course of my life.

Gobber swings the door of the van open and leaps out like he's probably practiced it a million times while watching a marathon number of episodes of *Cops* in his bedroom. Next, Tarzan follows in a similarly hyperbolic fashion, brandishing a rather dangerous looking spirit level and I'm wondering: out of all the tools in the van that could be used as likely weapons, how in the name of Zeus did he manage to choose that one, before admitting that now really isn't the time to criticise my closest ally, considering he's just saved me from at most, a possible physical assault and at the very least, further excruciating embarrassment. "Fuck yous lookin at cunts? Fuck off out a here before I batter yis" Gobber shouts and I manage to stand up and dust myself off, extremely impressed by Gobber's commanding presence. The four boys immediately understand that they're out of their depth in this particular encounter and they all stand in an anxious silence before the one who I suspect kicked the ball at me says, "Here relax man, we weren't doin anything. Yer man fell off his fuckin bike an all, we were just laughin like. It was funny an all, relax like." The three girls have also been stunned into silence, but I can see that two of them are actually grinning, presumably because they're enjoying the scene, safe in the knowledge that if any physical violence does erupt, none of us will sink as low as to strike a member of the fairer sex, and it irks me that they are deriving some form of perverse and voyeuristic pleasure out of the entire precarious scenario. "Just fuck off lads, I mean it!" Gobber roars, as Tarzan in a paradoxically inexplicable yet typical action of his, steps from behind him and strikes the spirit level off the ground, which duly smashes in half as some kind of gesture of our combined strength and willingness to use force. The four boys walk grudgingly and silently away, although one of them courageously turns around and shouts "Fuckin wankers" at us when they're almost out of sight, as they turn into a nearby lane. The three girls also begin to move away while Tarzan waves at them and one of them actually smiles and waves back, causing myself and Gobber to exchange looks of incomprehension. Gobber bends down on the path to pick up his broken spirit and turns around to Tarzan. "What the fuck was that about ye headcase? Fuckin 'odd job' out a *Goldfinger* over here. That's comin out of your wages by the way." Tarzan just laughs and says "Sorry Gobber, it just felt the right thing to do at the time. I was just feelin the moment man, just feelin the moment, ye know what I mean?" "Yeah whatever Taz, I know you're always gonna be a showman at heart. And you, fuckin head of operations." Gobber turns an accusing glare and pointed finger at me. "Learn how to cycle a bike will ye, ye looked like an absolute clown, except it wasn't funny, it was just pathetic." "It was pretty funny though" Tarzan interjects before Gobber starts laughing in acquiescence. "Ah no it was, fuckin hilarious. Wish we hadda got it on camera Taz, send it into Jeremy Beadle an shit!" My two associates' obvious glee at my recent misfortune causes the gratitude and respect I had so recently felt for them to dissipate as I am consumed with a hatred of them bordering on the pathological. "You mean to tell me you both saw the entire episode?" I ask struggling to hide the distress, nay, hurt coming through the elevated pitch of my voice. "Of course we did" Gobber says, "we were only parked in the driveway over there, in the Mooneys' gaff. Saw it comin a mile away. We were gonna beep the horn an give ye a lift back the rest of the way but we had a feelin that youngfella was gonna kick that ball atcha, too good to resist brother, I'm sure ye understand. You were seriously pantin on that bike man, you'd wanna give up smoking all that crazy sheeeet." My two associates start laughing once more as I try to ignore them and walk over to inspect my bicycle as it lies in a sorry looking condition on the footpath. I lift it into an upright position and I can tell the front wheel is buckled as well as there being some superficial damage to the paintwork of the frame. Gobber walks over and takes the bike from me, obviously noticing the look of dejection on my face that I'm sure must be visible, judging by my current emotional condition. "Come on, gimme that" he says, "I'll throw it in the back of the van and give ye a lift down the road. It'll be no bother to you to get that fixed anyway with the amount of money you must have stored away at this stage of the game, wha'?" Gobber walks to the back of the van and opens the two back doors. His comment about me having money stored away, takes me aback slightly, and I look in Tarzan's direction to see if I can detect any sign of prescience on his part vis a vis Gobber having any knowledge of the Running Away Fund, but Tarzan looks lost in his own little world, so I put Gobber's comment down as being a mere turn of phrase. The three of us pile into the front of the van and I somehow end up squashed in the middle, also noting the lack of seat belts in the cab and I decide to voice my objections to the current seating arrangements. "Could I not just sit on the outside Taz, seems I'll be getting out less than 500 metres down the road? Surely that would make a little more sense?" "Nah, don't like the middle Dosser to be honest. Anyway, we're in now so fuck it." Gobber pulls off in his customary *Dukes of Hazard* style, while blasting Oasis's *Acquiesce* from the tape player with both windows open, nearly giving a pair of heart attacks to an elderly couple walking an even more decrepit dog on the footpath. Gobber barks out the window at the cowering canine and at this point I'm looking forward to a nice night in, in front of war torn Europe like a British officer, festering in a Japanese POW camp, must dream about returning to his home village in Oxfordshire and sipping pims while watching his local cricket team, after the eventual ousting of the imperial forces of Nippon from south east Asia, and the subsequent liberation of his POW camp by combined Allied forces. "How come you were both in chez Mooney anyway?" I ask, eager to engage myself in some kind of conversation in order to pass the short journey and take my mind off my current uncomfortable circumstances. "I needed Taz here to help me move a piano in the gaff there. Couldn't shift it by meself, so I had to call in the big man for a bit of muscle." Gobber says this while igniting a John Player Blue with a Zippo lighter that has the name "Shauna" emblazoned across its metal exterior. "Do Pianos not normally have wheels on them?" I wonder out loud more than anything. "What? And wheel the fuckin thing all over me brand new floor? I'm a craftsman Dosser not a fuckin cowboy. Get some sense into ye man will ye?" Gobber says this almost indignantly. I think he always feels that I don't give his occupation the credit it deserves which is far from veracious, and by now I haven't the energy to continue this confabulation, but luckily we've just arrived at my familial homestead. Gobber parks the car right outside my house, pulling up onto the path in the process and blocking the passage of yet another elderly couple that he either fails to notice or simply chooses to ignore. "Oh by the way Dosser" he says while lifting up the handbrake with an abrasive jerk, "you might not need to get that bike fixed for a while now cause he's got the motor." "Who's got the motor?" I inquire, not fully understanding his meaning. "He's got the motor. Taz like" Gobber replies with a wide grin on his face. "I've got the motor" Tarzan says proudly. "You've got the motor?" I ask reluctantly acknowledging the factual nature of the statement. "He's got the motor" Gobber, repeats just to clearly reinforce the general message he is trying to convey, id est, Tarzan is now in possession of a fully functioning motor vehicle. "Nice one" I lie. "When the fuck did you start speakin like ordinary people? Get the fuck out of the car will ye" Gobber says while opening the door and walking around to the back of the van.

As the van pulls away Tarzan's head protrudes out the passenger window and he says "Pick ye up tomorrow then Dosser, about 8.20" and I turn to walk around the side of my house, wheeling my bike solely on the back wheel, with the buckled front wheel elevated into the air. As I open the side gate leading into my back garden, I actually can't remember the last time I felt so happy to be home and then I notice a familiar and hideous fiat punto parked on the road that runs alongside my house. I shove my dismembered bicycle into the shed and enter the house through the back door, where my mother stands at the cooker, preparing our evening repast. "There's the little gardener now" she says, as she comes over and tossles my hair with her hand. "What happened your little face? There's a big scrape on your cheek" I trace the length of my left cheek with my left hand and feel the unevenness of the skin. "I actually performed an unintentional dismount of my bicycle just there. I must have obtained this facial abrasion as I skidded on the footpath. Hadn't noticed it, so it must not be life threatening, I hope." "Ah, are ye all right? I don't remember ye fallin off your little bike before?" "No, no I'm quite all right I assure you. What are we having for dinner then?" "I did a nice stew on account of the cold weather. Dwayne's staying for dinner as well by the way so be down in about twenty minutes if ye can." I look up to the heavens as I walk out of the kitchen and cry "Oh stew, my most loathed of conglomerated nutritional substances, could this day get any worse?" "What's that chicken?" my mother calls over the noise of a beeping microwave and I simply reply "nothing, nothing" before carrying on out the door. I look into the front room before mounting the stairs and see Dwayne, studiously watching the television, sitting on the section of the sofa predominately utilised by me, with my sister's feet on his lap, while she lies the length of the sofa with her head at the end nearest the door. "Evening all" I mange to say, hiding my utter disdain for both of them, "what's this you're watching?" Obviously I care about what they are watching on television about as much as I care about the plight of orphaned guinea pigs, but if their activities are going to interfere with my planned night's viewing, it will not pass without retribution, and I'm thinking mainly of the alloyed wheels of a nearby Italian hatchback at this point. "Watchin America's Dumbest Criminals, gas it is man" Dwayne replies, with a ridiculously idiotic grin on his face. "Oh very cerebral indeed" I say and Dwayne looks at me with a confused look on his face. "Just get out will ye?" my sister says, without even deigning to turn around to look at me and I retreat from this bastion of the intellectually damned and make my way up the stairs. I make it to the landing and I notice the door is ajar in my parents' bedroom.. I can see my father sitting up on his bed, fully dressed above the waist in a rather spiffing argyle jumper, but wearing only white fronts in the lower half of his corporeal frame. There is a plethora of betting slips scattered beside his prosthetic limb and he is perusing the Racing Post by the dim light of his bedside lamp. The curtains of the room are drawn and he is bouncing a ball point pen from the side his mouth as he contemplates the recent form of various equine athletes, he then withdraws the pen from his pursed lips with a rapid motion and decisively underlines the name of a horse on the page open in front of him. I approach the stairs which leads to the converted attic where I lay my head at night, hoping to evade his attention, but I am sadly foiled as a loud creaking noise emanates from my footfall on the carpeted floor. "Ah, is that you son?" he yells, swivelling his torso around in the bed and catches my eye as I grimace at my flagrant carelessness. "Come on in here son and pick an aul winner for your aul da. The national's on Saturday remember?" I slide my bag of my shoulder and rest it on the floor before entering the dominion of my conception. I recall as a child, I would annually select a horse at random for the Grand National with my father and it strikes me as odd that I have not even thought about that aged ritual for many years. "Ye used to be a goldmine for pickin a winner for the national" he continues, "Jaysus not like your granda, I swear he musta been backin three legged donkeys most of the time. Lost his feckin arse he did. Don't think he cared either way, that was his problem. That and the drink of course." He extends the pen towards me with an almost supplicating expression on his face and I prise the disposable writing implement from his hopeful grasp. I scan the list of names on the page in front of me and mark an astericks beside one of them, I believe completely at random, although there is a musical quality to the horse's name that I feel strangely drawn towards. I look at my pater familias and express a knowing nod, as though I'm a member of some kind of horse racing cognoscenti and turn to exit the room. As I mount the stairs in order to change from my uniform and into civilian attire I can hear him muttering under his breath "Bindaree, not a chance, but ye can't win 'em all I suppose."

Dinner passes with no major incidents, although after I have practically force fed myself an unnecessarily large bowl of stew, I am dealt quite a serious blow to my morale with the discovery that there are only two Penguin bars remaining in the biscuit jar; one of which is given to my father due to his position as head of the family, and the other to Dwayne because of his position as defiler of my sister, which seems to me a somewhat dubious set of cultural mores. Consequently, I am forced to accept a brace of ginger nuts which are hardly an adequate replacement for the chocolate flavoured goodness of our winged Antarctic friends, but will suffice nonetheless. I duly excuse myself from the dining table, carrying a large mug of tea in my right hand while holding the two ginger nuts between my lips so I can open the door of the front room with my left hand. I eagerly make my way towards the front room to settle down for my planned night's viewing, thankful to at last enjoy some silent repose after a most hectic and taxing day's exertions. I enter the room and place the mug of tea on the floor beside my usual sitting position on the couch, resting the two ginger nuts on the arm of the cushioned sitting device. I walk towards the television and crouch down on the floor to extract the requisite tape from the shelf underneath the video player and a pang of anxiety sweeps through my veins as I realise the tape I took great care in carefully labelling "World War Two in Colour, please refrain from manual interference" is no longer where I had stored it. I push the flap at the exterior of the slot where one inserts tapes into the machine in order to ascertain if there is a tape currently occupying the space and my inability to push the flap all the way in enlightens me to the fact that there most certainly is. Obviously at this stage I am beginning to fear the worst. I press the "eject" button on the machine and as I watch the tape emerge from its mechanical Bastille, I see my inscription before me, in the manner in which a more than slightly annoyed bull must view the rag of a tormenting matador. I actually feel the sensation of a watery build-up behind my ocular sensory organs as I push the tape back into the machine, press "play" and see a black and white picture from a CCTV camera in a service station somewhere in Oregon, as a would-be thief wearing an American football helmet on his head, mistakenly attempts to exit the building through a full pane of glass he erroneously believed to be fresh air, while carrying a full tray of hot dogs. Just as I'm beginning to have thoughts of genuinely committing murder, Dwayne (just one of my potential victims)pokes his idiotic cranial structure into the room and says "Aw I love this one! Here, wait till ye see what he does now! Ha ha, look, he's concussed or some shit. Look at him runnin around, he doesn't know where he's goin!" I turn around in an attempt to meet his gaze, with an expression on my countenance which I hope will convey the level of contempt in which I hold him and also express the serious physical danger he has placed himself in. Of course, the fucking mongoloid is unable to divert the trajectory of his visual concentration from the television screen and my menacing scowl goes unnoticed and the inherent elliptical threat therein, unheeded. My sister arrives behind the potential future progenitor of a clutch of children, whose level of intelligence I would prefer not to even think about and says "Here come on you, are ye gonna take me for that drive now or what?" in a way that's grotesquely suggestive, while wrapping her two arms around his midriff in a disgustingly flirtatious manner. I fight against the urge to projectile vomit on the pair of them and instead compose myself to launch into a tirade about the heinously villainous recording over of my documentary series, but instead all I can manage to summon from my rapidly diminishing energy reserves is to ask "How did you end up using that tape to record that utter tripe? It was clearly labelled. Can you not read? It says "No manual interference. NO MANUAL FUCKING INTERFERENCE!" Just as the words leave my mouth my mother walks by the room. She leans her head over my sister's shoulder who is still standing at the threshold of the room with Dwayne so that it feels like the three of them are preventing me from any possibility of escaping from this escalating situation. "My God I never heard such language in this house! Wouldn't hear it on a building site. You better watch yourself mister. Good job your father's till out in the kitchen. A heart attack he woulda had if he'd heard those words come out of your mouth. And in front of Dwayne as well?" "They recorded over my documentary mam" I retort, "I needed to watch that for History class. You know it's very important for me to do well in school now don't you?" I say this in order to regain some higher ground in the battle between me and my sister for the greater share of our parents' respect and love, and I can see that it has achieved some success, judging by the softening expression on my mother's face. "Well it doesn't excuse that kind of language" she says before turning to my sister to deliver, in my opinion an extremely half-hearted reprimand, "And you, don't be recordin over your brother's documentaries, you know they're very important for his school work. I'm sorry about all this Dwayne. Ye must think we're a mad crowd altogether over here." "Ah no, it's grand Theresa, don't worry about it" Dwayne says, actually looking a little nervous and I can sense there's a bit of an awkward moment, when we all realise that that must be the first time he has addressed my mother by her first name, and my heart sinks to think of how ridiculously interwoven he is with the fabric of our familial existence. My mother walks upstairs as I plonk myself down on the couch, emitting an exhalation of exasperation and shaking my head at the cruel reality of the impossibility of my current living conditions. My sister evidently waits until she hears the bedroom door of my parents' room close and turns to me vindictively and says in a kind of harsh whisper "Yeah, you're a weirdo by the way. Who watches all that stuff about out wars an all? No wonder ye don't have a girlfriend, ye loser!" She storms out the front door with Dwayne shuffling tentatively behind her. I simply call "Biaaatch" as they exit the building and take a most unsatisfying mouthful of tea from my mug, due to the fact that it has decreased in temperature to an almost unpalatable level. I take one of my two ginger nuts and dunk it in the tepid liquid, and just as I'm putting the moistened biscuit to my mouth, the be-dunked part separates from the rest and drops into the tea, like when you see large chunks of ice bergs in the arctic circle breaking off and landing into the sea, shown on television as an ominous portent of our planet's ultimate demise due to global warming. I calmly replace the mug of tea back on the floor beside the couch, and have a moment of brief silence as once again I can feel that same watery build up behind my ocular sensory organs, coupled with a shortness of breath in the back of my throat. I can hear my mother dismounting the stairs and she enters the room yet again. "I heard what ye said to your sister you, ye little pup. After everything I said to ye just now. Well I really didn't think I'd still have to be doin this at this stage of my life but for the rest of the week ye won't be goin anywhere. You're to be straight home from school at four o' clock. No gardenin; nothing. It's really time for ye to grow up and not be behaving like a child do ye hear me now?" I simply nod despondently as I stare at the television screen and see an African American trying to steal a police car, not realising that there are still two police officers sitting in the front, polishing their nightsticks with which to beat his African American posterior. As my mother walks once more upstairs I resolve to try and remain positive; especially since I still have the *Nazi War Machine* recorded on another tape, so I have ample material for a quality night's entertainment. I initiate action stations by recovering the necessary tape from the tape drawer and placing it in the video player. I assume my customary television watching position on the couch and watch the screen fill up with images of Stuka dive bombers descending on convoys of fleeing Polish refuges and I affirm in my mind that yes; World War Two simply is the best war ever. I begin to feel a slowly but steadily rising tiredness permeate from my legs to my torso and decide to lie down on the couch on my left hand side, so that my eyes are still facing the television screen as Winston Churchill inspects the ruins of a recently blitzed London, while sticking his two fingers up at everyone he sees. It occurs to me that that's the attitude I need to have from now on; fucking fuck everyone. It's not enough to just have thoughts about what I'm going to do to so and so, or what revenge I need to exact on a particular somebody. I have to become more pro-active. Did I actually just say that word? But that's the truth of the matter. I know that in my heart of hearts, there are too many people walking all over me. I know that it has to stop. I know what I have to do, and just when I'm about to tell myself what I need to do, my mind goes blank.

I wake up with a start and I realise that I must have drifted off as I was watching the aftermath of the bombing of Coventry. I sit up suddenly and rub my hand roughly over my face to reinvigorate myself. I feel something strange on my left temple and as I run my fingers across my nose to the general area of this peculiar sensation, a disc shaped object falls to the floor and I can see that it's that second ginger nut, which has obviously been stuck to my face during my unplanned siesta. I look down on the floor to see where it has landed and discover to my horror that I have kicked over my mug of formerly hot, but by now cold tea, complete with the soggy remains of half a drowned ginger nut, which has mingled with its liquid sarcophagus and spilled out all over the carpet. I can hear voices in the hallway and I'm fairly sure that it was the sound of the front door opening and closing that probably roused me from my slumber initially. I look down again at the mess on the floor and ask myself for what I hope will be the last occasion in this twenty four hour period; if this day could get any worse. It is then that I notice that the voices outside are uncharacteristically joyous. I can detect a shrill of girlish excitement in my mother's tone and my father is laughing heartily. It is only then that I can detect a third voice, a voice which at first piques my curiosity until the shattering realisation of the identity of its proprietor assails me like a swarm of angry bees. I begin to shake my head and I even mumble "no, no, no" to myself, unapologetically, not caring that such behaviour must raise serious doubts about my sanity. It is then that the door of the room opens, in a slow and painful movement, and any equivocation with regards to the identity of the caller which may have been lingering in my subconscious quickly evaporates as the voice from the hallway accompanies the opening door and says "Hey Dennis." I turn my gaze from the tea stained carpet and look into my brother's face.

Tarzan's Story (Number Two)

Sorry I haven't talked to you for a while, but I've been fairly caught up with a lot of stuff lately. Things have been getting pretty hectic around here, what with me finally getting The Beast off my ma and everything, I've had tonnes of shit to sort out; like sending off insurance forms and shit like that. Well, obviously not doing it myself or anything, but you know, making sure my ma has all that sorted so I won't get hassle from the guards or whatever. Now that I've got my own wheels, it means I'll have a lot of freedom I suppose. But I'll just have to see where all that freedom can take me. School has gone pretty well this week. I haven't really got into trouble once, although Mister Johnson did make me take the blame for him nearly setting the science lab on fire, but there's nothing new in that is there? It all happened because all last week, Dosser was grounded by his ma, so I had to help Mister Johnson in the lab every day after school. On Wednesday I think it was, I was in there helping out with the production of this new fake-cocaine stuff that we're working on and Johnno was heating up some of that white shit using his Bunsen burner cooker thing and the flames started to get a little out of control. He actually ended up singing his hair and shit, and the cooking pots went all black and all so the whole room ended up full of smoke and it even started going out into the corridors and all. That's when the smoke alarms starting going off. Luckily enough, school was over at that stage but there were still a few heads knocking around in after-school study and shit like that. And all the head honcho teachers, the year heads or whatever, were still in their offices doing work and shit so it did cause a decent amount of chaos. Mister White was still there of course, and as we were all legging it out to the yard, I could see him giving me dirty looks and all, even though I didn't have anything to do with it. Well not really, it was pretty much Johnno's fault for the most part, although I did kind of have a small part to play in the whole thing, but Mister White didn't know that, he just assumed it was me because he doesn't like me. Or else he just needed somebody to pin the blame on. Either way I couldn't care less. Nothing he could do will ever really have any effect on me because I'm just not scared of him or of anybody else in the school really. Anyway, when all the smoke had finally cleared, Johnno collared me and asked me if it would be all right if he told the head honcho teachers that I had set the alarm off by mistake. He said he'd sort it so that I wouldn't really get in trouble or anything, and that he'd explain to the head honchos that it was just a freak accident. He said he'd just say that I'd left a lab coat too close to the Bunsen burner or some shit and that it had just gone up in flames. He said that it'd make him look like a bit of an eejit in front of the head honcho teachers if they thought he'd started the fire so I just told him I didn't give a fuck. He could say whatever he wanted. I'm not just saying that to be mad or anything, I really couldn't give a fuck. I don't really need school with the amount of money we're making at the moment. Plus I've got a couple of secret little side projects of my own going on that not even Dosser knows about, but I'll talk more about that later. The fire was a bit of crack though. I say it was a fire but it was only small, it was never going to do any major damage or anything. I say it wasn't really my fault but it kind of was as well. I just get so bored sometimes, I just find myself doing stuff, just to pass the time really. I need to kind of like, entertain myself I suppose, because I mean what else are you supposed to do with yourself in this country? The weather's shit, there's fuck all to do in general, so you have to something, don't you? So that was really all I was doing last Wednesday, it was just a way of relieving the boredom of working in there, especially seems we have to wear those masks which means we can't even really talk to each other. When me and Johnno were working in the lab that day, all I was doing was washing utensils and shit, if that is the right word. It's like Dosser and Johnno don't trust me to do any complicated shit so they give me these fucking boring jobs to do. So when Johnno was boiling that shit up on the cooker, I was just waiting for him to go into the backroom to get something, and when he did, I legged it over to the cooker and turned up the gas on the Bunsen burner. Just enough so that the pressure or whatever would build up, like gradually. So, by the time he had come back out of the storage room, the flames were just starting to get a little bit higher, until they started rising up around the cooking pot and I could see the grey metal starting to go black. Johnno was carrying this big plastic tray and he just panicked and froze and dropped the tray on the floor. But I had all this planned out you see, so as soon as I could see the shock in his eyes, even through those big goggles he wears, I grabbed the little mini fire extinguisher off the wall, jumped up on the desk and starting spraying all that white foam shit on the fire, like I was in *Backdraft* or whatever. Of course by then, the smoke had already gone into the hallways and all, and the smoke alarms had starting going off, so the havoc had already begun, but the real danger was over. By then Johnno was all "Tarzan I owe you big time man. You really saved my ass just there" and I was all "No problem Sir, anyone woulda done the same thing. Don't sweat it", so after the whole thing I'd achieved so much. First of all, I'd entertained myself by creating havoc in the school, plus I'd made it seem as though I'd done Johnno a massive favour, so now he like owes me and all. And he's the fucker that thinks I'm only smart enough to wash pots and pans? It's like even with the Bunsen burner, I probably understand how they work better than even him because all I ever did in Science class for three years was mess around with the Bunsen burners on those long desks they have in the labs. Whereas when Johnno was in school, he was probably all like, paying attention and all so he doesn't have the same understanding of the pressure of them and all. Like I know exactly how much to let out, so that there'll be just a slight smell of gas in the room and everyone would be like, sniffing the air as if they could smell something, but they wouldn't quite be sure if they could? And then I know how much to let out so that everyone knows there's definitely a whopper smell of gas, so even the teacher has to admit it and let us out for a free class while they investigate the problem or whatever, and open all the windows and shit. Then I know how to control the flow of gas, so that I can light it and just a little flame comes out, and then I can write my initials in a savage design on my pencil case or ruler or something. Then if I want, I can let more gas out so that the flame gets bigger and I can singe the jumper of Eamon O' Doherty or some bum basher like that, or even get the flame real close to their face so that it gets them mad paranoid, but not close enough that it could actually do any real damage to their skin or anything, so I'd be able to deny doing anything if one of those bum bashers did try to rat on me or whatever. Of course, it depends on what teacher you've got for science in the first place. I remember in first year we had Mister MacDonagh and you couldn't get away with anything with that fucker. He was just one of those cunts that was real strict and intimidating and stuff, and he had eyes popping out of his head like a hawk or whatever. In a weird way I kind of actually enjoyed his classes because they made a bit of a change from having to mess all the time. It was actually kind of relaxing I suppose to just sit there in silence for a while. But that's probably just because I was only a little kid then, if I had him now, I'd probably end up killing him or something.

But yeah, that was the only major thing that's happened in school for a while. Things have been heating-up a little bit more outside of school though. Last weekend, Dosser wasn't allowed out at all, as I said before, but myself and Gobber had some crack, just messing around all over the place. I even went into town with him on Saturday night. Dosser doesn't drink you see, because it's illegal and all. He says he won't drink until he's turned 18 but even then he's not sure he'd want to start because it's what everyone else does. I don't think it's really stuff being illegal that bothers him, it's just that he wants to be different to everyone else you see in the street. Don't get me wrong, I can see his point of view and I believe in it as well and all; there are a serious amount of bum bashers around the place, but sometimes you know, it's just good to do something normal once in a while, like hitting a few pubs in town with Gobber and trying to get stuck into a few birds or whatever. But I suppose that's the thing; even when we try to do something normal like going into town or whatever, something mad does always happen. I reckon weirdness just follows us around I suppose. But even before we got to Saturday, we'd some good crack on Friday. I bunked off the last two classes after lunch. For some reason we've got PE followed by Religion for our last two classes of the week so I hardly ever go to them. Stupid of them really to organise it that way, you'd think they would have copped on by now that half my class must be missing, but I suppose it's probably something to do with that Mister Murray, the Principal. He is a serious odd ball, even by my standards. I reckon I could probably walk into his office in the nip some day and he wouldn't even notice. In fact, I reckon I'll definitely give that a go before the school year's over. What's the worst that could happen sure? But where was I? Oh yeah, Friday night was a bit of a laugh all right. I bombed it out of the school in The Beast at about half two, and I met Gobber down at this gaff he's been working in for the last couple of weeks. I just give him a hand with the flooring from time to time, and I'd been helping him out in this place all week, just moving furniture and carrying shit and all. He doesn't really pay me or anything. It would be a bit stupid seems me and Dosser pay him for selling our shit on the street, so he'll normally just buy me a few cans or we'll both just smoke a load of Catnip and Dagga joints and get fucked up together, which I suppose isn't really like getting paid, but when you sit down for a nice smoke up together after a hard day's graft, it does kind of feel like it for whatever reason. Plus, some of the aul ones in the gaffs do make up some serious feeds sometimes and there's always plenty of tea and shit on the go, so all in all it's deffo worth doing. The aul one in this gaff actually, Mrs. Mooney her name was, made us dinner and all last week: burgers, chips, fries, everything. Totally savage food. I could take that for payment any day of the week but of course I am only messing when I say that. I really do realise the importance of money. Yeah actually, she also had this quality daughter, went to Our Lady's and all. Total fucking ride. If I could have the likes of her involved in one of my little side ventures that I was telling you about, it could mean a serious amount of cash for me, but I'll come back to that later. I still haven't told you about the fucking weekend. Jaysus, Mister White must be right; I really do have the attention span of an epileptic goldfish.

As soon as we finished up in Mrs. Mooney's, I bailed it back to my gaff to get cleaned up and shit. That's the one thing I hate about working with Gobber, you always get covered in all this sawdust and all, plus I'd forgotten to bring any change of clothes so I had to do it all in my school uniform. When I walked into my gaff, I went into the kitchen and my ma was all "look at the state of ye!" and I was all "yeah whatever like, it's only a bit of sawdust, it's not like it's muck or anything" and she was all just sighing and shit and she told me to stick my uniform in for washing straight away. I just got stripped right there and then in the kitchen and it was only when I'd taken off my shirt and jumper and was just starting to take off my shoes, socks and trousers, that I remembered I'd forgotten to put on any underwear that day. But at that stage I reckoned, so what? So I just whipped off my cacks and threw the whole lot onto the floor beside the washing machine. My ma was standing at the cooker at that stage and when she turned around she was like "Jesus will ye put some clothes on ye!" and it was then that my da decides to arrive home from work. He just walked into the kitchen and looked at me, with that look he always gives me, like he just hates my guts and wants to kill me or something. It's because he knows there's no way that I'm his real son. I've got four older brothers who all almost look like those albino blokes, with like, totally white skin and mad blonde hair and all. Gobber and Dosser and everyone really think it's like I don't notice and shit, but of course I do. It's just that there's really no point in talking about it is there? With all the money I'm making I don't really need anyone, so my family's just not that important to me. I don't care who my real da is, it makes no odds. He's not going to put petrol in my car or sort me out with any new threads or anything so what difference does it make? Anyway my ma was rushing around trying to find a towel or whatever to wrap around me and I was all "Relax will yis for Jesus' sake, I just need to get me phone out of trousers for a second, then I'll be off." I went over to where my trousers were on the floor and bent down to like, rummage through the pockets or whatever. The phone wasn't in either of the pockets, so I thought it must have fallen out when I threw the trousers onto the floor or something, so I started looking underneath my shirt and jumper and all. I could feel my da was just staring at me, even though I couldn't see him and I was actually taking a deliberately longer time than I needed, just to make him even more angry. Next thing, I heard this like tap, on the back window and I looked up from the ground and I could just see Gobber standing there in the back garden, right next to the window and he was waving in with his left hand while holding what looked like my phone in his right. He was shouting in through the window and it was hard to make out what he was saying but I could tell it was something like "YOU FORGOT YOUR PHONE" or "I HAVE YOUR PHONE." He had this real shocked look on his face and my ma was all like "Oh my God, will ye cover yourself up!" Because we've got the greenhouse out my back garden, the lads always just call around the back way to my gaff, so it's pretty normal for Gobber to give a knock on the window. Obviously though, I'm not normally standing in the kitchen in the nip with my arse up in the air with my ma and da just standing there looking at me, but I suppose, it's shit like this that makes everyone think my family's a bit weird. Not that I could care less either way. Anyway, I was having a good laugh at this stage, so I went out the back door and went over to Gobber to get my phone back. He was just like "What the fuck is goin on here? You doin your ma while your da watches or something? Fuckin Oedipal shit goin on here man, Oedipal shit." I had no idea what he was talking about but I didn't bother to stop to ask him because I was planning something in my head while he kept banging on. "You left your phone back in Mooney's gaff. Only noticed after you'd gone. I went after ye in the van but even I couldn't keep up witcha. You'd wanna slow the fuck down man. Anyway, thought I'd just drop it back to ye. Obviously got a little bit more than I bargained for, d'y know what I

mean? Didn't expect to walk in on the middle of a real life Greek tragedy."
I just said "Yeah whatever, just hand over the weapon before it blows up
in your hand or somethin" and as soon as he gave it to me, I gave him a
big bear hug and I was all "Thanks so much Gobber" but in like a bum
basher's voice. Gobber started going mad and he was screaming "Get away
from me ye fuckin weirdo, get away from me to fuck!" But I wouldn't let
go of him and I dragged him out on to the grass and like rugby tackled
him on to the ground. I managed to pin him, face down on the grass, even
though he is a wriggly bastard and I kind of like got on top of him so that
it looked like I was going to ride him up the arse or whatever. He was just
screaming "Cunt! Fuckin cunt!" during the whole thing but I was just
laughing. As I told you before, I just do this for a bit of entertainment. I
don't mean anything by it or anything. Anyway, in fairness to Gobber, he
managed to swing his elbow around and hit me straight in the stomach. It
was actually a savage move and all the air was knocked out of me, a bit like
when you do an American dream I suppose. That's another thing I like
about Gobber. You can do this kind of shit with him because he's tough
and he's always up for a bit of a laugh like that. He was supposed to be
an animal goer back in the day when he was hanging around with Stevie
Smith and all the head honcho scumbags around the area, but obviously
we've never gotten too serious with each other or anything, so I've never
really seen him in that kind of way. If I ever tried to have a mess fight with
Dosser like that, he'd just end up crying or something because he's such a
small little wind bag.

But anyway, after all that messing around the place, I was fairly tired so I
just headed up to my room for a bit of a nap. Whenever I want to go to
sleep like that during the day, I always bring a cup of tea up with me and
then sprinkle in a load of Scotch Broom leaves, and it knocks me out cold.
It tastes a bit weird at first when you're not used to it I suppose, but it is
good shit. Sometimes though, it can give you mad dreams and all. I
remember that day I had a seriously mental dream about me and Dosser
being attacked by a big giant tortoise. I normally don't really remember
everything that happens in my dreams, but for some reason, this one just
really like, stood out and all. I'd been kind of having dreams about us
being chased around the place by giant animals for a while; sometimes
they were rabbits, sometimes they were big spiders or guinea pigs or
something, but this was the first time it'd been a tortoise. At the start of

the dream, we were in the greenhouse in school, I think it was, and this mad green tortoise with crazy red eyes appeared out of nowhere, and was roaring his head off above us, like *King Kong* in the film but except it was a tortoise. He started pounding on the ground with his big mad foot thing, and every time he did the ground would shake like in *Jurassic Park* or whatever, and me and Dosser would end up being fucked around the greenhouse because of the impact, with all the plants and watering cans flying all over the place as well. Every time the giant tortoise smashed his foot on the ground, he was getting closer to the greenhouse, and we were all shouting and screaming because we knew he was about to smash the greenhouse with us inside it and all. Eventually Dosser was all like "The plants! Give him the plants! That's obviously what he's after. Tortoises eat plants, just give them to him!" As soon as he said this, I turned around to him and I was like "What d'y mean, give him the plants? They're fuckin ours. We need them to make money and all." Then next of all I could just hear this big smash and we both looked around and saw the tortoise's big massive foot had crashed down at the end of the greenhouse. We obviously started running for the door, but it felt like the greenhouse had become like, never ending and we kept sprinting to get out, like we were running down the big corridor to the front door in school after the bell's gone for the summer holidays or something, while behind us the giant tortoise's foot kept smashing and smashing until eventually the end of the greenhouse opened up like a miracle, and the two of us jumped out onto the grass and we knew we were safe. When we got up and like, dusted ourselves off, it was as if we were a mile away from the greenhouse and we were just looking back from a safe distance and we could see the tortoise munching away on all the plants and tearing into them like a Tyrannosaurus Rex eating like, a cow or whatever. I just turned to Dosser, put a Catnip joint to my mouth, struck a match off the side of my face, lit the joint and said "Well he's certainly having a smashing time" but in like, a real kind of cool way and all? But Dosser wasn't having any of it. He was all trembling with rage and stuff, and he had that look on his face when he gets real angry but in like a nervous way. Like he's trying to make you afraid of him but it actually just ends up making him look more scared than he did in the first place. Anyway, he was all "We need to mount a counter attack! We simply cannot afford to relinquish an area of such strategic importance and economic value!" We both kind of nodded to each other, like we both knew we'd have to get our crow hunting equipment, but instead of us having to like, go and get it, it just like, appeared in our hands like in a computer game or whatever. Then, just as we were about to start running towards the giant tortoise, these like, horses just appeared underneath us and before I knew it we were galloping at full speed and it felt like I was on a motorbike or something, except like, bumpier and Dosser was right beside me and he kept shouting "Yah! Yah!" and he looked like he knew what he was doing so I tried to shout "Yah! Yah!" as well, except when I tried to say it, it came out sort of as "Ee Aw! Ee Aw!" like a kind of donkey noise or something. Anyway, we got right up to the tortoise, but it was like he hadn't noticed us, and he had his head buried in all our plants that were like, strewn all over the ground? I kind of like, stood up out of the saddle of the horse, put my dart gun to my mouth and nailed the fucker straight on the chin. Dosser flew by him and let off a few rounds of stones from his slingshot but they just bounced off the tortoise's shell. He did start to get really like, annoyed and shit though, and he started going mad, twisting his neck around the place and throwing his two front feet up into the air and all. Me and Dosser started riding around him in circles, just lashing him out of it with arrows and stones and we could see that he was beginning to like, tire. Just when we thought he was looking like he was about to collapse, out of nowhere a big massive load of crows came flying across the sky. There were so many of them, it was kind of like a big black cloud, except instead of being like, gas or whatever, it was just a big load of crows. They kept getting nearer and nearer, and you could just here this big mad sound like "Ca Caw! Ca Caw!" and it got louder and louder, the closer they got. Dosser was like "I hate to say it, but this reminds me a great deal of the Red Army's final approach to Berlin, just before they administered the coup de grace to the crumbling body of the vanquished Reich." I just told him to shut the fuck up and keep firing, even though I was getting kind of worried myself. The crows at this stage, were right above our heads and I think we both knew exactly what they were planning to do. It was pretty weird, but we could hear all of them begin to count to three, but in kind of like, crow voices, so it was like "Wahhn, Toooee, Traayyy." As soon as they'd finished saying "three" a big load of bird shit came pelting down out of the sky, except instead of being just like, normal size bird shit, it was all big massive drops of kind of white and black shit, and I could feel it landing all over my face and making my clothes all wet and all so it was hard even to move. Next thing I knew, I was knocked off my horse by this one big drop of bird shit and I ended up on my back, looking up at the sky, like when you're a kid and you're staring at the clouds and trying to see if they look like anything? Then I looked beside me and Dosser was on the ground as well, doing exactly the same thing as me, just looking straight up at the sky, and looking like he was about to fall asleep or something. It was then that I could see the crows weren't just normal crows at all, but they were kind of like, half-man, half-crow things and they were all carrying these kind of spears, and they were sharpening them up as if they were about to close in to finish us off or whatever. Then I noticed that they seemed to have this one kind of leader bloke, and he had this mad beard and looked like your man out of that film *Flash*. Except as they got nearer and I got a closer look at him, I could see that it wasn't your man out of flash at all but that it was Gobber. Then it got to the stage where the half-man, half-crow things were just above our heads, and their leader/bloke out of Flash/Gobber was doing this mad deep laugh-while-you-speak thing and he was just like "Finish them off." Next of all, all these spears just came lashing down on top of us and I could feel all these little like, pricks on my skin, but not in a gay way or anything. I turned on my side to say something to Dosser, but when I looked around he was lying with his back to me. I started shaking him on the shoulder and shouting "Dosser, Dosser!" Suddenly his head just kind of flopped over to the side, so that I was face to face with him, but I could see that his eyes were rolled up like, to the back of his head and there was this mad trail of gooey blood coming out of his mouth and running down his cheek. I just kept shouting his name over and over and over again but he just wouldn't wake up and there wasn't anything I could do to help him. Next thing I knew, all I could hear was my own name being called over and over and over again. I opened my eyes and it was weird because I was totally awake whereas normally it takes me about half a day to wake up after being asleep. I looked straight above me and all I could see was my ma's face and she was poking me with the fingers on her hand and saying "Come on chicken, your dinner's getting cold." I just sat up in the bed and said "Thanks" and she just shouted back as she was walking out the door "And for the last time, will ye put some feckin clothes on ye!"

Well after all that I suppose I was feeling pretty weird, but I still managed to destroy a load of munch when I went down for dinner. After I'd finished eating, I got a bit of *Home and Away* action in and then I rang Gobber. Gobber answered the phone and I could tell straight away that he was still kind of like, annoyed at me or whatever for what I'd done early on and he sounded real like, lazy and like he had no energy or whatever. I asked him was he still going to come over to the greenhouse for a bit of Friday night madness and he said he still was after being kind of quiet for a while. I was glad he was still coming over. Even though I said I don't really feel like I need anybody anymore, you do still need a couple of heads knocking around the place to have a bit of crack with now and then, and Gobber in fairness to him can be the best crack ever sometimes. I told him to come over to the greenhouse at around half eight, so that gave me around an hour and a half to sort out a few things for that side project of mine that I was telling you about. *Home and Away* finished just as I got off the phone to Gobber, but because I was kind of concentrating on talking to him, I kind of didn't really catch what happened in the end which was obviously a bit annoying because I like the way all the episodes always end with something like, mad happening and the music goes all mad serious and all. Plus, the birds in *Home and Away* are all fucking crackers, which is probably one of the main reasons why I want to go to Australia as soon as I finish school. That and the fact that it's so hot over there, you could grow all sorts of mad shit and you wouldn't even need a greenhouse or anything. I obviously haven't told Dosser anything about this. Sometimes I think he wants us to keep the business going forever, but I don't really see things happening that way. At first, when we started out and we were younger and all, I really needed Dosser's help, especially with all the gardening end of things. You see, I've never really been good at school and I'm not really into reading books or anything but Dosser laps all that shit up, so he used to learn how to like, plant shit and how to grow everything and what like, food all the different plants would need for us to be able to grow them and then I'd just do whatever he'd tell me to do. But now we've been at it all so long, it's like I know everything myself now, so it's like I don't need Dosser like, giving out to me and ordering me around all the time like I'm some kind of fucking eejit. So I'm thinking, fuck it, I'm getting out of here and moving to Australia as soon as I can, over to all those hot chicks and sunny beaches and barbeques, and I can live my life whatever way I want to, so that everyday will end in some mad way, just like it does in *Home and Away*. The one major problem I have is that Dosser's the only one of us who gets to deal with El Diablo Rojo. You see, I don't know if I've told you about this before but this bloke called El Diablo Rojo is the one who sends us over all the mad plants that we want to start growing and really without him, we wouldn't have been able to get the show on the road in the first place. When we first started with the Gardening Club in school, Father Whatshisname gave us the details of the place where he used to get any gardening equipment or seeds that he needed but then when we rang the place up, it turned out that the bloke who used to run it had died and the place just shut down because there was nobody else to keep it going or whatever. Anyway, Dosser had to tell Mister White this because we were going to be given an annual budget every year from the school for running the club and I suppose they wanted to know where all the money would be going. Dosser managed to convince Mister White that the real future of shopping for gardening supplies was in shopping over the internet and asked would it be all right if we used this website that Dosser said had "the most reputable appellation in on-line horticultural retailing." Anyway, Mister White is a real push over and he didn't even ask Dosser to explain himself even though I'm pretty sure neither of us knew what the fuck he was shiteing on about, so we had the green light to go ahead with doing things this way. But anyway, the main problem with me and this El Diablo Rojo bloke is that he only speaks French, even though I'm fairly sure his name's like Italian or something. So Dosser has to email all our orders in French and I never did French in school, I did German, and I was banned from doing that by Miss O' Riordan after my Junior Cert because I told her she had a bigger moustache than that Adolf Hitler.

But I suppose I don't really have to worry about any of that shit right now, Australia is a fairly big country so I'm sure I'll be able to make a few contacts of my own to get myself set up over there when I have to, so I suppose I'll just keep telling you about my weekend then. As I was saying, on Friday night I had an hour and a half to get cracking on my side project before Gobber showed up at the greenhouse, so I headed up to my bedroom and got my new jacket that I made last week with the Tiger skin lining and the green and yellow check outside and grabbed the keys to The Beast, snorting a couple of hits of that new shit we have while I was up there and sticking a pre-rolled Dagga joint in my pocket for when I was cruising in The Beast. I headed out the back way, even though I keep The Beast out front because I wanted to check on the prison hooch I had brewing in the greenhouse. I had the stuff in a couple of black bin liners at the back of the greenhouse and when I opened it up, the smell was so intense that I actually pulled my head back and banged the back of it off the shelf where we keep the watering cans and a load of them fell on top of me. One of them still had fucking water in it and it spilled all over my new jacket, but luckily, I made the jacket reversible so I was able to just turn the jacket inside out so the Tiger skin was on the outside which was pretty cool anyway. At least I knew the prison hooch was ready so I legged it out the back gate and ran around the lane, back out onto the road and up to my driveway where I angered The Beast and ripped it out of the driveway and headed up to Saint Aidan's Crescent to pick up Susie, my Number One. I remember I actually saw Peter and Paul Smith on the way and it was kind of weird because when I waved at them, they didn't wave back and they were standing around this savage white Mercedes, kind of like hunched over and talking to some bloke in the front of the car, but I couldn't really see who they were because the windows were like, tinted and all. I suppose those two are always up to some kind of trouble, but I don't know, it sounds weird like, but I'm pretty sure they saw me waving at them, but it was like they had this look in their eyes when they saw me, almost like they hated me or something. Anyway, I obviously couldn't let it worry me because I had to get on with sorting my shit out. I pulled up on Saint Aidan's Crescent, still a good bit down from Number One's gaff, just so her ma or da or whatever, wouldn't be able to see me picking her up when she walked out onto the road. I gave her a bell on the phone, but hung up before she could answer it because it saves a fortune on credit and that's how we always do things anyway. I waited in The Beast and had a look around the road, to check if there were any other young ones with potential knocking around, but all I could see was some aulfella, bringing his dog for a walk, but the dog had stopped walking and was just pissing up against a tree. I remember I started thinking about that dream with the tortoise again, and I started laughing to myself, when next of all I could just hear this knocking on the window and I nearly jumped out of my seat because it came out of nowhere and all. Anyway, I looked around and it was just Number One knocking on the passenger window, so I reached across and opened the door for her, because you can't open the door from the outside, which I suppose is kind of like a fault or whatever, but I don't really mind because it kind of gives you an extra bit of security if some honcho was trying to get into the car to like, whack me or whatever. Number One got in and I have to say, she smelled amazing and I actually felt myself starting to get a bit of a stalker. She was wearing a kind of black leather jacket and a real short black skirt, but it was the smell of her that was the best part. She was just like "Jaysis, it's a bit fuckin easier this way. Used to be a bleedin nightmare havin to go on that bike all the time. Me arse'd be in fuckin ribbons and I wouldna even got to the fuckin house yet!" Obviously she was talking about The Beast and how like convenient it is and I was just like, "Yeah a bit easier for me as well, ye fat bitch. Nearly gave me a heart attack having to cross bar you around the fuckin place all the time" but I say it with like a smile on my face, so it's just like a joke and she laughs and all because she doesn't really get offended when you say shit like that. So I angered The Beast again and started bailing it down to Saint Michael's Avenue because that's where I had to pick up Maeve, my Number Two. On the way down Number One was talking on her mobile phone, which was kind of annoying because it's sort of rude and all? Plus, her voice goes through your head after a while, but luckily I had that Dagga joint in my pocket, so I sparked it up just as she was shouting down the phone to her friend saying "I'll kill that bleedin young one, bleedin state of her! I never went near her fuckin fella, the fuckin state of him as well!" As I said, I was lucky to have that Dagga joint with me. I rolled up to saint Michael's Avenue anyway and gave Number Two the same missed call treatment I gave Number One. As we were waiting in the car, Number One took off her shoes and put her feet up on the seat and started like, rubbing in between her toes and then smelling her fingers. I just turned away in like, disgust, and then out of nowhere she put her hands up to my face and was like "Here d'y like the smell of that?!" and I pulled away but hit my head on the side of the car on the exact same spot where I'd just hurt myself in the greenhouse. She started laughing and saying "The state of ye!" which seems to be like, the only thing she ever says and I actually felt sick that I was on a semi-stalker when she first got into the car. I just gave her a look, like I was going to kill her or whatever and she actually stopped laughing and said "Ah I'm only messin wit ye Daddy, sorry ye banged your head" and she looked kind of like, real sorry and all. I just said "Remember who's paying your wages Number One" and then she said something back to me but like, under her breath and I didn't even bother asking her to repeat it because just then I could see Number Two walking down the road towards The Beast, and I wasn't happy at all because she was dressed in this like, real knacker tracksuit. Number One opened her door and got out of her seat to let Number Two get into the back of the car and I was all like "What the fuck are you wearin? Are you tryin to fuckin ruin me or something?" And then she was all like "What?

Your man likes it he does, fuckin asked me to wear it up tonight. Isn't that what ye want me to do Daddy, keep the customer happy?" Then Number One was all "She can wear what she wants you ye bleedin tick ye, look at her sure, she's gorgeous" and then she like turned around and put her hand on Number Two's face and was all "Don't mind him babes" and I was starting to wonder if this Number One was worth all the hassle at all. By that stage I couldn't even have been bothered talking to them anymore so I just headed off to pick up Katie, my Number Three. Number One and Number Two kept banging on to each other, about like school and shit and I suppose like, all these birds that they know that they hate or whatever. I polished off the last of the Dagga Joint and was raging I hadn't brought something stronger because the two girls started singing together when Number One realised the radio in The Beast didn't work and she was like "The state of your bleedin car!" and the two of them started laughing even though neither of them have a set of wheels of their own. After what seemed like the longest five minutes of my life, we got to Katie's house. Even though I call Katie my Number Three, she was actually the first bitch in my stable and I actually broke her in myself. And if the truth be told she's the only bird I've ever rode, even though I don't feel that bad about it because Dosser's never even kissed a bird, even though he says he met a couple of birds down in Wexford before which is obviously absolute bollocks. Once I'd ridden her, I thought I'd be banging birds left right and centre, but I suppose I just got caught up in our whole business venture, and in fairness, spending your weekends drinking prison hooch and smoking weird plants in a greenhouse with Dosser and Gobber, isn't exactly the best way to go about your business, if you're looking to get a ride every now and then. Katie got into the backseat beside Number Two, after Number One letting her in by the passenger door. At first, I thought I could see Katie making her way to my door, as if she was expecting me to get out of the car and all, but I kind of gave her this look that just said, "Not a fuckin chance love" and I gave her this kind of like, grin. I don't know if I've told you this before, but it was Katie that I used to get that Mister Delaney bloke that me and Dosser used to deliver the papers for arrested. Dosser doesn't even know about this, probably because I never told him but I planned out this whole mad like, operation to get Mister Delaney nicked, so we could make a load of money, get to keep his push bikes and I suppose it was really all just a bit of a prank as well if I'm to be honest.

It was around that time that I first started seeing Katie. I used to like, see her down the shops and stuff everyday when she'd be hanging around outside with some of her friends, not the likes of Number One and Number Two but like, nice girls. I'd normally be going in just to get like, skins and cans of coke and shit like that and I kind of started to notice that she was like, staring at me all the time. It must have been around the summer holidays, before I'd gone down to the country to stay in my granny's, when I came out of the shop one day and walked past Katie and her mates who were there as normal, just like hanging around and eating ice-pops or whatever and as I was walking out of the car park, back home towards my gaff, one of her mates called out "Here, will ye meet her?" and I turned around and the girls were all like, giggling and shit and I could see that the girl meant Katie when she said "her" because Katie was all scarlet and like, hiding her face and all. Anyway, being the smooth bastard that I am, I turned around and started walking back towards the girls and they were all like "Oh my God! Oh my God" but I was like, loving it. Anyway, as I got closer to them, the girl who had called me back in the first place ran out to me and she was all "Here, will ye meet my mate. Her name's Katie. D'y see her over there in the denim jacket?" and she was like, pointing over to where Katie was standing, but this time she wasn't really hiding her face, but she was kind of like, standing to the side and talking to one of her friends so that it looked like she wasn't really taking any notice of me but I could still get a good view of her for myself. Well obviously I was all like "Yeah, cool, whatever" and so the two of us went down the lane behind the shop and started like, kissing. I remember I tried to get a feel of her tits as well but she was all "No, your hands are too cold", even though it was like, summer and they were actually probably sweating. Then I tried to get a feel of her gee and she was all "No, it's my time of the month" so at that stage I was just like "Yeah, I'm out of here so". But then when I walked away, she said she wanted to see me again, and it was the days before we all had mobile phones so I told her I'd just meet her down outside the shops the next day. And it just kind of took off from there I suppose. Really, if I'm to be honest, she was mad innocent back then and after a while she'd do anything I'd ask her to do. We used to even get fucked up together, and it was cool because she always used to say that she never wanted to do drugs and that like, her ma and da would kill her if they ever found out she did, so I used to be always like "These aren't drugs, there's nothin illegal about them, relax" which I suppose was fairly handy, and it wasn't like I even had to tell any lies. I actually used to ride her a good bit, normally up the arse at first because she was afraid of getting pregnant, but then it just got to be like, anything goes because we'd normally be so fucked up together on urinal air fresheners and mushies and whatever me and Dosser had going at the time that she wouldn't even be like, capable of worrying about things like that. She kind of started to act mad weird and all after a while. Like, sometimes she'd start crying when we were riding and saying things like "You don't even like me" and "Why are you doin this?" which was kind of off-putting if the truth be told. But then other times I'd be walking home alone after being over in the park with Dosser or whatever and out of nowhere she'd like, jump on me and drag me into a lane and start ripping my cacks open, and start sucking my mister like she was some kind of rapist but like, in a woman way. Then she'd always be at me to get her more stuff, like mushies and prison hooch and shit to smoke, to the point that I almost started to worry about her. Then when me and Dosser started delivering the papers for Mister Delaney, I realised that she'd gone so weird that I'd probably be able to use her in my scam.

I started to notice that Mister Delaney seemed to always go up to The Millers at about 10.30 every night, and I don't know how he managed it but he'd come home around 12 and most of the time he'd be fairly sozzled. So one day when I met up with Katie, I asked her if she'd mind doing a favour for me, and that if she did it for me, I'd sort her out with a nice big present for our like, six week anniversary or something. Anyway, I told her she'd have to get properly dressed up the following night, as in with a skirt and high heels and like, loads of make-up and all, and to meet me down at the corner of Saint Michael's Avenue, where the church is, which is exactly where Mister Delaney's gaff was and that I'd tell her exactly what I wanted to do then. Well when she went down to the corner that night, I met her there and she was all done up, looking properly quality in all these stylish threads that she'd robbed off her sister or some shit like that. Anyway, as soon as I went up to her I started explaining to her what I wanted her to do, and I'd even brought this like, goodie bag, of all sorts of mad shit that I promised I'd give to her as soon as she went through with her side of the like, bargain. Anyway, we waited there for a while and it started to get all dark and all, and she was asking me to give her something to like, calm her nerves to make it easier to do what she was about to do. Of course, I had to say no because then she might not have gone through with it all and I had to keep her wanting that goodie bag to keep her like, keen. Eventually, as I kept refusing to give her what she wanted, I could see Mister Delaney coming down the opposite side of the road out of the corner of my eye. It was fairly obvious that he was pretty scooped because he was all kind of, wobbling all over the path and all. Anyway, I shoved Katie off in the direction of Mister Delaney and as soon as she saw him, she kind of turned around to me with this real horrified look on her face as if to say "Please don't make me do this" so I just waved the goodie bag in front of her to remind her of what she'd be getting if she just did this one simple thing for Little Old Tarzan. Eventually she just kind of turned around and you could see on her face that she realised there was nothing else for her to do so she walked over to Mister Delaney who seemed to be leaning against a wall for like, a bit of a rest and he was breathing all heavy, the way fat aulfellas sometimes do. I remember as she was walking over she looked real awkward, like she'd never walked in high heels before and I realised that that was probably a bad idea on my part because if she like, fell and broke her ankle or whatever, the whole game would be well and truly, up. Then when she got to the other side of the road and she was stepping over the kerb, up onto the footpath, I nearly had a heart attack because she went over on her ankle because the heel of her shoe like, broke. But in the end it actually turned out for the best because then Mister Delaney was coming over to her and he was all like "Aw, are ye all right love" and all, and in fairness to her she really played her part well and she was all real like, flirtatious or whatever, and before I knew it, the two of them were walking down the road towards Mister Delaney's gaff with their arms all linked and all, and eventually the two of them walked into the house together and I was obviously thinking, nice one. Then it was fairly simple after that. All I had to do was walk down to the phone box and ring the guards, but when I was talking to them I put on this mad like, deep voice and all, and I told them that I was a concerned parent from the Whitefield area and that I had suspicions that there was a paedophile currently living in the area, who at this very moment had an underage girl in his house at 29 Saint Michael's Avenue. Then I just went into a lane, on the opposite side of the road to where the house was, lit up a Catnip joint and waited. After a while, a squad car pulled up and two guards, big massive fuckers as well, went up to the door and started knocking on it real like, aggressively. From there, the plan couldn't have gone any better. Mister Delaney answered the door and he was just wearing this kind of vest thing on top, but even better, he was only wearing his boxers down below, and I'm not even sure if he was wearing even that because it was kind of hard to see past the two big mullahs from where I was watching. But there was definitely no difficulty in seeing what happened next, when out of nowhere, Katie came out of the gaff and burst past the two coppers, only wearing her knickers and she was all like, hysterical and all. Well after that, what could the coppers do only slap the old love bracelets on Mister Delaney and try and like, calm Katie down and stop her from going all mental and all. Well really after that those bikes were ours, and as far as I'm concerned, no major harm was done. Mister Delaney must have gotten a least a blowie of Katie (I never asked for any details to be honest), which must have been like, fairly savage for him because he probably hadn't even kissed a bird in ages, me and Dosser got to keep the bikes and all the takings from the previous two weeks (I actually managed to get into his gaff as soon as the guards had taken him down the station and took the money, which was obviously a savage bonus to the whole thing, plus, the stupid boggers had actually left the front door open, so I didn't even have to break in which means I didn't do anything illegal, well not that illegal anyway), Katie earned that goodie bag she wanted so badly, and she wasn't allowed out of her gaff for about a year which meant I didn't have to like, go out with her anymore, which was good because she was starting to get all kind of clingy and all. Then when it turned out that Mister Delaney had been overcharging all of his customers anyway, I was all like "Fuck it, cunt deserved it. He was a criminal anyway so let him stew in the pen if he has to". It is funny though, that Friday night as I was driving along with Number One cackling in my ear and Number Two tearing little bits off a tampon and throwing them at me while I was driving, I looked at Katie in the mirror and she was just kind of looking out the window, real quiet like she always is, and nipping away at a naggin of vodka that she always keeps in her handbag. It was then that I noticed that she was wearing that denim jacket, the same denim jacket she was wearing the first day I ever met her, but the funniest part of it all is, I actually cannot remember if I even gave her that goodie bag I promised her. And if I'm to be honest, I'm fairly sure I didn't.

But anyway, I dropped the three girls off at the houses of the three different clients I have going for me at the moment. I dropped Number one off at this aulfella called Digger's gaff and obviously I was seriously glad to get rid of her because she was really starting to get on my tits by then, and it pisses me of that she seems to be able to really get like, under my skin and all. I have to say, that's the one major problem with working with women, because even though Dosser can annoy me sometimes, I can always kind of like, threaten to hit him if he does, and that'll usually stop him from doing whatever it was he was doing that was annoying me in the first place. Whereas with the bitches, you can't really go around hitting them because then they'd be all bruised and the clients wouldn't like fancy them anymore, kind of like when you go to buy like, apples in the shop, you don't want ones that have any marks or bruises or anything on them, you want ones that are all smooth and look all nice and all. So instead you have to just put up with all the shit they give you because I suppose it's just easier in the long run and in fairness, it is making me a serious amount of cash at the end of the day. In fairness to the girls, they are fairly serious looking birds, the three of them that is and now that I think about it, I should probably try to up my prices once I get round to talking to the three clients who I haven't actually spoken to in ages with me being so busy with our new product and Dosser being grounded and all. I could probably do with adding one extra bitch to the stable though and I am on the lookout at the moment for any potential candidates. I have it down to a tee at this stage. Once I manage to find a bird that I reckon could pull off the job, I just use exactly the same method that I used with Katie and Mister Delaney. You just get to know them, find out if they're gamey or not, or if they're the type that would do anything if it meant they could get off their faces at the end of it, then you just get them dressed up real nice, find some sad old fucker who looks like he hasn't had a shag since the age of the dinosaurs, and then just set the whole show on the road, it's so simple really, I don't know why everyone doesn't just do the same. Especially if you can manage to land yourself someone like Number One. I swear to God, that girl actually enjoys what she's doing. That Friday night when I dropped her off at Digger's gaff, she was actually proper giddy when she got out of the car, just like a kid on their way to a birthday party or something. I know she wrecks my head and all most of the time, but she is a true professional when it boils down to it, not like Katie, she still seems to be moping around all the time, but I suppose at this stage she's just so used to the money that now she couldn't do without it. Once I'd dropped Number One off that night, I dropped Katie off next at this new client I found only a couple of weeks ago called Mister Cleary. Word on the street is, the bloke used to be a butcher, but that now he's retired and all he's got fuck all to do so I knew straight away that he'd be game for a bit of this kind of carry on. I think he used to be married as well, but the missus left him and ran off with some Spanish bloke or something, which is a bit mad because he looks mad old, like a proper granddad and all, and it's kind of hard to imagine people his age getting up to those kinds of shenannigans. When I dropped Katie off, she had that mad like, depressed look on her face, but Number Two just gave her this smile and kind of like, touched her hand and said "See ye later babes" which seemed to make her look a little happier. I was just glad not to be left on my own with Katie in the car because last week that's exactly what happened and it was really just, mad awkward and all. Once I'd gotten rid of Katie, Number Two just sat in the back talking on her phone which was grand because by that stage I really didn't feel like having to talk to anyone. I know it sounds mad, but sometimes I do start to feel real tired and stuff, like that maybe there's an easier way to live your life, especially when I think of the look on Katie's face when she walked away from the car towards Mister Delaney's gaff, but whenever this happens I just think of the new life I'm going to make for myself in Australia and a big beautiful smile just like, stretches across my face.

Once I'd dropped Number Two off at this bloke, Terry Steele's house, the rest of the night was mine and I knew exactly what way I wanted to spend it. I got back to my gaff around 8.30. I put The Beast to sleep in the front driveway but then I legged it around the back way to get into the greenhouse because I really didn't feel like walking through the house, in case I ended up bumping into my da or whatever. As soon as I got into the greenhouse, I got my hooch-drinking jug from the cabinet beside the big rose bush we have growing at the moment, and wouldn't you know it, but I managed to scrape myself in about six different places trying to get it out of the fucking thing and I decided there and then that the roses would have to go. I put down the hooch-drinking jug and got a secateurs and a pair of hard, black gloves out of my tool box, but just as I about to start attacking that fucking rose bush, I heard this mad kind of like, blurting sound and it gave me such a fright that I actually jumped and when I turned around to see what was going on, all I could see was this big hairy arse on the outside of the door, and it was only then I realised that it was obviously Gobber and that he must have just farted on the greenhouse glass, and that that was what had made the mad sound that made me jump. I opened the door and let him in and he had the usual big smile on his face, and I could see by looking into his eyes that he'd been drinking since I'd last seen him because they had that mad, red kind of glow to them that they always have. At first he was all like "Yes! Bring it fuckin on! Gimme the fuckin hooch man, gimme the fuckin hooch!" but he wasn't just saying it normally, he was kind of singing it and dancing around at the same time. Then he went real quiet for a second and he was like "Here man, are you mad in the head or what? You've got a fuckin scissors hangin out of your hand!" I was all like "What?" because I didn't know what he was talking about and then he started staring and pointing down at my hand. I looked down and the secateurs I was going to cut the rose bush with, was actually stuck through my left hand and it looked really cool because I still had the black gloves on and the blood from my hand was starting to like, seep out and it made it look like Darth Vader's hand or something. I was just like "It's not called a scissors ye clown, it's called a SECATEURS!" and I was all delighted with myself because Dosser and Gobber love nothing more than like, correcting me when I say something wrong or whatever. Then Gobber was just like "I don't care what it's fuckin called man, it's gone through your fuckin hand! You're gonna have to go to the hospital ye big black lunatic!" After he'd said that, there was actually just this mad awkward silence, because although we always slag each other all the time, neither Dosser or Gobber has ever called me black before, because in fairness none of us is really sure what I am. I was just like "Nah, I can't be bothered with that. This hooch will go off if we don't get it down us now, I'll tell ye what. After we've drunk this shit, I won't know what the fuck is going on, so you can pull this secateurs out of my hand and I'll be as right as rain. What ye reckon?" Gobber was just like "Whatever man, it's your fuckin hand. I suppose it is only your left hand so at least ye won't be without your one true pleasure in life. As long as you're still able to get fucked up, I really don't see any problem!" but he said the last part in a mad kind of like, posh accent. Well anyway, the rest of the night is a bit of a blur if I'm to be honest, but he must have done what I told him to because I woke up the next morning (in my own bed of all places) and the secateurs was out of my hand, and not only that but it was all bandaged up and shit as well, although don't ask me how that happened because not even Gobber had any memory of the night after about his fifth cup of prison hooch and he doesn't normally forget anything.

Well after Friday night's madness, we decided that we should probably take things handy enough, and seems as though Dosser was still locked up in his gaff, we decided to hit town to see if we could get ourselves a couple of hoochies, because we'd deffo had enough of the hooch by that stage anyway. It's weird, but even though Dosser was only grounded for like two weeks, I was actually starting to kind of miss him, and I deffo would've loved to have gone for a good old-fashioned crow-hunt that Saturday afternoon, but instead myself and Gobber hopped on the 15A nice and early and headed into town, which wasn't such a bad thing to do instead, I suppose. It was a beautiful day and the sun was actually beaming down, so I wore out these killer new shades that I managed to kind of like, design myself. I just got a really cheap pair in Penneys, and put all these mad like, designs on the frames from this kit I got in the post. When Gobber saw them he was all like "What? You cannot be serious!" but in this mad like, American voice but I just ignored him and in fairness he was just like "Well, I suppose I should be used to it at this stage" which was probably the best response he's ever given to any of my designs. Apart from that, it was just standard khaki combats with purple suede shoes and yellow mesh-vest, what on account of the good weather and all. We had to get off the bus a little early than planned because Gobber was saying that he was beginning to feel a bit ropey, so we started off drinking in some pub down in Rathmines, but to be honest it was a little bit boring. It was just full of all these aulfellas sitting at the bar, drinking Guinness, but it did occur to me that it might be a good place to go if I ever needed to get more clients for my side project. I wasn't really sure what to drink, so I just drank Heineken because that's what Gobber was on. I have to say, I've never really been that into drinking, mostly because I've never really had to be, what with all the alternative life-enhancing products that I've got to hand, as Dosser likes to call them. But as the day went on, I was really starting to get into it, and even Gobber had to say that he was impressed by my like, stamina, which was good to hear because normally all he does is slag people all the time. We went to a couple more places in Rathmines, mostly all still just full of aulfellas. Gobber seemed to know a few of them here and there and in this one place, this aulfella sat down beside us for a while and started talking to us about all kinds of shit, but it just got real annoying after a while because he wouldn't leave us alone. He kept talking about America for some reason, and it turned out that his son lived over there and he was just like "Everything is absolutely amazing over there lads, I'm tellin yis. They have everything over there and we have nothing. I'm tellin yis, yous are young men and yis should get out of this kip of a country before it drags ye under the ground. I'm tellin yis, I visit my son every summer and everytime I leave I say the same thing; it's like leaving heaven and going into hell, I'm tellin yis lads; leaving heaven and going into hell." Obviously, me and Gobber were looking at each other and thinking, "What the fuck is this guy on about?" And as soon as he got up to go the jacks, we necked our pints and headed for the door, because even though he was annoying the shit out of us, we didn't want to be like, rude to the bloke because he was so old and all. Just as we were walking out the door, he came back over towards the table where we'd just been sitting and he shouted over to us and he was all, "I'm tellin yis lads; leaving heaven and going into hell, leaving heaven and going into hell", but we just kept walking because at that stage he was kind of starting to embarrass even us, and I can't actually remember the last time I felt embarrassed about anything. Anyway, the day just kind of continued like this until it started to get a bit late, and finally, there were a few hoochies beginning to knock around the place. By the time we'd made our way into town I was starting to feel pretty drunk, but compared to Gobber I seemed pretty ok because he was completely off his rocker by about 10 o' clock. When he gets drunk like that, he just never shuts the fuck up talking. But it's not just like, normal talking, it's kind of like he just talks and you just listen, if you know what I mean? We were down in this pub called The Foggy Dew and Gobber was like "I'm tellin ye. The English league is just pure fuckin shite. It's all just pure hype man. All the clubs over there think they can just buy success, but you know what kid? The game doesn't fuckin well work like that. You need proper homegrown players to add a bit of backbone to your team, cos they're the only ones that are ever really gonna give a shit, d'y know what I mean? Now obviously I'm not denying that one or two big name signings can add a huge amount to a side: Platini, Van Basten, our very own Liam Brady and of course Maradonna being cases in point. But the thing is with those lads, they were special cos every other cunt on the fuckin team was still from the fuckin mother country. D'y know what I mean Taz? Of course you do, what am I saying? You're a good lad kid, a good lad. And the bottom line is man, nine European Cups have been won by Italian sides with an all-Italian final on the way this year, plus three world cups for the glorious Azzurri compared with those English cunts' fuckin one! I mean, the facts don't lie Taz, I'm sure you'll agree, the facts

DO NOT FUCKIN LIE." And then he'd just keep going on like this about whatever idea might come into his head, so I'd just keep nodding along even though I'd stopped listening to him about two boozers back because it was just easier than trying to come up with anything to say back to him. But then it was kind of weird at one stage of the night because he went kind of real quiet and got this mad serious kind of look on his face and he looked at me and he was like "Here, you boys must have made a fair few quid for yourselves at this stage, what? I' mean yous have been at it long enough, how much have yis made would ye reckon?" As soon as he said this, I almost felt sober all of a sudden, because I was wondering if maybe he had an idea about The Running Away Fund and where it was hidden and all. So I was just like "I don't really know to be honest, I just kind of spend it as I get it I suppose, I'm not really thinking too much about the future" which was obviously a lie but I don't want to like, tell Gobber about my plans for Australia because then he might tell Dosser and I deffo don't want him finding out. Gobber just kind of nodded, almost like he was disappointed and I thought he was going to keep on asking me about it, but luckily he noticed that his glass was empty so he just asked me if I wanted another drink and headed up to the bar.

Later on, we headed to some club in like, Temple Bar and it was it has to be said, full of savage birds, but it was real dark and the music was real loud and I don't know but, I just felt real weird inside the place, like I'd just done an American Dream and I was about to collapse, but not in a good way. By then we were drinking these drinks that Gobber was calling Screwdrivers, but really it's just like, vodka and orange juice. We must have only been there about ten minutes before I completely lost Gobber and I just ended up walking around in circles to see if I could find him but I couldn't see him anywhere. I tried to go up to a few hoochies to like, chat them up, but whenever I'd go over to say like, hello or whatever, they'd just turn away and keep talking to their friends, or start dancing like I wasn't even there. Well after a while I just got pure fed up with the whole thing and I was starting to get that feeling of like, breathlessness again, so I headed for the door and just legged it out of the place. It was only when I got out onto the street that it hit me how fucked I was and I was struggling to even stay on the path while I was walking. At one stage, I kind of like, wandered out onto the road and I just heard this mad beep and there was this like, taxi man shouting out of his car at me but I was just like, whatever.

I kept on walking and to be honest I don't really know town that well so I wasn't even sure where I was going. Eventually, I got to this big purple pub and because I like the colour purple so much I was like, fuck it, so I went inside to get another drink and just to see what the crack was like in there. When I got inside, the first thing I noticed was how well everyone was dressed, there were some serious threads on show, kind of like the shit I'd come up with myself down in my Granny's gaff. The music was pretty cool as well, kind of trance kind of shit, which is exactly the stuff that I'm fairly into at the moment, even though Dosser never lets me listen to it when we're working in the greenhouse. I made my way over to the bar and I was looking out for any hoochies that might be around the place, and it was weird but I couldn't see hardly any birds at all, just mostly blokes wearing savage threads. The place was fairly packed so I had to kind push my way through everyone to get to the bar. When I eventually got there I kind of didn't have a clue what to ask for and the barman was looking at me like I was some kind of crazy person. Then I was trying to think of the name of the drink that I'd been drinking with Gobber and then I looked at the barman and I was like "Oh yeah, a Screwdriver." The barman gave me this kind of nod, like he knew all along that's what I was going to ask for, and then when he gave me the drink, this bloke came up to me and he was like "Snap!" and he like, clinked his glass off mine. The guy was a bit mad looking in fairness. He had this mad, spiky blonde hair, but his face was real kind of tanned so there was kind of like, this mad contrast or whatever. At first I was kind of like "What the fuck is going on here?" but then when I looked down at his shoes, I noticed that they were almost the same as mine. Then I was like "No way man, lookit. We have the same shoes" and then I suppose I wanted to kind of like show off so I was like "Except I designed and made mine myself of course." Well whatever it was about what I said, this guy just went mad all of a sudden and he was like "OH MY GOD! You're a fashion designer? That is like SO amazing. Hi I'm Greg by the way", except he had this mad accent accent, kind of like he was from Northern Ireland or something. Then I was like "I'm Tarzan" and I put out my hand and Greg shook it but he was like "Oh you're so formal Terence, please you'll have to come over to meet my friends" but he said it with this big smile on his face and then he wouldn't let go of my hand and kind of brought me through the crowd like your ma does when you're a kid and you're walking through a shopping centre in town or something, but I was happy enough because it was deffo much easier to get through the crowd that way. When we got over to his friends Greg was all "Hi everybody, this is Terence, Terence this is everybody" then everybody came over like, individually and gave me a hug and they were all like "Hey, Ternece, you look fab" and I was just thinking that it was great to finally get some praise for my designining skills. They all told me their names but I couldn't remember any of them and I didn't bother like, telling anyone that my name wasn't really Terence because it just seemed too complicated to like, correct everyone. Well anyway, the night just kept going on and in fairness to Greg and his mates, they were all fairly sound blokes, just real nice fellas. Like, they were always just hugging each other and stuff and they definitely enjoyed their music, and their drink. All the gang kept coming over to me and asking me about what kind of stuff I was designing at the moment and if I'd ever designed anything for anyone famous or whatever. I was like "Well only for myself" and they just fell around the place laughing, even though I didn't really see the funny side to be honest, but I just laughed along anyway because they were all such nice fellas. Then after a while, Greg went to the jacks, but when he walked out of the kind of circle we were all standing in, he put his hand on my shoulder and he kind of like, whispered in my ear "Make sure you're still here when I get back" and I was like "Yeah of course I will" because in fairness I was actually having a great laugh with the boys and I really didn't want to head home yet. Then when Greg was gone, one of his mates came over to me and he was like "I think Greg really likes you Terence" and I was just like "Yeah, I think he's a top man as well" and then his mate started kind of giggling and getting real excited and stuff, and whispering to the other lads, and then they all started giggling as well. When Greg got back from the jacks he was carrying two Screwdrivers in his hands and he kind of like, nudged me with his elbow and he was like "One for the road?" and he held out the glass and it was obvious that he wanted me to like, take the drink. I was all "Yeah cool man" and then Greg started telling me there was a party on in one of his mates gaff's, and that it was just down the road if I wanted to like, go and I was like "Yeah cool". Anyway, myself and the whole gang all legged it out of the pub and started walking down the road and they all started singing that song that goes like "We are family! I've got all my sisters and me!" but Greg just kind of hung back with me and he was like "The state of them" but he was only saying it in a mess kind of way, with a smile on his face, not in a slagging kind of way like Number One does. When we got back to the gaff, we all went into this like, living room and the lads just got the music going again on this big stereo, and bottles of Vodka just started appearing out of nowhere. The lads were all up and dancing with each other and then one of them, who must have like, owned the gaff pulled this little plastic bag out of a drawer under the stereo, opened it up and put it on this table in the middle of the room. All the boys started digging into the bag like when you're a kid and someone has a bag of sweets or whatever, but it was obvious that the bag was full of like, yokes or whatever. Greg turned to me and he was like "Do you want one?" and it was obvious that he meant a yoke, but I was just like "No, I've never touched one in my life" and he just gave me this big smile and he was all "No, me neither". Then he was like "I know where there's a bottle of poppers, if that'd be more up your street?" and I was like "Yeah, I'd hit some of that" even though I hadn't had poppers in years because I drank a full bottle of it one time and I actually got sick so badly, that even the sight of a bottle would get my stomach going again, but I was willing to give it another go seems Greg was being so nice and all. So, we left the living room and I just kind of like, followed Greg up the stairs and then he brought me into this bedroom and he was just like "Just lie on the bed and make yourself comfortable, I think the bottle's in here" and then he started looking through the top drawer of the like, bedside cabinet. I just lay down on the bed and took my shoes and even my vest off because it was actually starting to like, chafe my nipples a bit. Then Greg turned around towards me and he had the bottle of poppers in his hand and he was like "Found it" and I was like "Cool". Then he was like "Sit up for a second and take a sniff" so I sat up in the bed and Greg took the top off the bottle and he put it up to my nose and I swear I must have inhaled half the bottle because I couldn't see for about two minutes and I just got a mad fit of the giggles the way you do. Greg did the same and the two of us were just laughing like mad, and I was like "Here, will ye put on some music?" and Greg was all "No problem babes" which is weird because that's what the bitches from my stable always call each other. He stuck on what I'm fairly sure was a Kylie Minogue album, on this mad old CD player that was beside the bed and then I was like "D'y wanna lock the door as well?" and he was like "Oh look at you giving all the orders, you're so domineering. *I really like that*" and I was just like "Yeah, whatever" so he went over and locked the door. Then he came back and he kind of like, perched himself up on the bed and started kind of rubbing my face with his thumb. Then, he started feeling my chest and stomach with his two hands and he was like "You're *so* beautiful". Then he started kissing my neck with these real like, soft kisses, and he started doing the same all down my body; real softly. Then when he got down to my bellybutton I was like "Take off my belt" and he was just like "There you go again, more orders" and he just started undoing the big buckle on the front of my belt and then just slowly, slid it off from around my waist. Then when he was just about to undo the button and zip on my trousers I was like "Just hand me over me belt there for a sec will ye?" and he looked up at me and he was like "What?" I was like "Just give us me belt there for a sec" and he had this mad weird look on his face but he handed it over to me anyway. As soon as he gave it to me I just sat up all of sudden and said "Well that was a fuckin mistake wasn't it?" And Greg kind of jumped back because he wasn't expecting to me to sit up like that and I just started laughing and cracked him a proper slap across the head with the belt buckle. I obviously split the skin with the first whack, because a load of blood kind of squirted off his face as his head turned to the side. Greg was all like "What the hell?" but he said it in a way that it was kind of like crying, and I was just like "Shut your bum bashing face or I'll kill ye" and then he started screaming "Help! Help!" and he ran for the door but I just pulled him back, cracked him over the head a couple of more times with the belt until he kind of sank to the ground and curled up in a ball, and I knew then that he wouldn't be making any more runs for it. I turned up the volume on the CD player as it was blasting out that Like a Virgin tune. The fucking bum bashing cunt just stayed on the ground and I just kept whipping the fucker with the belt, mostly on the head, but after a while I started working the body a bit more because the blood was starting to get all over my trousers. Eventually the belt started to hurt my hand for some reason, so I just started dancing on the fucker's ribs and grabbing him up by his spiky hair and crashing his bum bashing face down onto the floor and all the while the cunt's screaming out "Please, please stop. Just stop hurting me!" After a while, I don't know how long, he just gives up struggling and goes real quiet and just lies there on the floor, panting like a little dog. I check to make sure he's still awake. He is but his eyes are all kind of glazed over, kind of like Gobber's when he's had a few too many to drink I suppose. Anyway, once I could see he wasn't going anywhere it was like, plain sailing. I looked out the window of the bedroom and luckily enough, the gaff was like one of those real old red-brick houses and the drop to down to the street was nothing at all. I stuck my shoes and vest back on and opened the window. I got kind of half way out and I took one last look at the bum basher lying on the ground and I just said "Here, Greg. D'y wanna do this some other time or what?" and I just started laughing so hard that I nearly fell out of the window. The bum basher just kept panting away and I turned around and made the easy jump down to the street, checking before I did that there was nobody down below because I obviously didn't want to hurt anyone. I kept walking until I got back onto the main road, and I have to say, I really did feel seriously happy for myself about what a good night I'd had. I actually don't think I can remember ever having as much fun. And you didn't really think I didn't know Greg was a bum basher did you? How stupid do you think I am?

A Brief Biography of Mister Brian Johnson

Mister Brian Johnson is a good teacher, not a great teacher, and he knows this only too well. He is standing at the top of the Biology Lab in St. Leonard's College, taking a deliberately longer time than what is necessary to tidy the books on his desk in order to allow his final charges of the week file out of the room in a semi-orderly yet quite chaotic fashion, and although he knows he has undoubtedly done some good work, he also knows that he could surely have done much more. The Easter holidays, are he must admit; a godsend and he intends to take full advantage of these two weeks off for some well earned rest and relaxation. He has arrived at a point in his life where each passing day of the school year nears him ever closer to the end of his teaching practice, and he greets the clanging of the one o' clock lunch bell with a grateful but not overly celebratory smile, in much the same manner as a prisoner marks the completion of a day of a long sentence with a notch on his cell wall, content that he is a step closer to ultimate redemption, but resignedly prescient of the adversity still to come. Mister Brian Johnson knows that he is a good teacher and not a great teacher because he is frighteningly aware of a clearly defined dichotomy between evidently positive and evidently negative characteristics of his professional attributes. On the positive side, he feels that on most days, the majority of his students learn at least one important fact through the dissemination of his own personal knowledge of the curricular material dealt with in the subjects of Junior Certificate Science, Leaving Certificate Biology (both almost certainly to a standard somewhat approaching Higher Level) and that of Ordinary Level Junior Certificate Mathematics, although in the case of the latter, he did suffer one unfortunate moment in a second year class, when through admittedly gross negligence and incompetence on his part, he completely forgot how to illustrate graphically, information from given sets between three Venn diagrams, a failing which was immediately noticed and commented upon by several members of the relevant second year class, and has consequently and unequivocally damaged his working relationship with this particular group of students. Although he is positively pleased in the knowledge that most of his pupils are acquiring at least a diurnal modicum of information from his tutoring, he is quizzically aware that the vast majority of what he says in class, is knowledge that he acquired when he himself was a secondary school student in this very same educational establishment, listening intently to his teacher as all good students do, and propelling himself forward, in a literal academic sense of course, into the esteemed corridors of University College Dublin. Indeed, he notices that hardly any of the august scientific expertise he imparts in class was garnered from the lecture halls of the science building in UCD and at times he wonders if he did actually learn anything of scientific value in those three years of undergraduate scholastic ramblings, and concludes that he almost certainly would have made a better teacher as a callow yet assuredly self-confident eighteen year old, than he can manage to be now as a world weary and nerve-shattered wreck at the relatively mature age of twenty three. He wonders why this must be so, but laughs at the absurdity of his preposterous pondering after a nanosecond of time has elapsed, because he knows really there is no need for any deep, solipsistic and introverted questioning of the existential nature of the self in order to find a logical explanation for an answer to this question. The reasons why he managed to learn so little science while studying for his science degree are so banally cliché that he can barely bring himself to consider them. Although his attendance at lectures was in fact, above the average attained by his fellow aspiring Mendelevs, for Mister Brian Johnson, or simply Brian, or perhaps Johnno to his old school friends (of whom there were few) as he was then known, lectures were more suited to the perusal of tabloid newspapers and the autobiographies of Association Football players than they were to the detailed learning of the fundamental workings of the natural world. Aside from the very obvious difficulties he encountered in his lectures, he realised after only a matter of weeks as a full time student, that he actually spent at least twice the amount of time he spent studying (in inverted commas), stacking shelves in the pet food aisle in Dunnes Stores while attending to his supposed part-time job. Indeed, as the chiming of festive bells heralded the end of his first semester of First Science, he felt as though he would struggle to point out UCD on a map, let alone deliver a concise synopsis of everything he had learnt over the last three months at Ireland's second most prestigious third level educational facility to his proud and eagerly inquisitive parents, yet he could name the six different varieties of tinned Pedigree Chum, along with details of the calorific content and nutritional values of these products while having a wet dream about Marie Lynch, the checkout operator whose radiant beauty once caused him to knock over an entire shelf of Whiskas kitten food with his protruding engorged penis, as he tirelessly endeavoured to ensure an ample selection of feline, canine and piscine cuisine, remained at an arm's reach of the animal lovers of south west Dublin. Owing to this situation, coupled with a number of disparate yet paradoxically related contributory factors which we shall consider in due course, Brian never felt truly as though he were a student, and in fact, felt himself much more to be a simple working man, who toiled in a department store to earn money, and then in whatever leisure time he may have had, pissed the financial benefits of his labour up against the proverbial wall. This somewhat adopted, or as it may have been viewed by others, contrived attitudinal vision of himself was further reinforced by the fact that he continued to consume vast quantities of alcoholic beverages in the largely working class hostelries of the Crumlin and Tallaght areas, as well as spending almost five nights a week in the Station or Portobello night clubs in Rathmines. Aside from these two night clubs, where the clientele could be admittedly a little more diverse on occasion, he was generally surrounded by tattooed apprentice tradesmen of the booming, building industry, postmen who had traded in their bicycles for spanking new green vans and warehouse workers, who drank still clothed in the vestments of their industrial labours and who more than likely slept in them as well. As he sat and slurped among them, shoulder to shoulder and knee to knee, his naturally modest Dublin accent became fortified with the clamour of the building sites and the factory floors, and was given a guttural tone due to the habitual imbibing of a famous brand of traditional Dublin porter, a substance he practically forced down his neck, as the semi-digested contents of a mother seagull must be regurgitated and propelled down the gullets of her fledgling offspring, compelled as he was to maintain face in front of his drinking companions. A casual observer, who may have strayed into The Cuckoo's Nest on a Super Sunday afternoon would surely not have detected the presence of real life cuckoo egg amidst the smoke-filled scene before them, for not even the most astutely perceptive minds would acknowledge the presence of a callow boy genius, a scholarly revelation no less from the multitude of young faces before him. For in truth, that was what the young Brian was, an academic sponge no doubt, who had a mental capacity fit for any purpose of esteemed portent that one could imagine. And as Brian would heartily laugh at jokes as crude as those which must be told among the denizens of an institution for the incompetently insane, he was indeed, acutely aware of this fact. Because unbeknownst to his companions, his comrades of the daily struggle to suppress the vomiting reflex of one's stomach, who would unquestionably spend the long remaining years of their simple lives entertaining themselves in this very same fashion, he had a plan up his sleeve and he was fucked if he was going to tell any of them about it.

The last member of Mister Brian Johnson's third year science group has left the class and he finds himself once more in a state of solitude, staring into the space beyond the teacher's desk against which he leans. For a moment, he drifts into his daily reverie, watching the years of his boyhood play on a loop among the empty chairs and desks before his eyes. Still at times, even though he has been teaching at his alma mater for nearly eight months as well as having done a stint as a substitute two years previously, he is caused to shake himself into an awareness of reality as he meanders through the corridors, forgetting for minutes at a time his age and new found existence as a figure of authority. For it seems like only yesterday when he first arrived on the steps of St. Leonard's as a wary and indeed, frightened child, searching across the faces of fellow grey-clad first years, for a familiar set of eyes to catch his unsettled gaze. Now as he closes the door of the biology lab behind him, he grins furtively to himself, as the absurdity of the present state of affairs hits his consciousness like the impact of a meteor on the surface of the ancient moon. For even if he never teaches again, this period in his life will always be there for himself and others to remember, and look back upon in their secret, private minds, as if the moon was only theirs to see in a sky of otherwise featureless black. The school is now closed for the Easter Holidays, a half day has been granted to the students on this Friday before Easter Week, and all staff are required to attend a brief meeting in the staff room although he is debating whether to bother going or not. As a student teacher, whose working days never extend beyond lunch hour anyway, he is not strictly required to attend and he concludes that surely his absence would not be noticed. Mister Murray, or Kevin as he should now address him, although the uttering of these two syllables still makes his cheeks turn red, turning him back into the shy and awkward twelve year old on that far off day in late August, probably wouldn't even notice if he decided not to turn up for class for the rest of the year, let alone comment upon his absence from a presumably pointless meeting before a two week hiatus, so he decides to make a break for it and run. He puts his light jacket over his shoulder and places his solitary blue pen in the front pocket of his shirt. He could, if he were assiduous or conscientious enough, bring home some textbooks with which to prepare some exciting and novel lesson plans for the final term, but as all his inspections from Miss O' Loughlin, the old hag, have been completed, he resolutely decides against it and leaves all the books in a semi-neat pile on the teacher's desk. He quickly locks the door of the biology lab and peers over the heads of the throngs of giddy adolescent boys, down the length of the corridor towards the back entrance of the school to look out for any possible obstacles to his making a clear getaway without the raising of disapproving eyebrows from any senior members of staff. He looks down the other direction towards the front entrance and he can see Mister Murray, or should he say Kevin, standing at the threshold, high fiving the students as they race past him into the yard, and laughing to each other about the unbelievable actuality of how they ever managed to end up in a school with such an insanely incompetent principal. He looks back to the opposite direction and although he can see Mister White, or Old Chalky as they used to call him, sitting in his office with the door open, he should still be able to make his way to the back entrance without encountering any serious problems. He begins to make his way down the corridor, walking briskly and manoeuvring between the jostling crowds of students, keeping his eyes fixed on the light shining in through the open double doors, the portal to two weeks of unadulterated rest and recuperation. He can almost smell the fresh spring air when he encounters his first obstacle, as Sharon O' Neill meekly attempts to shout at lads who are oblivious or otherwise, to the fact that they are blocking her path as she desperately tries to make her way down the corridor in the opposite direction to Mister Brian Johnson, while also hoping to avoid making eye contact with her sometime lover. Brain sees Sharon and can tell straight away that she is trying to avoid meeting his gaze, and instead of helping her attempts to make her way through the uniformed hordes by maybe calling the attention of the high-spirited students to the struggling female in their testosterone dripping midst, he simply walks on, allowing her to continue her struggle alone, yet affirming to himself the certainty that he will contact her via the medium of drunken text message in a matter of hours. The next hurdle to traverse is the open door of Chalky White, the old prick, who if he sees Brian skulking his way out of the building, will not necessarily call him back to inform him of the incumbency upon him to attend today's meeting, but will certainly use this escapade as ammunition for future looks of scoffing disapproval. Brian quickens his step on approaching the open door and as he passes by, he sneaks a seemingly perfunctory glance inside the office of his former, current and potentially future nemesis, and to his considerable delight he spies Old Chalky, hunkered on the ground with his back to the open door, searching for a pen no doubt, that has slipped from his tyrannical grasp and nestled its way into a particularly tricky spot beneath his desk. Mister Brain Johnson almost squeals with a girlish excitement as he comes within a matter of metres to the exit, opening up onto the front yard, and from there into the outside world and freedom. He casually slips his leather jacket off his shoulder and dresses himself in its moderately warm embrace, imagining himself as a James Dean type figure, ready to do battle with the entire established order of the world (for a two week period anyway) when he suddenly emits, like an erupting Vesuvius, the grossly offensive profanity of "Cuuunnnnnnnttt!" He cannot believe his own stupidity, but he appears to have left his bag of personal and rather incriminating substances, not only within the walls of the school building he was so desperately trying to escape, but within the confines of the staff room no less, the very place where upon each occasion of entering, at least a little, but sometimes a very substantial piece of his soul dies. He ceases the animalistic articulation of his immense despair and rather embarrassedly observes a number of parents parked in cars, looking at him as though he were carrying the severed heads of their blessed children. He also notes that he is completely surrounded by the stunned faces of numerous students, some of whom also share the petrified countenances of the adults sitting in cars, so he holds his hands up in an apologetic plea, mouths somewhat gauchely, a word that should be intelligible as being "sorry", turns dejectedly around on the concrete step that had so recently served as a tangible vestige of his Houdini like feat of endeavour, and resignedly re-enters the school building.

As Brian's years in university continued their passage of time consistent with the fundamental rubrics of the earth's celestial orbit, he found that he was beginning to drift into a state of almost semi-normality on the one hand, yet in a different and clearly more visceral context, he felt a burning desire within his body and soul to remove himself from his surroundings in both a literal and transcendental sense. His life had in truth, become one big elaborate compromise with the predominating forces of normality. The man who was the boisterous life and soul of the party with eight pints of Guinness and four double southern comfort and red lemonades inside him in The Submarine Bar on a Saturday night, struck rather a meek and unimposing figure among the rugby jersey-clad hordes of UCD. Indeed, Brian had noticed very early on in his journey through third level education that he seemed to be the only person in the entire college who spoke with an accent anywhere near approaching one which could be described as being Working Class. This debilitating epiphany condemned the boy genius into an unprecedented laconic state at the best of times, and an unseemly muteness at its worst. And in these times of hardship he felt a growing hatred, of the south Dublin elite by whom he was surrounded, and even a contemptuous loathing of the self began to assail his once self-assured mind, causing him to reminisce about times bygone, better times no doubt. He remembered his old school days when he sauntered through the corridors of St. Leonard's College, impervious to sling or arrow, stick or stone as he paraded himself, master of the fine balance between being admired by those in establishment, and respected by his peers. Imprisoned like a wasp in a beehive in the lecture halls of UCD, his mind would begin to take him back to the halcyon days of St. Leonard's, where life was easy and nothing was difficult, when reposing at the back of class with his chair leaning against the back wall, he would scoff at the absurd attempts of his less academically able classmates, as they struggled like beetles stuck in melted tar to grasp the most elementary ideas of Euclid and Pythagoras, before raising his hand in a perfunctory and nonchalant manner, to relieve the obvious distress on his teacher's face as he grew alarmed at the inability of his charges to understand his Aristotelian diatribe. Then as the nights out in Rathmines grew longer and images of the occasional yet all-consuming sexual conquest began to pulse from his inner eye, down through his chest until he could feel it mingle with the alcohol still tearing shreds from the lining of his stomach, it was he who found himself staring at power point presentations as though he were staring into the void of an empty universe, a place without the light of the sun or the subtlest twinkling of a distant star, as he realised that the boy genius was really not a genius at all, but was just another bee in a hive. But as all the other bees, busied themselves around him, burdening themselves to do the queen's bidding, ignorant as they were to their own ability to fly away, he felt the wings on his back, twitch and fan and search for space to fly. And when he felt this urge tingle the length of his still stretching spine, he knew that it would serve him well, but he knew for certain, that he must not serve it yet.

When he thought back to his day's at St. Leonard's, he would wonder what on earth he had managed to learn there, aside from the obvious propensity for alcoholism and misogyny, the twin illnesses he could see destroying the lives of his old companions, although their lives were perhaps being destroyed through a wonderful series of blissful moments, as the more enjoyable each weekend became, the greater part of their mental and emotional well being was chipped away and turned to dust. In university he realised beyond any doubt, that the most important lessons he had learnt at St. Leonard's had been those imparted to him by old Father McEvoy. The aged priest had a terrible reputation amongst the student body, owing to his very noticeable eccentricities and the peculiar gait he cut as he strolled around the modest grounds outside the school buildings during class time, when the boys in different rooms, much to the distress of their would be educators, would en masse arise from their seats to point and laugh at the acolyte of Christ, knocking on the windows of their classrooms like caged barbarians as he bent his back beneath the shade of a willow tree, to pluck a solitary fallen leaf from the ground and place it delicately on the lapel of his jacket, or pausing to smell the beauty of a hydrangea blossom, as its pink hue attracted his searching eyes as they surveyed the scene before them, hoping to glimpse upon a burning vestige of the beauty of God's natural world. Even now, as Brian moves awkwardly and even morosely towards the stairs that lead to the staff room, he brings to mind the memories of he and Father McEvoy, working like two peas in a pod in the old priest's allotment behind the priests' house. For it was there that Brian stumbled upon a beauty he would carry with him through his life. It was the beauty of an idea, the beauty of a young dreamer's vision being fermented with the liquor of reality. For Dosser Doyle and Tarzan were not the first two dreamers to strike a blow for the subversion of the established order of things via the medium of the St. Leonard's Horticultural Society. All things have their genesis, and all beauty has its creator. In Brian Johnson we can see the genesis and the creation, encapsulated in the meandering mind of the boy genius. Our contemporary heroes of the cultivation of mind altering substances are not aware of who their God, their provider, their genesis is and *that*, he considers is *true* beauty. That is the beauty of God. That is the beauty of the boy genius.

As he mounts the stairs that lead to the staff room, Brian can hear the rattling of tea cups being taken from shelves and the metallic rumblings of sugar spoons in drawers cut through the din of unfamiliar chatter. He braces himself to enter the domain of that infernal noise, but just as he is about to push the door that will lead him from what he considers to be reality into a morass of madness, he is violently accosted by a smiling figure, steaming from the other side of the divide like a train emerging from a dark tunnel and into a blinding summer sun. "Ah Brian my boy, what are you still doing here you old dog? Surely there are some fluffy little tails out there you should be chasing, what? A young man like you, by God I can tell you if I had my youth again this is the last place I'd be. Australia maybe, Canada perhaps, or even the searing and suffocating heat of the Niger Delta would have suited me better than this old place. But we are the consequences of the choices we make Brian and there is nothing surer than that I can tell you. But it's not all bad I suppose; I have my health, I have my beautiful children and well, my not so beautiful wife if the truth be told, but by Jesus I have the one most important thing still in my life and do you know what that is Brian?" "No I don't Sir, I mean Mister Murray, I mean Kev, I mean Kevin." "Ah go on, a bright boy like you, you must be able to guess. Have a look at me there now and try to think to yourself; what's the one thing that that old codger wouldn't be able to live without?" Brian effects a ponderous gaze into the far off nowhere behind Mister Murray's back, searching for a clue that will never reveal itself, but searching nonetheless. "Golf Sir?" he questions more in hope than anything else, inwardly cursing himself for unceasingly regressing at least twelve mental ages every occasion he finds himself unfortunate enough to have to converse with his current employer. "The boys of course Brian, the boys! Jesus Mary and Joseph. Golf, ugh, can't stand the game Brian. A good run ruined, as Jack Kennedy used to say. No

Brian, it's the boys. I couldn't live without them Brian. Their eagerness, their energy, their dedication to the school colours on the sports field. It all makes me choke up with tears to bear witness to their youthful exuberance you know. Even this year, when we lost that match by that record score, what was it again?" "152-nil Sir, I mean Kevin" "Yes that's it, 152-nil, trust you to remember the score Brian, you were always so good with numbers. Yes, 152-nil, but the way they just kept going. Beautiful I thought. Called to mind the majesty of Leonardo and the glorious 500 as they defended the gates of Rome against the Egyptian hordes, don't you think? But do you know what makes me happier than anything in this life Brain? It's to see boys like you, good St. Leonard's boys who choose to return to our hallowed and humble halls and join us in the educating of the future guardians of the morals and values brought to us by Jesus himself when he appeared to St. Leonard and commanded him, to educate the young boys of Dublin and ensure that our capital city should not fall foul of the purveyors of Judaism and the disciples of various other miscellaneous voodoo claptrap. The words of Our Lord himself Brian, the words of Our Lord himself. Now, here, listen to me going on like an old broken gramophone, what is it you're looking for Brian, how about our beautiful Miss O' Neill perhaps? Sweet Jerusalem what a corker eh? One of the best we've ever had here I'd say, what do you think? Serious set of baps on her, as the boys would say eh? Oh don't look so surprised Brian, I'm not such an old fuddy-duddy you know, I'm down with the lingo, have no fear." "Well Kevin, I was of course just making my way to the staff meeting. I am required to attend am I not?" "Staff meeting? Ah bollocks to that Brian. Get yourself a few pints somewhere in the name of God, young man like you. Go and paint the town red. We've two weeks' off for heaven's sake. Paint the town red like the ground beneath the body of the hanging Christ on Mount Sinai must have been stained crimson by the blood which oozed from the wound in his jugular. In the words of King Lear Brian, Get thee to a pub!" "Oh thank you Kevin, I really appreciate that. It's a shame to miss the meeting and all but I suppose you're right, a few pints wouldn't go astray." "Hahaha, wouldn't go astray. I like it Brian, I like it; you're a man after my own heart, a St. Leonard's man through and through. Well what are you waiting for Brian, get a move on for goodness' sake." "Yeah, I just need to get one thing from the staff room there Kevin. It's just a bag, that's got a few papers I need to correct in it. You know, so I can get a bit of work done over the break." "Work be damned, but I suppose if you really need it. Listen, you wait here Brian, I'll go in and get it. Don't want the rest of them seeing you in there or else they'll all know I've let you off early. They're not all St. Leonard's boys you see Brian. We've got to look out for each other you know. Now, where is this bag of yours?" "It's just on the ground beside where the toaster is Kevin. It's just a plain black, leather bag." "Rightio, I'm on the case. Hahaha, do you hear me? I'm on the case, oh lord. Right beside the toaster, theses bloody teachers Brian, nothing better to do with themselves than eat bloody toast all day." Brain waits a few solitary seconds in a state of mild trepidation, although he is somewhat befuddled by his recent conversation so he feels more in a state of bafflement than anything else. Presently, Mister Murray appears at the door, holding up the leather case and slapping it with his hand as if to signal the completion of his mission. "Nothing in here I should know about is there Brian? No *Playboys* or copies of *Loaded* magazine or anything?" "Oh nothing like that Kevin, I keep those somewhere much safer." "Hahaha, by God you're a card Brian, a card I tell you. Just get out of here you old rascal before you kill me with the power of your witticisms. Now, high five that shit." Mister Murray raises his right palm above his head and Brian duly slaps his hand against it. He retreats quickly back down the stairs and once more enters the corridor that will lead him to the freedom of the outside world. He breathes a sigh of relief so strong, that it feels like a gale force wind escaping from his lungs and he wonders if it may even have been audible to his colleagues incarcerated in the staff room for at least another hour. As he strides down the corridor he is overcome by a childish giddiness so that he almost skips out of the door and into the bright spring day. He places the strap on his bag around his shoulder, taking a brief glance inside to ensure that everything remains in order and walks briskly around to the front of the school to collect his bicycle. As soon as he reaches his bicycle, he performs his daily check to ensure that the air has not been let out of his tyres and that his brake cables have not been severed and once he is sufficiently content that there are no life-threatening mechanical booby-traps awaiting his cycle home to Rathmines, he sets off in a leisurely enough pace, as he wishes to savour the feeling that a moment like this can bring. As he skilfully negotiates his way out of the school gates, he cannot help but turn back to look at the old priests' house and his mind is once again cast back to those days spent smoking dried dagga leaves with Father McEvoy and listening to his stories of performing exorcisms in mud huts in Sierra Leone. "Da black man be a good man, but a mad man" the old priest used to say, and the young Brian could see in the priest's eyes, that he believed life was better in Africa than it was here in what the old missionary would call "civilization", as though the madness of the African was really something beautiful, as though it was a quality of human existence that had been strangled out of the westerner's life, and that we had replaced it with another set of considered beliefs, culminating in the need for twenty-seven different varieties of toilet paper on supermarket shelves. As a 16 year old boy, Brian Johnson believed he had stumbled upon an idea, as he pottered around the greenhouse and the plant beds in St. Leonard's College. He knew that he could attempt to live as a wandering spirit, drifting in a smoke filled haze towards the mud huts of the African jungle. On the other hand, he could also sense that there was money to be made, and he had the perfect way to do it. If only he could cultivate huge amounts of the Dagga and sell the produce to his peers, promising them the experience of drifting across the oceans and mountains towards the glorious vistas of foreign lands. But for Brian there was one obvious hurdle he had to overcome and in his heart of hearts he knew he could never realise his dream. For Brian Johnson, then as now was truly a loner. Although, as he drifted through life he had his companions and he undoubtedly possessed the ability to sustain entertaining conversation for hours on end, for some reason unbeknownst to him, he never experienced what might be called "true friendship". Really his solitude was not something that was inflicted on him due to any kind of natural unsociability, rather it was something he chose for himself, as it allowed him the freedom to usurp the spinning world as it passed before his discontented eyes. And when he was young he had a vision of what it would be like for two young allies to form their own horticultural society, or more accurately who would be able to bring the aspirations of his spirit to fruition. At an early stage he enlisted the help of two young spectacled first years, to see if they would have the inherent capabilities to create a dynasty of his vision. Yet by the time Brian was preparing to leave sixth year, the raving homosexual tendencies of the two boys, coupled with their evident disinterest in indulging in any kind of mischievous behaviour, clearly demonstrated to him the folly of his ways. He still believed however, that two young boys would eventually inherit the true ideals of the St. Leonard's Horticultural Society as sure as the meek would inherit the very Earth itself. He could not say for certain why he was so sure in his belief; his faith in this became an all consuming fire within his soul. He knew how it would come to pass. He saw himself as a seer, a soothsayer, a prophet, perhaps more John the Baptist than Jesus, but a prophet all the same. Two young boys would grow to be men from the bounty of God's green Earth. In plain words, two head the ball young fellas would eventually cop on that you could possibly make a lot of money out of making legal drugs and selling this produce to anyone who was willing to buy it. Brian's years in UCD passed by as a mere formality, present he may have been in body but his mind was always on the future. As soon as he had finished his degree, he understood what had to be done as the Mayfly that emerges from its pupae state, understands its destiny to soar above the river of its birth and to procreate. He returned to his old school with his parchment in hand and dressed in the finery of a freshly purchased second hand suit. A tendency towards the teaching profession? Of course. A belief in the moral and social vision of the school's founding fathers? You better believe it. So when the boy genius returned to the corridors of the place where he felt he was created it didn't take him long to notice, the disciples and vehicles of his prophetic vision. He almost wept with delight when he saw them, walking through the school with an air of that *something* about them. That something which cannot be described but can only be understood. That ineffable beauty of *knowing*. And most of all it was in their eyes that he could see that he was right. In that intricate mingling of blood vessels and organ, where blues and browns stand out from a shade of seemingly futile white, it was there he could see the shared vision, of a world that was somewhere else, but not here. And as the year continued he watched them, closely. Like a lioness guards her cubs from the caprices of roaming lions. In the science labs he saw them, exchanging looks of excitement and hope. And in the computer rooms he studied them, as they searched the infinity of hyperspace for the God that in truth was walking in their midst, breathing the same air that passed in and out of their lungs. But he knew that two could not be enough to fulfil the dream. He understood the majesty of the triumvirate, the strength of the triangle and the mellifluousness of the chord. There must be three, each holding their share of the power, their part of the weight of the world, or sounding the beauty of their voice to the infinity of the universe. And it was to the world that he knew he must go. And so, he voyaged, from the gardens of the Pyrenees to the oasis of a Kibbutz in the Holy land, from the deserts of New and old Mexico to the ancient jewels of the Amazon. It was in this world beyond the corridors of St. Leonard's, away past the streets of Whitefield or Kilnamanagh, of Camden Street or the Rathmines Road, that he found the true path to happiness, and the true road to redemption. On his journey, he compiled and collected the various treasures that the one true God had bestowed upon his chosen people and sent them back to his awaiting disciple. He learnt the languages of the vast continents and the ways of the multitude of tribes that scavenge the soil of knowledge for thought-sustaining roots. Although his wanderings did not last forever, he endured as long as was necessary, for he felt the breath of prophecy blowing on his neck, warning him of the need to see it all through to fruition. And now as he pedals along the happy roads of a brightening Dublin, he allows a smile to bridge the space between his two ears, content as he is that the moment of destiny is almost upon him. This moment will be his ascension to the right hand of God, this will be his apotheosis. This will be the culmination of every bead of sweat that has poured from his brow, forming a life-sustaining river that will flow its beauty for years to come. For he knows with the certainty of one that is accustomed to understanding, that two boys who have enacted his vision will keep the monetary fruits of their labours in a place they feel to be safe, a place where they both go, where nobody else knows, like two young lovers in a love song. He can see it before it has even happened. Soon he will take what is rightly his. He knows where it will be. He knows they would not keep it in the school grounds; that would be far too risky. He knows it will be in Tarzan's greenhouse, the same way he knew the meaning of the fiery look in Dosser Doyle's eyes when he first saw the scrawny inconspicuous scamp in St. Leonard's. Knowledge he concedes, is a beautiful thing, and the beautiful thing is he knows what to do. And just like Christ who strode stoically to fulfil his written destiny, he is drawn to the symmetry of the foretold; it must happen on Good Friday. That is the day he was brought on this Earth to live, and so it must be and so it will be so.

As he arrives at his abode, Mister Brian Johnson dismounts from his bicycle with the delicate ease of a consummate artist and carefully places his Earth-friendly vehicle on the railings beside the large rose bush in his front garden. He steps through the front door of his house half expecting a wild-eyed Mister Murray to jump out at him, brandishing a rusty chainsaw, although he concludes that this would probably be preferable to the prospect of actually having to talk to the old cunt. He climbs the stairs to his bedroom, conscious of a tiredness creeping over him, as the earlier enthusiasm on being released from work for two weeks begins to subside. He walks into his bedroom and throws himself, face down on his bed like he's just been hit in the back by a tomahawk wielding Apache, before rousing himself to look at a photograph on the wall. It is a picture of him in a small Peruvian village, one that he passed through while on a four-week long trek of the Andes. The ground beneath his feet is muddy from recent rains, yet the smile on his face is great, almost boyish and it visibly shows an inner enjoyment he is not sure he has ever felt before or since. Also pictured are two local men with equally broad smiles across their hard, brown faces. One of them, an old man by all accounts, is pointing to Brian's chest, examining the crest of an old Man United jersey he had brought along on the journey, as a sop to the boyhood football fan within him. He remembers how he had to explain the meaning of it all to the villagers in his broken Spanish, but how after all his seemingly unintelligible ramblings they incredibly seemed to get the gist of what he was trying to say. He smiles as he thinks about that moment when he realised he had been understood, it was the moment the old man turned to him to christen him forever more, "El Diablo Rojo".

Pictures of Whitefield come to her, like flashing lights in a far off distance, warning of impending doom as she feels the sensation of speeding inexorably down a motorway at night time. And as she approaches these lights, these images before her eyes spark a terror in her heart, a terror that she knows she has felt before but one that she cannot fathom as a feeling of any natural humanity. Such terrible fear, sparked by the vision of distant and as yet unknown lights cannot be a vestige of sanity, she ponders. Surely such a feeling of animalistic, nerve shattering terror, must purely rest in the domain of the mad, or perhaps even the un-dead, as they lie caught in a sleepless slumber of restless paralysis, fighting the urge to fall backwards into a bottomless pit of darkness, while simultaneously seeking the certainty of the dark and fighting the invasion of light into a world unused to the ineluctable march of its all pervasive truth. But then, as the sensation of moving along a darkened highway begins to subside and dissipate into the far off ether of some forgotten hope, she remembers a beauty she had ceased to let herself believe existed, as memories of her mother's face breathe a joy into her bloodstream, like the tributaries of the overflowing Nile must sparkle and cleanse the once desiccated and eviscerated, sacred earth of the African plains. Hope is all she has now, but hope still remains only an idea in her mind, and the warmth of maternal love embodies this idea, this belief in the reality of an existing world beyond the boundaries of her shrinking mind, embattled by the fire of life and death, yet frozen in a never ending universe inhabited by herself, alone. And as these images of her mother's playful laugh and eyes of sparkling light come before her, like an apparition of the Virgin Mary dressed in the blue of the sky and the purest of whites, she sees her own child-self, gazing into the brilliant blues and whites of her own mother's eyes, as she calls her to walk hand in hand, barefoot through the summer grass soaked with virgin dew, as yet untouched by the flesh of man. And she sees her child-self, rushing with a graceful alacrity to her mother's side as she entrusts her tiny hand in hers and hopes for the certainty of peace. There she can see her child-self with her mother, as the two of them together once more, begin dancing on a full but misty moon that shows itself in the morning's enlightening haze as they wrap themselves in the sanctifying embrace of the setting sun. But it is in these images, these very same images of a majestic space beyond the realms of her old, earthly existence, that she is once again brought to Whitefield. Whitefield is but a dream, but its life breath flows into her body like a saccharine elixir, suffusing her every pore with the memories of life. Whitefield is but life, it is existence itself. It is cigarettes and vodka, bubble gum and cheap perfume. It is six inch-heel boots and dark brown roots, and

151

the sunshine of adolescent eyes, crying for a life that never will be. Whitefield is where her eyes need to rest their anguished gaze and Whitefield needs to feel the light of those eyes on it. It is a place where the souls of the unborn wail for the love of virgin mothers, and the ghosts of the happily living, mingle with the pulsing hearts of the indifferent dead." Take me once more to Whitefield" she begs. Take me once more to the sun-heated steps of childhood, where the memories of the forgotten are one with the hopes of those yet to come. For it is in Whitefield that life is meant to be lived, and not on some ethereal cloud of despair where a mother dreams of her baby's demise so that they both may dwell in an eternal sleep.

The haze of that sun-filled vision begins to vanish, as she fights to lift her unmoving legs from this torturer's rack, to return to the living world once again, and to the roads of Whitefield, as they twist and turn their merry dance around the souls of the ignorantly blessed. She knows now, like she knows that the breaking voice that often sounds a tearful prayer into her sorrowful ear, can only be that of her father's, that she must return from this precipice of separating and clashing universes, this unending orbit of deathliness and once more join the spinning earth of the living. She will try and hope and fight, to raise herself up from this place where she has been left to lie, by the mindless phantoms that still assail the visions she conjures in her inner-eye, unconsciously as though it were the act of breathing itself. She will try and hope and fight to be once again, walking on the long tarmac path, that stretches its meandering course to the top of the hill, from where you can see not only all of Whitefield, but nearly all of the city of Dublin itself. There from the foot of the Wicklow hills, where not so long ago, wild animals roamed and Fenains marched into battle with equal measure of fire and fear in their hearts. There, there are roads older than America that lead to public houses older than Australia, and it is there, listening to the old stories that her father told her when she was young that she wishes to be, and longs to be, and needs to be. From there, on that hilltop path you can see not only the whole of Dublin, but the entire world itself, as it stretches out from the blue waves of the Irish Sea, bringing people to lands who have taken souls from that very hilltop for generation upon generation. She remembers when as a young girl she would ask her father "how can a road be older than America, or a pub older than Australia?" and he would reply with a knowing nod and a comforting hand placed on her shivering shoulder that "Australia and America are just ideas my love. They existed before anyone thought of an Australia or an America as a country, a place that people would belong to. Before the idea, there was just land that people lived on, but the land had no name to bind them together, so that it would mean something more to them than fields of rock and clay." She never understood what her father meant by these words, but now in her present existence she wondered if she had begun to glimpse the truth behind his strange words. For her, Whitefield was now something more than a piece of land she had lived on. It was a place she belonged to and her memories of this place reminded her of the life she used to have, and could have again if only she could rise up to grab the vision that fleeted before her once beautiful face. She summons a surge of energy from somewhere in the very depths of her soul. For the first time in a long time, she can feel her own body move. A body she at times believed no longer existed, as though she were just an intangible consciousness, floating between the orbits of the heavens in the sky. An excitement seems to grip her, as a flurry of adrenaline rushes through her veins and she realises without any doubt that she has a beating heart as it thumps in her breast like a primeval drum, summoning her spirit to rise up and shake itself from its corporeal incarceration. She feels a burgeoning energy, building up inside her and the whispering voice that she often heard in her ear begin to roar like a wild animal, as she realises she can hear noises that she felt as though she had never felt before. But as the noises grow louder and louder, she understands that they are the sounds of the world outside her. They are the sounds and smells of humanity, calling to her to awaken and join them in the morning light. She feels as though she is almost back with them, like she has just dived into a cold sea and is floating involuntarily back to the surface, bursting her head through the rippling waves to breathe once more, the air of life. But as she hears that once whispering voice booming and roaring in her ear, it evokes a weakness in her soul that she cannot overcome. The voice is that of an animal. It is the roar of one trying to take her blood into their mouths, to feed on her life so it will bring them strength. This weakness is another memory of Whitefield. In this memory there are no sun-drenched doorsteps, no views of the entire world shared with the shelter of her father's embrace. There is only the memory of the animals. The animals that did this to her and left her to die in a pool of her own hopes, reddened by the death of her bloodied dreams. Now, as her body lies underneath the surface of the cold sea, she sees the sun above her eyes, through the breaking waves overhead. But she will not push herself to crash through the water, to fill her lungs with the air of life and breathe among the living once again. Instead she will sink down

153

and down without end. She will not feel the certainty of the sea bed on her feet. She will only feel the continuous drifting downwards. And as she sinks lower and lower to a place where she will never see light again, she hears one word whispered from that tearful whispering voice in her sorrowful ear, and the word she hears whispered is "Revenge".

The Life and Times of
Gobber Gilsenan (Continued)

Aaaaagggggghhhhhh, that old familiar feeling again. There's a narrow streak of light coming through a little gap in the curtains over the window, and it has to be said, the comfort of this bed is un-fucking-believable. And I'd say the size of it is no accident either, the kinky bitch. I've been in a king size, more times at this stage than I can honestly recollect, and this monster outstrips any king size by a good 360 millimetres, give or take. I'm completely sprawled out like the bloke in that Leonardo Da Vinci picture, what do you call him? Oh yeah, the Vitruvian-fucking-man, and my hands and feet still aren't anywhere near hanging out over the edge of the bed. The shit she had me doing last night was more like an Olympic gymnastics event than sex. My back is completely in bits, my knees are red raw from giving it the old Her-Legs-up-on-my-Shoulders routine, and even my fucking dick is chafed to bits, but clearly I'm not going to start complaining about these minor drawbacks of playing in (and being incredibly successful at, if I may add) the best game in town. You can't win the Scudetto, or as in my case, a succession of the most illustrious title in world club football without picking up some injuries along the way; and it's this feeling, this feeling of utter, hung over, over-sexed contentment that makes all the training and the battling through the intensely gruelling fixture list, all so very worthwhile. What absolutely caps off the utter beauty of my current situation is that the bird's only gone off to work and left me in the peace and quiet of my own company, but only after administering possibly the world's best blow job to yours truly. So I'm about as chilled out as a young white male can be at the moment, without of course having taken some kind of mind altering substance. And I suppose that's the beauty of sex man; it's the best high in town and it's all completely free and natural. Well at least most of it anyway. I reckon some of the manoeuvres I was pulling last night might not have been in the big man's plan when he was designing the less glamorous sections of the human anatomy, if you know what I mean, but fuck it. As I always say; "If it fits, stick it in", and it's a motto that's served me well enough up to now I can tell you that without any hesitation at all.

The bird was I have to admit, an older piece, but she was kind of one of those real sexy aul one types, and I'd say back in her day she was a proper stunner. She had a bit of a look of your one, Liz McDonald from Coronation Street about her, but much, much better looking. I managed to pick her up down in one of those seedy wine bars on Leeson Street. I have to say, even I find those places depressingly fucking creepy, but when you're a top professional as I obviously am, you'll stop at nothing to get the job done, and cement your rightful place as one of the best (if not the best) players in the business. I mean, not every game can be at home in the San Siro to Real Madrid in the second leg semis of the Champions League, do you know what I mean? I mean, you still have to go out and play away to fucking Atalanta on dreary winter nights from time to time, but you still have to perform and come away with a result because if you're losing those games, everybody will just write you off and think you're a mug. But having said that, any bird who's drinking on their own in some shit hole wine bar on Leeson Street on a Wednesday night has to be as gamey as fuck, so really this kind of result should be easier to pull off than let's say, hitting Temple Bar on a Saturday night, when every amateur in the city is out polluting my streets with their weak-stomached vomit, and clogging up my fast food restaurants with their gangs of annoying mates, all barely capable of reading the neon menus in front of them. But that's the nature of the hunt. You have to pick your terrain and your targets very carefully. It's like, if you want to go out and hunt deer let's say, you can't just go out and buy a shotgun, and randomly start walking around the countryside in the hope that you'll see one of the fuckers. You have to know where the cunts are hanging out, and which ones are going to be the easiest target. It's like when you watch those nature programmes about lions or leopards or cheetahs or whatever. When those big fearsome cats go looking for antelope to fuck up, they choose their targets carefully. Like, as soon as they find a herd of those antelope cunts, they see which ones are the weakest, obviously the oldest or the youngest, or maybe the sick or the injured and then they pounce on them because it's a piece of piss compared to going after the adult males who are fast and strong, and can cause some serious damage with their antlers and what have you. It seems to me, that these are exactly the same principles that we human beings are working under, except for us city dwelling westerners, the only hunt we're ever actually engaged in, is the hunt for the members of the opposite sex. Obviously you've still got tribal players in Papua New Guinea and shit, who are out there hunting animals everyday with spears and bows and arrows out of pure necessity, using the exact same skills as the big cats, because it's like an innate instinct, if you know what I mean. And that's the whole point, we players who are living in the city have exactly the same instincts in our DNA, but we no longer have to play that game. But we still have to release all that pent up, naturally instinctive energy because if we don't, we'll all end up going mental and so instead of hunting animals, we just hunt each other. And instead of using spears and arrows, we're obviously using our cocks. And I suppose, that kind of explains the problem with those nut jobs in the states who walk into their schools and start shooting everyone up and then blow their own heads off. All those guys are players, who just weren't up to the game, who would've had zero success with birds all their lives so they never got to release all that pent up, predatory energy, so eventually it just explodes in a moment's madness, culminating in their own deaths, which is like, the complete opposite of what the aim of a hunt should be, which is killing something else. So the way I see it, going out on the piss with the aim of ending the night engaged in casual and fantasy-satisfying sex, is the only logical path to achieving true happiness, not just on a personal basis, but for the whole of mankind in general. Instead of telling kids not to drink and not to have sex in school, we should be fucking encouraging the young to start as early as possible, so they can be well trained up for the rest of their lives, and I put myself forward by the way for teaching them. It'd be twice as fucking useful as half the shit you learn in school anyway. It'd almost be a work of pure charity to go into the schools and show the young players how it's done. I mean, at this stage, I'm obviously a pure diamond at this malarkey, but sometimes when you see young players out, trying their best to pull and being about as successful as a manager of the English national side, it's clear that the idiots just haven't been getting the necessary training in, and you'd almost feel sorry for the fuckers if their total car crash attempts at chatting up birds weren't leaving a few open goals for an expert such as yours truly to slot in with the ease of the natural striker. Just like the big cats, this game is all about watching what's in front of you, assessing your options, waiting for opportunities and knowing when to pounce at the right time. It's like this piece from last night. As soon as I walked into the place, I spotted her straight away as a potential target, but did I move in straight away? Did I fuck, because that wouldn't be the right way to go about things, would it? Just like the big cats, who can spot a physically vulnerable antelope, we human beings have to be able to spot emotional vulnerability, unless of course you're a totally sick fucking rapist or something, who will actually prey on cappers, but thankfully, that's never been a low I've had to sink to, and if it ever happens, you have my full permission to rip my balls off. I walk into a place and I see an aging but still radiant beauty, sitting quietly on her own at the bar of a complete kip on Leeson Street, those basic details alone scream, emotional vulnerability. And then when I see her eyes wandering around the bar half the time, and the other half, staring down at the dingy carpet, like she's looking at the massive void in her life, I'm obviously thinking "I can fill that void my dear, I can fill that void with my big, throbbing erect cock." But as I said, you have to look at everything that's in front of you, just like a leopard has to look at the jungle around him before he swoops on a stray piece of meat that's lost its herd. I would probably have to say that in a situation like the one I found myself in last night, there are three very distinct questions a player should have to ask themselves; first of all: *1. Are there any other leopards knocking around the place, trying to bag your target for themselves?* Yes, there were two Franco Baresi type players in bad suits, standing at the opposite end of the bar, but not too subtly, making their way towards the sexy aul one at a slow but gradual speed. *2. Do / Does this / these leopard/s have much chance of bringing down this animal?* No, unless the bird was going to turn out to be a brazzer, neither of them had any chance whatsoever of pulling this chick, mostly due to the fact that they were both old, bald, fat, completely paralytic, and by the time they got down to where she was sitting, she was staring at me as if pleading for my help, but also clearly undressing me with her eyes. *3. Should you stop the other leopard/s from attempting to bring down your potential kill?* This is a judgement call, depending on the terrain in which you find yourself. For instance, you have to consider if there is an easy escape route for the animal, if the other leopard/s fail in their attempt/s, will the animal simply bound away in a panicked fright? Or will they simply run straight into your path, weakened by its recent entanglement with the other members of your species, thus making the kill easier for you? In this case, the place was poky, with only one exit that I was sitting beside, so if she were to find the approaches of the two Franco Baresi players to be so disgusting that it would necessitate her immediate departure from the place, she would still have to walk by me, and more importantly my magnetic charm and perplexingly interesting good looks, therefore leaving her like a fish in a barrel and me with the sexually attractiveness equivalent of an AK47. So in this case, yes, the other leopard/s can be allowed to attempt a kill on the potential quarry, as you have judged that their endeavours will in fact, ultimately work towards your benefit. So as you can see, the whole process is really fairly easy to understand. So easy that you really could teach people how to do it in school. But of course, it can't all be learnt as if it was the ten times tables or something. You still need to have that certain *Je ne sais quoi*, and unfortunately kids, I think you've either got it, or you don't, but luckily enough for me, I most definitely and certainly have.

But that's basically the way everything went down last night. It was a good job I decided to head in there for one last throw of the dice, to think I was almost about to hop in a joer and go home with my tail between my legs! Fucking hell, even I have to admit that you need that bit of luck sometimes. You can prepare as well as possible, perform to the utmost of your ability, but at the end of the day, you need that spot of good fortune to be with you or else you could be left a very disappointed bunny. I finished a deck I was doing up in this gaff in Kilnamanagh, near the shopping centre, unexpectedly early, so I'd been at it from about five. It must've been close enough to two by the time I rolled down Leeson Street way, so it certainly was a last minute clincher. But I suppose that is the Italian philosophy; stay patient, keep it tight at the back, prevent the possibility of any major catastrophes and hopefully nick a goal while you're at it, if you can.

I'm lying here now in this massive bed and I'm beginning to wonder where the fuck I actually am. I give the old ball sack a good molesting and stick my fingers to my nose and inhale the scent of gee through my nostrils, so deeply that I momentarily forget to breathe back out and end up coughing like I'm bloody drowning or something. The smell is fucking beautiful, but I do wonder if I detect a hint of blood, indicating that the bird must've been in her flowers. But then I realise that it's probably just my imagination, almost like I'm trying to convince myself that she was young enough to bleed, when the reality is, there's a strong possibility, if not a certainty that she's gone past that stage in her life. I say fuck it, and I manage to haul myself off the monster of a bed and I head over to the window. I draw back the curtains and look out the window. I'm obviously in the master bedroom of the upstairs of a semi-d, looking out the front of the house but unfortunately, I can't see any shops or the numbers on any bus stops that might give me some clue as to my whereabouts. I seem to be in the middle of an estate because all I can see are other houses, and I've been around the block enough times at this stage to make an educated guess that I'm in Artane, judging by the style of house and just the general vibe I'm getting off the place. I pull back the curtains to let a bit of light in, but I make the mistake of pulling them back a little too much at first so it's like an acid attack on my eyes or as though I'm a vampire, and I audibly wince with the shock. After I recover my vision enough to once more function as a human being, I stumble around in search of my clothes and it's then I notice that my knees are so raw, I've actually broken the skin and I'm bleeding in little spots, and the only thing the makes me feel better is that if my knees are this bad, she must be a fucking paraplegic after that session of intense riding. I see my clothes are all in a neat, folded pile on a chair beside the wardrobe, and it's obvious that the bird must have done that before she left for work, which tells me that I must've made a serious impression last night if she's already cleaning up after me. I notice a narrow door beside the wardrobe and when I open it up, I can see it's a full en suite, with a shower which is fairly fucking swish for Artane I must say and I'm wondering if my senses are beginning to betray me. I'm wondering if I should take a shower or not. Normally, I like the leave the scent of a female on me for a day or two if possible because I reckon it definitely increases your attractiveness to birds. I know you might think it sounds crazy, but I'm convinced that birds can smell the scent of another female off you, even if it's only on some sub conscious level, thus making you irresistible to them because they know straight away that you're a man who's deffo able to tango. It's like when you're younger and you're going out with a bird, and other birds start coming over to you when you're out and chatting you up, even though you haven't even shown the slightest shred of interest in them. It's the fucking scent man, as I keep telling you; we're just the same as the animals, surviving on our instincts. Luckily enough the days of the steady relationship are firmly behind me, those were my young and foolish days, before I'd realised the great truth in life and committed myself to The Way.

I give myself a quick sniff under the armpits, and I have to say I am absolutely reeking, and I realise that I am going to have to have a shower for reasons of pure hygiene. Plus, Artane is a two bus home job, and I don't want to get thrown off at any stage for being mistaken for some kind of homeless person. Now that I've decided to deffo take a shower, I'm debating with myself, whether I should take my celebratory dump before or after cleansing myself of the smell of half a week's work, sex and alcohol abuse. My trade mark calling card is to always take a dump before I leave bird's gaff, but to make sure I don't flush, just as a kind of a Marking of My Territory ritual I suppose. The best is when you end up in some shite apartment where there's about five culchie birds all living in it, because you can maximise the amount of emotional trauma caused by it if one of the birds you didn't do is the first to walk in on it. But it works on any kind of level really, as long as you've got a digestive system in as bad a state of disrepair as mine. So now I'm thinking, it's kind of pointless to have a shower and then unleash this load of day old beer and Burger King because then my arse would just be pure filthy again, after me spending so much time giving it a proper old scrubbing. But on the other hand, it's kind of going to affect my enjoyment of the shower if that load is stewing in the toilet beside me. Eventually, I decide on the ingenious plan of just taking the dump and then using as much shower gel and shampoo as possible, in the hope that it will drown out some of the evil smelling fumes coming from the jacks pot. So, I do the necessary in the toilet, and thankfully it's not as unpleasant as it normally is, and I'm wondering if all the orange juice I'm drinking in all those screwdrivers is helping my stomach, what with all the Vitamin C and shit that I must be getting into my system. After a naturally thorough wipe, I hit the shower and luckily enough, there's a load of different gels and shampoos stacked on this little shelf underneath the actual hose, all women's stuff, but at this stage I'm stinking that badly that I'm not really bothered about all that and in fairness the shit smells beautiful. Plus, really if you think about it, it's all just fucking soap at the end of the day. I mean, just because Mister fucking Nivea, or Mister fucking L'Oreal or whatever has decided to make soap products gender specific so he can make as much money for himself as possible, doesn't mean we all have to go along with it. But now that I've said that, the aroma in the shower as I'm lathering this sweet, luxurious gel on my body, truly is reminiscent of the scent of a nubile young female, so much so that I start to get a boner. I contemplate having a wank as I'm starting to get fairly hot and bothered in this steamy, sex smelling enclosure. But after a few tentative strokes, I realise that the old weapon's a little bit sensitive after such an intensive work out after what occurred last night, and I realise that I'll have to knock that idea on the head, so to speak. I'm just finishing up in the shower when I notice there is actually one bottle of Lynx shower gel hidden behind a bottle of fake tan and moisturiser in one, but I've already washed myself completely so I don't bother taking any, even if I do wonder how the fuck it got there in the first place. But I suppose she could have had a fella around here before, I'm not that naive to think I'm the first bloke she ever brought back to her monstrous work bench. I have to say, fair play to the old bird, she's certainly keen enough to keep looking after herself which you really have to admire in a woman of her age. I mean it's better to burn out than fade away as they say. And that goes for women just as much as it does for men in my opinion. I am a proper fucking feminist really. I want women to enjoy all the same sexual freedoms as the males of our species have done for centuries, if not millennia. Especially when you think of all those Roman and Greek cunts, and the shit they used to get up to. They used to have proper orgies man, men and women, altogether, fucking hundreds of them all shagging each other. Can you believe it man? That was real liberation if you ask me. That's the problem with young Irish birds you see. They're still all sexually inhibited, deep down like, because of the terrible truth that they've all had at least some form of Catholic upbringing. Even if their parents weren't religious, they're still getting it in school or just from the general vibe that's going around the place. And then, they're watching all these American programmes on telly, like do you see that Friends and Sex and the City and shit, and they want to emulate the shit they're seeing going on in New York. Now obviously I'm not complaining too much, because clearly I'm cleaning up out there, but see some times when you shag a bird, and the next morning you can just see this pure guilt in their eyes? Like they can't believe what they've just done and they look at you like you're some kind of sexual deviant piece of shit? It's because they're not really properly comfortable with it. They don't really belong in the tough, no holds barred world of Serie A and it's only when they go out and play against the big boys that they realise how out of their depth they are. Like sometimes, you even get birds crying after sex. I mean, what the fuck is that about? Talk about putting a man off his dinner. But what can I do, they keep just lining up in front of me and I keep just sliding it between their legs and hammering it home. I'm a natural born goal scorer, and once the opportunity presents itself, I don't have time to think about the heart ache that my scoring is going to cause the opposition. As I said before, I'm running on pure instinct out here because I am an animal, nothing more and nothing less.

I step out of the shower, and I have to say I'm feeling seriously refreshed, almost as if I hadn't been drinking and shagging all through the night at all. I take a towel off the rack in the en suite and step back into the bedroom, closing the door quickly behind me as I don't want to be drying myself right beside the festering shit in the toilet bowl. I stick on the radio on the bedside locker as I'm giving the aul groinal area a good going over with the towel, as it's obviously important for a tradesman to keep all his tools in peak working condition. There's some talk show on RTE Radio One, which the radio is obviously permanently tuned into, full of aul ones talking bollocks about how the country's gone to the dogs and young people are out of control, all the usual bullshit, but I can't be bothered trying to tune in another station so I just leave it on and decide to go for a bit of a wander around the house. As soon as I step outside the bedroom I can see that there's a couple of other bedrooms on the top floor and I'm thinking that the bird could hardly be living on her own in a three bedroom house and I wonder if she's renting out the other rooms or what. It even occurs to me that there could be some young Spanish student behind one of the doors, lying on her bed in her knickers, just fantasising about being de-flowered by some roving Irish stallion of Italian heritage, but I reckon that'd clearly be too good to be true, because I of all people know the world doesn't exactly work like that. There are three doors around me, and I know the one to the back has to be the main bathroom so I decide to check out what should be the back bedroom. I open up the door and straight away you can tell that there's some young chick living here because the room's covered in all these posters of pretty boy, boy band members and a couple of that abomination to the world of Calcio, namely David Beckham. It's obvious that whoever's staying in this room is clearly not renting and must be the aul bird's daughter which is absolutely fine by me. I've no problem doing birds who have kids. This is all just one big game and anyone's allowed play as long as they're fit and ready for action. I do wonder though, if the kid was in the room next to us while we were banging away last night and, even I reckon that'd probably be a little out of order, especially seems as though she was never asked to join in, what! Then I remember that the Easter holidays must be on and that's why Dosser and Tarzan want to go and play a bit of pitch and putt up in Bohernabreena today. Maybe the girl's gone off on some little holiday, or over to her da's or something, and that's why that kinky aul one of hers was out prowling the dive bars of Leeson Street last night. I can tell from the little desk in the corner of the room that the girl must be in fifth or sixth year in school, because I can see the old maths book I used to have myself when I was doing the Leaving, well allegedly doing the Leaving anyway, even though I probably spent more of sixth year drinking flagons over by the river in the park then I did in class. I remember that book so well because me and Stevie Smith used to always smack lads over the head with it when we were walking down the corridor. I remember one time, me, Stevie and another one of my old mates Damo Steele, gave this kid a serious going over in the Junior toilets, just using the fucking maths books. I can remember the crying out of the little chap and the terrible part when he pissed himself. Makes me fucking sick looking back on it to be honest. Little cunt didn't deserve any of it, but what you going to do. We were young and stupid and I'm sure that little nerd's a fucking millionaire banker or something somewhere, living in some proper massive gaff in Kildare or some boring shit hole like that. Last laugh was on him eh? I look at the bed and think wouldn't it be classic to jump in and wank all over it, but then I remember the precarious state of my banjo string and regretfully put the idea out of my mind. I look over at the mirror that's hanging on the wall over the desk and I can see all these photographs are stuck around the edges, obviously of the young one and her mates or whatever. I go in for a closer look at them, just to see if the bird's any use, and I can't believe my fucking eyes but she looks exactly like *her*. It actually takes my breath away, the resemblance is that strong, I even stumble back a little, like I'm just after being pushed by a ghost from my past. My heart starts pounding and I begin to feel real light headed, and it gets so bad that I think I'm going to faint right there in this kid's bedroom. It takes me a few minutes to get myself back on track, and I have to concentrate really hard on my breathing, just trying to slow it all down, taking really deep breaths and telling myself to relax, over and over in my head. I focus again on the face in the photograph. The girl's obviously on holidays because she's on a beach, sitting on a rug with some youngfella who looks like he might be some kind of boyfriend. Judging by the light of the picture, it looks like it was taken in Ireland, probably in Wexford or somewhere like that. For a moment I think about taking the picture and bringing it with me but then I decide no, that'd be too fucking mad. And anyway, I don't need any more reminders of *her*. *She* is a weakness. A stupid childish fantasy I have to get out of my head. *She* gets in the way of my game. I cannot let her effect my performance, out there in the gladiatorial arena where I thrive and become something greater than I have ever been or ever could be with *her*. *She* will bring me down.

I back my way out of the bedroom and I put all that stupid shit out of my mind right away. I walk over to the door of what should be the box room, and fucking hell, but what do I see when I walk inside, only a room that's obviously being used by some little girl because the bed's covered in these mad pink, Barbie bed sheets and there's a load of cuddly toys and dolls lined up on the floor, leaning against the wall like a little army of mini-pretend humans and teddy bears. I don't hang around too long because in fairness it is only the bedroom of a child and I'm not so sick that there could be anything of interest for me in there. I walk out of the room and head back into the main bedroom and by this stage I'm pretty much fully dry. I start to feel a bit peckish and I realise that I haven't eaten anything since I got that Burger King around five bells yesterday. I check the clock on the radio beside the bed and it says 10.45. I'm supposed meet the two boys for pitch and putt around two, so that gives me plenty of time I reckon, to raid the old fridge downstairs to see if I can get a bit of breakfast going for myself. I chuck the towel on the floor and I'm so lacking in energy from the lack of proper sustenance in my stomach, that I literally can't be bothered getting dressed until I'm properly fed, so I just grab my phone and fags out of my jacket pocket because I'll need to ring the lads after breakfast to see what the situation is with the pitch and putt. I mosey on down the stairs and head into the kitchen to give the old fridge the once over for any nosh and wouldn't you know it but the aul bird's got the works: sausages, rashers, black and white pudding and even a few tomatoes which I reckon I'll grill up to add a bit of colour to the plate, even though I probably won't even eat the fucking things. I panic for a second when I notice that I can't see any eggs knocking around the place, but then I spy this porcelain hen on the counter, over beside the microwave and when I lift the chicken's head off, there's a mountain of eggs inside, so luckily enough for me, it's a case of crisis averted. I decide that I don't want to take any kind of liberties here because in fairness the aul bird has only been extremely generous to me, wake-up call blow job being a case in point, so I settle on just having the standard three sausages, two rashers, two bits of white pudding, two bits of black pudding, two fried eggs, one grilled tomato, two pieces of toast, a full pot of tea and because I'm such a nice bloke, I reckon I'll hold back on raiding the biscuit cabinet for afters and I promise myself that I'll wash up once I'm finished, but I suppose we'll just have to wait and see if I'll actually go through with that in the end. I take everything I need out of the fridge and thank god, the cooker's gas and not electric, so I won't have to worry about the possibility of any disasters, like I had with this French bird one time, when I promised her I'd cook up a storm in her gaff in Rathgar, using all the knowledge I'd acquired from spending half my life looking at Ready steady Cook and Jamie Oliver, and when I turned up, the cooker was electric, which I'd never used before, so I ended up having to order pizza, and even though I forked out for the whole fucking thing, she still wasn't gamey for a ride! I mean, what can you do with a bird like that? I suppose I can only really blame myself. What was I thinking, going over to some French slut's house to cook for her? Serious mug material that, makes me sound like a fucking yuppie or something. I suppose I was young and all so, what are you going to do? Definitely wouldn't catch me doing anything like that anymore. I'm not showing up for any fucking friendly matches I can tell you that, it's the real deal or nothing. I'm not getting my boots all oiled up for a piss around the park, do you know what I mean?

I get the cooker going anyway and luckily enough, there's a CD player in the kitchen so I get some tunes pumping to keep the old morale up. I'm looking through the CD collection, and fuck me but the aul bird's got a serious taste in music. She's got nearly everything Paul Weller's ever made, from the old Jam days, right up to the all the latest solo stuff, plus a load of Baggie and early 90s dance compilations, but there are a few dodgy ones in there like Duran Duran and Whitney Houston, but I suppose for a bird, it's a fairly amazing CD collection overall. I get a bit of the Happy Mondays spinning and before you can say "You're twisting my melon man" I've got the fry, fully cooked and ready to go. And amazingly for the Red Tomato team, it's all done with ten seconds to spare!

I bring the fry, plus the teapot and toast into the living room, leaving the doors open as I do so, so I can still get my groove on to the pumping tunes, and luckily all the seats are black leather, because I was conscious of not skid marking anywhere I might want to sit down. I take a seat on a nice, big black motherfucker of an arm chair and start tucking into my breakfast, a little more tentatively than I normally would because I'm sure it's got to be a serious shock to the old stomach and I don't want to puke my ring up all over the clean carpeted floor. It's weird but knowing there's a little girl living in the house, has made me kind of more respectful of it for some reason. If I knew the aul bird was living on her own I'd probably be dragging my arse up and down the carpet like a dog trying to scratch himself, but you can't be carrying on like that when there's a little kid to come home to the place, you know what I mean? You've got to draw the line somewhere, and fortunately a man as sensitive as myself, is well aware of exactly where that line is. I suppose it's partly because my own da's not at home anymore that I'm thinking about the little girl and how tough it must be for her to grow up without a father figure around the place. I mean it's all right for me, I was fucking glad to see the back of mine, the useless waste of space that he was, well still is. But it's different for girls though, isn't it? It fucks them up in the head when they don't have a proper relationship with their da, but now that I mention it, I don't know what I'm complaining about. It's women's fucked up relationships with their aul lads that's the number one driving factor behind the success of marauding sexual hunters like myself! I'll have to actually take note of where this gaff is when I leave it so I can come back for the little chick when she's older and ready to fill the emotional void left in her life by her absent father with hours and hours of meaningless, filthy sex with me! I have to say, that the fry is up there with some of the best Morning-After-Sex fry ups I've ever made. I suppose it's all down to the quality of the produce really, but I have to give myself, just a little pat on the back for my culinary expertise; Introducing Ireland's very own Naked Chef!

I start mopping up all the egg yolk and grease from the plate and then I kick back with a nice hot drop of tea, putting my feet up on this little table in the middle of the room with all these glossy magazines piled onto it as I do so. I look around for an ashtray but there doesn't seem to be any around the place so I'm guessing it's probably one of those No Smoking houses, even though the bird was scabbing smokes off me all last night.

Then I realise that my fags are out in the kitchen anyway, but I'm far too comfortable at this stage to bother getting up, even to feed my chronic nicotine addiction, which obviously says a lot about the quality of this fucking chair. I think about taking a look at some of those glossy mags, just to see if there's any filth in it like, but then I notice the remote control for the telly is on the floor beside the leg of the small table, and luckily enough, the telly's on standby so I can turn it on without having to get up and press the little button on the actual television set itself. I blast up the bad boy, and fuck me but the bird's only got the works on the thing, full satellite package with Sky Sports, movie channels, the whole fucking deal. I'm thinking at this stage that she really is a quality catch this bird: top notch gaff replete with en suite master bedroom (although it is still admittedly on the north side), exceptionally class CD collection (perhaps with a few exceptions, but if I'm to be honest, Duran Duran actually have some serious tunes), savage kitchen (especially with its user-friendly gas cooker) and a proper load of channels on the old goggle box, perfect recreation for a bloke who has a lifestyle like mine, spending at least five days a week, sitting on his arse in a fragile hung over state, capable of doing nothing more energetic than vegetating in front of the telly watching celebrity chefs make stuff with rocket in it all day. Jesus, it'd almost make a man want to settle down, but of course, the kids would be a serious drawback to the whole deal. I just couldn't be dealing with that everyday man. No way fucking José. I have to say, the one annoying thing about having all these channels on your telly is that you can't just bloody relax and watch something. I'm finding it too difficult to decide what I want to watch because every time I try to settle on something, I'm still thinking about the possibilities of what might be on the other channels and it's actually wrecking my head. Eventually, I have to just say fuck it and I whack on a bit of Australian Rugby League on one of the Sky Sports channels. Obviously, the game doesn't have the finesse or beauty of Serie A standard Calcio, but all that flicking around was giving me a migraine so it'll have to do. I find myself beginning to feel a little bit tired, I suppose it's only natural, what with me literally getting about half an hour's sleep last night, so I try to fully concentrate on the game to keep myself alert. But it's no good, and I find myself unable to stay awake as I keep nodding off and my head keeps falling behind me, but I keep jumping forward before I properly fall asleep. It's scary, but that's exactly what my ma does in front of the telly every night, and for a weird moment I wonder how similar I must look to her right now, but of course, I don't have an empty bottle of vodka beside me so I haven't quite got that aul alco chic look, that she has so consistently sported for most her adult life. Suddenly, just as I feel myself drifting off to maybe a genuine sleeping state, this mad loud noise frightens the living daylights out of me. I spring up out of the chair like I've just been bitten on the arse by a Rottweiler and I spill my cup of tea all over the carpet, but really I'm not too bothered because I'm absolutely blessed not to have spilled it all over the aul work tools, so thank the lord for small mercies. I'm in a sudden state of panic, and my heart starts racing again, just like it did when I saw that photograph upstairs, and for a moment I feel like an absolute shell of a man, and that the pure hassle of life is going to crush me into the ground, like a fat, mean hearted child crashing his big fat feet onto a dying snail he sees frying on the side of the road on a summer's day. After a few seconds, I realise that there isn't a sound in the house except for the strong Aussie accents of the match commentators coming from the telly, and the background noise of The Inspiral Carpets coming from the kitchen. After a few seconds, I catch a glimpse of myself in the mirror above the fireplace and when I see the petrified look on my face I start laughing so hard, that I'm literally bent over double, cracking up over how much of a fucking mug I've just been. Imagine anyone had just seen me? They'd think I was a complete fucking nut job, and you wouldn't bloody well blame them either. Just to ease any lingering worries I might have, I step out into the hall way and I see the source of the noise that had so recently caused me so much pain and anguish. On the floor beside the front door, is a big pile of letters, that's obviously just come through the letterbox and it's mad to think that something like that could've caused such a racket. I go over and pick up the pile of post and then I peak through the window beside the door to see if I can see the postman anywhere. He's just a couple of houses down, propping his bike up against the low wall that runs along the front garden. He's a beardy cunt, so I open the front door and I shout out at him "Here ye beardy cunt. Fucking relax with the way you're putting these letters through the fucking letterbox will ye man? There's people trying to sleep in here!" He just looks at me with this look of complete terror in his eyes, and you wouldn't believe it, but he says nothing back to me, because obviously he's a windy bastard, legs it out to his bike, mounts the thing quicker than I'd jump on Anna Kournikova bent over in the shower, and pegs it away on the yoke like he's Stephen fucking Roche! I mean, just a smidgen of an over-reaction if you ask me. People here still have letters to be delivered to them, and he's running off without finishing his job? I was only having a bit of a laugh with him for Jesus' sake. I'm just like any dog man, my bark's nearly always worse than my bite. Just as I'm about to head back inside, I cop this aul granny who's out trimming a little hedge in her front garden, a few doors down staring at me, and she's looking at me with the exact same expression of pure fear that the postman had on his face before he pulled a legger. I kind of half close the door, leaving it open just enough so I can stick my leg out in a seductive manner, and I give the aul granny a wave and say "yoo hoo!" in the kind of high pitched voice, favoured by performing drag queens. Well this takes the granny completely by surprise, and she reacts like I've just pointed a machine gun at her and asked her for her pension book and she lets out a scream like the proverbial banshee. I decide to play it cool and leave her alone, because I don't want the feds pouring into the place and making life awkward for me. I mean, I definitely don't want to end up with a record for indecent exposure to a geriatric woman on my cards. That certainly wouldn't do the aul street rep any good, something I can't really afford to have tarnished as a young entrepreneurial player, hugely reliant on his good name to sustain himself in business, do you know what I mean? I close the door over anyway, and I head into the kitchen, still chuckling away to myself all the same and I reckon I'll have a quick smoke out the back, give the lads a bell while I'm at it, and the get the flock out of here to kick some ass on the old P and P course. I bring the pile of post into the kitchen and leave it on this shelf in the kitchen where there's a few old letters already, so I'm guessing that's where they keep it. I grab my smokes and the aul phone, and pull across the sliding door that opens out onto the back garden. I tap a ciggie out of the nearly empty box of Johnnie Blues and I head over to the cooker to the light the bad boy off the hob. I head back over to the sliding door and stand there at the threshold of the kitchen and the garden. The day's actually hotting up nicely, which goes against my normal rules for P and P. The way I see it, you play should play P and P when it rains, because then there's hardly anyone else out on the course so you won't get stuck behind some group of cappers who can't even hit the fucking ball, and you can just get the round in, in lightening speed and get the fuck out of there. Then when it's sunny, I like to hi the snooker hall to do my famous Jimmy White routine because you're always guaranteed a table, and there's no useless cunts, clogging the place up and coming over to borrow you're triangle when you're about to take a frame clinching shot. But I suppose one round of P and P in the sun isn't going to kill me, and knowing this country it'll probably start raining later on anyway. I look out at the garden, and even though it's small I can't help but notice that the place is bloody immaculate, pure Green Fingers material, with loads of serious looking flowers along the back wall, and this fairly impressive looking ivy knocking around as well. They've got this nice little shed in the corner, and there's a little pink children's bike leaning up against the front of it. The only thing spoiling the tranquil beauty of the scene is a clothes line beside the shed, but I suppose it might even add a little something to the place, a kind of homeliness, if you know what I mean. There's no grass either, but instead they've got this nice patio stone work, so I suppose I won't bother asking the aul bird if she fancies getting a bit of decking done, because the patio looks like it's only been recently done. Better off anyway, best not see this bird again I reckon. I don't know if I could face seeing that daughter of hers for real, in the flesh like. I just couldn't be sure of how I'd react. And anyway, Onwards and Upwards as my aul motto goes. It's certainly a rule that's served me well enough up to now, so why change it? Onwards and fucking Upwards.

I find myself almost drifting off again, even though I'm standing up, smoking a cigarette, and then I remember that I have to give the lads a bell. I give Tarzan's number a go, but surprise fucking surprise, there's no answer so I'm forced to give Dosser a buzz, and I enjoy talking on the phone to that guy, about as much as I having my annual STD test, which is obviously not a lot. The little shit picks up after about two rings, so he's obviously been sitting around waiting on my call because he's a sad fucker with nothing better to do with himself on his Easter holiday, no fear of him getting any action anyway, that's for sure. I reluctantly say "Hello" and wait not so eagerly for the torrent of shite to spill from his mouth. "Gobber, is that you?" he says, because I always keep my phone on Private Number, well for a number of reasons really. "Yeah it is you little shit" I say, with just a touch of menace in my voice, just enough to keep the little rat bag in his place. "What's the story? When we getting goin with this P an P?" I continue, sounding a little annoyed like, I've been up and ready for ages waiting on him to get on to me, when really it's been the other way around. "Well as you well know Gobber, tee off time is due to commence at 1430 hours and Taz has kindly agreed to collect you from your official place of residence at precisely 1405 hours. So providing we don't manage to career of the edge of a cliff en route to our scheduled rendezvous, you will need to be awake, appropriately attired, suitably nourished and fully equipped with the necessary accoutrements of the game of Pitch and Putt, plus being adequately supplied with copious quantities of herbal, fungal and chemical life-enhancing products, all of which of course, contravene no laws of the state of The Republic of Ireland or Eire, as it is officially known in our native and ancient tongue. Can you fulfil all of the above specified requirements?" "Yeah whatever man, no bother. I'll see you then, right?" Just as he's about to launch into some other stream of bull shit, I hang up the phone just as he's saying "And don't forget to . . ." because I've seriously had enough of that conversation. I look at the clock in the kitchen and it's almost half eleven, so I suppose I better get a move on, right after one last smoke. I light another ciggie off the butt of the first one, then I stick the old butt down the drain because I don't want to just throw it onto the new patio, because it would spoil the look of the place. I then sit down on the kitchen floor, with my legs stretched out onto the step that leads into the garden. I see the pile of letters just to the right of the door, and seems as though I can reach them, I decide to take them down for a bit of a look, to see if there's anything a bit interesting looking. The first one just looks like a bill and it's got the aul bird's name Suzanne Lynch written on the front of it which is a bit of a surprise because I was convinced her name was Sandra, and I'm pretty sure she even told me that, but in fairness I'm no stranger to giving false names myself so I won't hold it against her, as if I give a shit anyway. The next one's for some geezer by the name of Gerry lynch, and I'm guessing that must be her ex-husband, and I suppose it makes sense that some post is still going to arrive here to him in his old gaff. But then when I look at the next letter and the next one, they're both for this Gerry bloke as well. Then the next one is for Suzanne Lynch again and I'm wondering how come she keeps on using her married name, assuming she's at least separated from this Gerry cunt. Next thing I know I hear another noise and I immediately recognise it as being the sound of a bunch of keys jangling, coupled with the sweet, high pitched tones that could only be the voice of an innocent young girl. Before I even turn around to look at the front door, I know exactly what's about to happen, almost as though I'm suddenly outside of my own body, looking down on myself. Or like, I'm an ordinary punter in a cinema, watching a film on the big screen, seeing Gobber Gilsenan sitting naked in a stranger's kitchen, smoking a John Player Blue and feeling more than a little anxious about what's about to happen. Because it all of course makes sense now. In this one split second, I have a moment's realisation, and I don't even need to see the two figures that are about to walk through the front door because I know exactly who it's going to be. The Sky Sports on the telly in a house, supposedly inhabited solely by females, the killer CD collection, the perfectly manicured back garden, complete with brand new paving. In this split second, my mind seems to have the ability to slow down the entire world, like I have the ability to slow down the rotating earth as it orbits around the big fucking sun that's shining on my outstretched naked legs. Because in this split second I'm able to take in more information through my eyes than Suzanne Lynch was able to take spunk into her big voluptuous mouth, and trust me, that was a seriously large amount. In this split second, I notice a wheelbarrow, sticking out from behind the shed, full of broken bits of unused paving-a sure sign that whoever did the job on the patio, lives in this house. In this split second, I look at the clothes line, hoping in a last ditch hope against hope that all I will see is a selection of women's undergarments and children's clothing with cartoon characters emblazoned on brightly coloured fabric. But instead, all I see is a load of clothes that are clearly recognisable as being those favoured mostly if not only, by people of the masculine persuasion. And in this split second, before that door opens and the person jangling those keys in the keyhole enters this house and shatters the beauty of my so recently perfect morning, I know like I know my name is Gobber Gilsenan that that person jangling those keys will be no other than Gerry Lynch-the guy who quite clearly lives in this house and is still obviously married to the obviously psycho-sadistic bitch who I repeatedly defiled in all three major orifices with my love truncheon last night. And as I finally hear that key in the keyhole turn, just as the earth once more begins to spin and the front door finally begins to open, as the shining sun splits the clouds over Dublin city, I know now, that there's only one thing that I can possibly do.

We are gathered here today for what should be a spectacle of sporting magnitude, the likes of which has not been seen on this island since the young Setanta, armed only with hurley and sliotar, did smite the blood thirsty hound of Culann in the legend of old. For today we may bear witness to three of the greatest exponents of the game of pitch and putt that Bohernabreena par three golf course has ever had the pleasure of welcoming onto its picturesque fairways and verdant greens. Our trio can now be seen walking with a sense of leisurely purpose towards the first tee. The model of consistency that is the young Dosser Doyle is weighed down with a golf bag and is trudging behind his two companions with a somewhat disgruntled scowl on his face. "I still don't understand why we have to bring this golf bag, I mean we only have two clubs each, surely it would be more expedient, let alone pluralistic, if we all simply carried what was ours and no more?" "Ah no, it's much better this way" interjects Tarzan, applying the final touches to a freshly rolled cocktail cigarette of catnip, dagga, fauxcaine and magic mushrooms. "This is just how we're gonna do it from now on. We'll all take turns carryin the fuckin bag man. It's just for this round, it happens to be yours." Tarzan's reasoning does little to placate Doyle, so in a charitable act of almost brotherly love, Tarzan passes the unlit cigarette to Doyle, allowing him the first inhalation of his latest concoction. "Here brother, you'll feel much better once you've got a bit of this into ye. Now don't say I never do anything for ye, me ole mucker." Doyle grudgingly accepts his friend's olive branch, but little does he know that Tarzan is beginning to feel the effects of a cup of magic mushroom tea, secretly consumed in a petrol station coffee cup on the somewhat perilous journey to the pitch and putt course. Tarzan in truth, is beginning to feel so overwhelmed by the psychotropic affects of the sacred fungus, that he literally could not bring himself to take the first drag from his freshly rolled masterpiece. Beside Tarzan strides the single minded Gobber Gilsenan who is beginning to feel a little more himself with every swig he takes from his first naggin of vodka, a second concealed in readiness in the inside pocket of his parka. Gilsenan is intent on regaining the title he lost in somewhat controversial circumstances to Tarzan on the previous occasion that these two titans of the game crossed nine irons, and he will not rest until he is crowned once more, the champion of the Tri-Annual Completely Fucked-Up Pitch and Putt Open and the focussed single-mindedness in his eyes is clear for everyone to see. He reaches the tee box before his two playing partners and by his body language and general demeanour, it is clear that he intends to take the honour of playing his shot first. "Nine iron" he commands without even deigning to look in the direction of Doyle, whose expression has changed from one of severe annoyance to that of a man content in a state of altered perception. He slowly draws Gilsenan's weapon from the bag and places it in its owners extended arm. Gilsenan allows himself a perfunctory practice swing before placing his ball on the tee with no evident shaking in his hand; a worrying sign for his two challengers. Gilsenan steps up and nails it straight onto the dance floor, congratulating himself with a long draught of his medicine, before prising the cocktail cigarette from Tarzan who has regained possession of his creation from Doyle, who searches in his pockets for the makings of another beastly concoction. Tarzan takes a pitching wedge from the communal bag, an alteration he was forced to make to his game after he rather regrettably, destroyed his nine iron against the trunk of an oak tree in a fit of rage, an act which caused him to be ejected from the course by a man on a ride on lawn mower. Tarzan addresses the ball without feeling the need for any practice shot and to his utter consternation, over hits the pin by a distance of around 100 metres, narrowly missing an elderly couple and their grand children, who are grouped together as a young bespectacled man takes their photograph. "Be careful would you for God's sake" shouts the specky cunt, gesticulating wildly in the direction of our happy trio. Tarzan simply glares back at his verbal assailant and even though there is quite a distance between them, the eyeglass adorned gentleman can feel the menacing aura behind those dead brown eyes, and decides it best to turn around conveying the posture of the vanquished as he does so. Dosser's initial tee shot is an aesthetic nightmare, and scuttles along the ground no more than ten metres, causing an eruption of laughter among his opposing players. "It's called laying up you ignorami. At least I have a perfect view of the green for my second shot, Tarzan doesn't even know if his ball is still within the confines of the course." "Yeah, but at least his shot didn't make him look like a gayer Dosser, I'm actually embarrassed to be playin with you right now" Gilsenan says, as he lopes nonchalantly towards his perfectly placed ball. As expected, Gilsenan slots the putt home for a birdie, while Tarzan is forced to take a penalty drop when he is unable to locate his ball and Dosser inches his way to sink the ball in eight. The entire front nine follows in much the same manner, as Gilsenan blasts his way into a seventeen shot lead. The game becomes so one sided, that Gilsenan launches into one of his world famous narratives, not even pausing as he takes his shots with typical aplomb. "Last night man, I'm tellin yis. This bird was a serious goer in every sense of the fuckin word. I'm tellin yis lads, fuck all that teenage girl shit, the mature lady is the way to go, especially when they're as quality lookin as this one from last night. I mean this bird coulda easily passed for twenty-five, but ye know what, I'm glad she wasn't cause a twenty-five year old bird wouldn't have had half the tricks up her sleeve that this one had man, seriously. It was a fuckin education lads; a fuckin education." Gilsenan's audience both nod their heads in knowing assent, a gesture that causes a scoffing grin to light up the speaker's face. "But seriously lads, that wasn't the half of it. Ye wanna see what happened this mornin. I'm literally lucky to be alive right now, not messin witcha or anythin. So, I'm there chillin in the kitchen havin a smoke right, when next of all, the fuckin front door opens and I'm obviously thinkin, what the fuck is goin on here? Cause your woman's never said anythin about her havin a husband or anythin right? So I'm just there thinkin, what the fuck am I gonna do, because on top of everythin, I'm standin there in the nip while I'm havin the smoke, but the worse part of it is, I can hear this little kid's voice as the front door starts to open, so ye know yourself, I don't wanna be getting a reputation as some kind of sicko so I'm fairly plankin it by this stage." As the story continues, Tarzan and Dosser give each other knowing looks as they realise this story could take a while, so they lie down in the middle of the eleventh fairway, and both set about rolling two more cocktail cigarettes to get them through to the eighteenth hole. Gilsenan, leaning on his nine iron continues. "So yis know yourselves, I'm fuckin able to handle meself with the best of them, so if it had to come to fightin me way out of there, it wouldn't have been a problem, but ye know how it is with the kid an all being there, don't wanna be whippin out the A material in front of a little kid, I'd scar the little shit for life an all so I realised I'd have to try an make a run for it. And then, when I saw the cunt comin through the door, ye actually wouldn't believe the size of him. He musta been a proper six foot five, no mess, and built to shit as well like he was some kind of body builder or some shit. Anyway, as soon as he saw me, all hell broke loose. The kid's voice I could hear before the door was even open, turned out to be the voice of this little girl and as soon as she saw me, she let out this mad high pitched scream and started shoutin 'Daddy Daddy, kill the bad man, kill the bad man!' and I was just there sayin 'relax will ye for fuck's sake, no need for anyone to be doin any killin, just let me get me shit together an I'll get the fuck out of here', but it was obvious the big fella wasn't havin any of it, an he was lookin at me like he was gonna make sausages out of me arse cheeks. Anyway, as soon as I realised there was no negotiatin with the fucker, I legged it out into the garden and what does your man do only leg it out after me, snarlin like a dog after a fuckin pussy cat. So he's there chasin me around the garden for a few minutes and then what do I notice, only the cunt's startin to get out of breath, and it's obvious that yeah the fucker might be built like Ivan Drago's big brother, but the cunt's got no stamina, no cardio vascular fitness, d'y know what I mean? So all I have to do is stop runnin, an deck the cunt, which is exactly what I did. Didn't even have to hit him twice. I planted him one solid in the face an he went down easier than his missus did in their marital bed only a few hours previously." Tarzan and Doyle, resurrect themselves from their supine positions as they perceive the narrative to be at least nearing its natural conclusion. "But that isn't the best part of it all" Gilsenan continues, much to the dejected bewilderment of his not so attentive listeners. "What do I hear next only more voices coming from the front door an I look in an all I can see are two coppers bailin into the gaff, truncheons drawn an ready to use them. Your man's still on the deck, holdin his nose like he's just been shot by a sniper and the little girl's havin a pure panic attack as the coppers push past her like she isn't even there. I look around me for some way of gettin the fuck out of there, an I see this motorbike that's been leaning up against the back wall the whole time, but i've only just noticed it now because I never had time to see it when I was tryin to get away from your man. I'm still in the nip at this stage as well, so all I can do is grab this dressin gown from off the washin line an I wrap it around me, quicker than superman could get changed in a phone box, an I leg it over to the motorbike. As soon as I get over to it, I can't actually believe my own fuckin luck but the key's still in the ignition! It's been a while since I was on one, but obviously by then, I wasn't really gonna let that get in my way. There's this gate in the middle of the back wall, an just from lookin at it, I could tell that it was only a bit of soggy old chipboard an that all I'd have to do was rev the fuck out of the bike an I'd blast me way through it, an that my good sirs, is exactly what I fuckin did. I was out of there like Steve fuckin McQueen man, cruising my way through the mean streets of Artane, and the rest as they say gentlemen, is history." Gilsenan finishes his tail with a contented smile but Doyle doesn't look convinced. "But what about the police? I mean surely it would have been easy enough to pick up a man riding a motorcycle through north Dublin, attired only in the garments of household leisure, and where's the bike now for instance? Did you drive it up to the mountainous southern outskirts of our city and set it ablaze or something?" "Eh yeah, that's exactly what I did actually, rang an old mate of mine then to pick me up an give us a lift back. Sound cunt actually, Mick Sheridan his name is. Yous boys wouldn't know him. Bit before your time an all." Gilsenan signals the end of his story by moving towards the eleventh green as howls of "Get a move on!" come from the members of a substantial queue that has begun to form on the eleventh tee box. Tarzan once again retorts in a non verbal method to the jeers of his fellow course users, by exposing half of his posterior, much to the chagrin of the same grass cutter he had previous dealings with who hums slowly by on his lawn mower and points with his thumb towards the exit to Tarzan, as though he is signalling that he wishes for our trio to vacate the premises. Tarzan chooses to ignore the command and instead exposes the other half of his posterior to the still screaming queue of people behind him. The three players approach the next tee as Gilsenan announces with glee "Ah yes, the glorious twelfth. Scene of my famous hole in one this time last year chaps. Remember ye the event well?" By this stage Doyle has seemingly lost all touch with reality and falls face first into a crying child who has somehow wandered off on his parents. Doyle is understandably startled, as the screams of the child pierce into his brain and he is duly challenged by a rather fearsome looking skin head in a Celtic jersey. "Watch were you're fuckin goin, will ye, ye bleedin muppet ye!" Doyle cowers away from the verbal assault as though he is looking into the eyes of the devil himself, while Gilsenan, completely oblivious to what is occurring behind him, blasts his ball out of the course and onto the road outside, although he smiles contentedly to himself as he believes the ball has once more sunk into the hole on the first attempt as he gleefully exclaims "What did I tell yis lads, the glorious twelfth!" and lifts his nine iron to his mouth and pretends to play it like a flute while marching in circles around the cowering figure of Doyle. The Celtic jersey wearing skin head eventually backs away from the scene, believing as he does so that Doyle was having some kind of seizure. Doyle eventually rises to his feet and notices just before the still marching Gilsenan realises what's going on, that Tarzan is running at a tremendous speed around the course being chased by a rather angry looking man on a ride on lawn mower. Doyle makes a feeble attempt at calling Gilsenan's attention to the whole scene when Gilsenan says "Yes, that's it. Game over. The championship is mine once again. We're deffo being booted out of here anyway. No more time to finish the course so the leader at this current juncture shall be declared the winner, that's what it says in the rule book eh Dosser?" Doyle looks Gilsenan in the eyes and moves his lips in response but no audible sounds emanate from his mouth. Doyle senses this, and instead communicates his intention to get the fuck out of there, by pointing in the general direction of the car park. The pair trot at a steady pace to the car park, where they can see Tarzan has already started the car, and is revving the engine as a means of conveying the very urgent need to get away from this place before we all get killed. Doyle and Gilsenan both jump into the back of the car and Tarzan shoots off down the road with the pace and accuracy of a well aimed missile. "Ah pick up the pace would ye Tarzan for fuck's sake" teases Gilsenan," this isn't Drivin Miss Daisy ye know." "I would drive faster Gobber, only I can see five roads from where I'm sittin, so I'm just choosin the one in the middle. Everythin all right back there Dosser?" By this stage Doyle has regained his voice and has even managed to take out a small amount of Alpha Chlorolose he had concealed in his sock and offers it around to his companions. "Absolutely top notch Taz. Any possibility of stopping by the old school greenhouse perhaps? I've a sizeable amount of Cysticus Scorpius stored there, that may add a little something extra to our night's festivities, if there are no objections of course?" "Fine by me old friend" says Gilsenan, as Tarzan steers the Beast in the direction of St. Leonard's College. Gilsenan climbs into the front of the car, nestling into the passenger seat with the gracefulness of a harpooned walrus and fishes for a tape in the glove box. "Ah yes you beauty" he exclaims, "here it fuckin is" and he proceeds to place the best of Dire Straits into the cassette player. "Told ye I'd be able to fix that for ye didn't I Taz? I'm tellin ye man, I know we slag the car an all sometimes but it's grand really. We're only messin witcha. Once you've got the sounds pumpin, that's all that matters." Tarzan nods in acquiescence and through the skewed prism of their mind altered state, all three can feel a closeness between them at that moment, as the adrenaline continues to soar through their bloodstream and the beautiful clanging melodies of Mark Knopfler soothe their rabid tendencies into a marvellous acceptance of the here and now. They drive for maybe an hour, maybe two, as Tarzan attempts to negotiate the multiple paths ahead of him, but it doesn't matter to anyone; not tonight, happy as they are to share the splendour of the moment. "Hey Gobber,"

Doyle inquires, "What's the thirteenth hole actually like on that course?" "I don't have a fuckin clue man" Gilsenan replies, "I've never got any further than the fuckin twelfth!" The three of them erupt in a laughter that is in keeping with the spirit of comradeship they have created in the haze of their own making. "Will it not be a problem getting in here with the school being closed an all?" Gobber wonders aloud more than anything. "Fortunately we have year-long access to the horticultural facilities Gobber, although we shall be required to scale a wall at the side of the school, but nothing that a man of your immense athletic prowess wouldn't be able to handle." "You are such a gayer" scoffs Tarzan, as yet another shared moment of laughter is enjoyed, even by Doyle himself, as the harmonious twinkling of human love becomes enrapt in the glory of boyhood dreams, as images of other worlds collide with the minds of our three heroes.

As they near the school a silence descends, at first the occupants of the Beast are not sure why it is so. Maybe it has something to do with the fact that the tape player has inexplicably ceased playing, or is it because Tarzan has slowed down to a speed somewhat approaching regulation? As they arrive at the gates of the school they become certain of the reason for their silence. It is the result of an innate perturbation, reacting in the heightened senses of all three to the disturbing vibes that could be felt in the immediate universe. At the gate of the school there is a fire engine, complete with blue lights flashing, and the yellow-headed figures of firemen busying themselves around the red mechanical monster. Without anyone speaking a word, they know what they will find. Tarzan brings the car to halt, as Doyle alights from the vehicle to bear witness to the eternal fire of hell. For over the wall they had planned to traverse, Doyle can see a panorama of dark-black smoke, billowing towards a heaven it will never reach, covering the sky with a sight so horrendous, it carries him to a sobriety he has never felt before. He is joined by his two companions, his associates, his friends, as they watch the flames still burning in the dusk-laden air. They do not speak or look for any explanation from those firemen or onlookers who share the vista but do not share their understanding of the flames. As they watch years of hard work evaporate as clouds of smoke, the colour of death, they are shook by a noise from behind. Doyle turns around, putting his back to the horror of a nightmare, to face the dawning of a reality that would breathe bad dreams into the minds of dreamers. Doyle watches a car move slowly but assuredly by, and the smiling faces and waving hands of Peter and Paul Smith can be seen from the back window. For now Doyle knows, that life cannot be everything one would like it to be; sometimes, life, is just that.

The Thoughts of Dosser Doyle (Volume Three)

Life at the moment is about as hard as it gets for a person dedicated to a just and righteous cause, such as myself. It all seems very clear now, that for the first time since our operations began we are faced with a very real enemy, vying for a share in our market as purveyors of life-enhancing products, who are also clearly intent on destroying our crusade by any means necessary. I am endeavouring to remain strong in the face of this perfidious adversity, and I am striving to maintain an air of calm assuredness in a world turning into a chaotic tempest of hate and dissolving ambition. Gobber has seemingly disappeared from the face of the Earth, well the face of Whitefield anyway, and Tarzan's mental state has unquestionably disintegrated to a level of instability, I haven't witnessed since the day he first realised his inferiority to me in the life affirming field of crow hunting. His moods have become erratic. He has become taciturn to the point of rudeness on the one hand, yet can also fluctuate towards a state of ultra excitement, as though his limbs have become possessed by the souls of a dozen rabid rats, fighting to liberate themselves from their prison of human flesh and bone, as his heightened state of anxiety manifests itself in his unpredictable bodily movements. Although this may be a worrying development for me and for all of us, I feel I know Tarzan well enough to allow myself to hope he will free himself from this sentence of panic; it is the absence of Gobber however that is causing me the most fear. His phone is turned off, and his van is no longer parked outside of his home. I have not tried calling to his door because there's simply no point. His mother would never answer the door anyway, inflicted as she is by the insidious and psychologically crippling disease of which I understand her son is also a victim, and his father has of course not been seen for many years I believe, indeed I have never actually seen him myself. Really, Gobber's evanescence is not something that should surprise me. Our relationship with him was only ever based on the harsh expediencies and practicalities of commerce. It was never a friendship in the truest sense of the word, and therefore we have lost nothing really, that cannot be replaced. The unfortunate incident in the school greenhouse is a setback, no doubt, but the reality is, it is merely a minor inconvenience as our main base of operations in Tarzan's back garden remains fully intact, plus with a few supplementary defensive measures recently constructed, it has become a veritably impregnable bastion, a Siegfried Line like fortress, ready to repel any onslaught from any potential assailants. We have wisely fortified Tarzan's back wall with a motley assortment of broken glass and nails, so if Peter or Paul Smith, or any other reprobate associated with their infernal clan should try to climb over it, their hands shall be ripped to shreds like rotten meat through a mincing machine, hopefully eventuating in their contraction of a life threatening disease of the blood, whether it be hepatitis, HIV or full blown AIDS, I sincerely have no particular preference. We have however left one section of the wall free of any jagged implements of war, so that a sentinel may be perched there at all times to allow us a reasonable vantage point for surveying the surrounding area. Although one may be tempted to board up the roof of the greenhouse with layers of wooden shields, my feelings on this issue are somewhat idealistic, possibly impractical, but unshakable nonetheless. I believe firmly that we must carry on as much as is possible, in the fashion we have grown accustomed to over the last number of years. Our beautiful plants require the nurturing warmth of our planet's sun, the very life force of creation, and the light from the sun they shall have. There cannot be any ceasing of our activities because if we cease to work, we cease to be who we are and I will not allow that to happen. As of now, I have implemented a Sentry Roster, in order to safeguard Tarzan's greenhouse, our stronghold; our foundation stone. There will not be a moment of an opportunity for our enemy to strike us there, for every second of the day and night we will stand guard and fight to the very death if necessary, in order to protect all that we hold dear and to preserve our way of life. Owing to Tarzan's obvious disgruntlement at the prospect of staying awake all night, I have enlisted the support of one Richard Grimes Esquire, who has been entrusted with the great responsibility of joining our security shifts, with the promise of earning all the Nepeta Catoria that one man could smoke, although I do fear that his capacity for the sacred flower, has potentially reached a level that could see our entire stock go for free, it is a risk I am willing to take. Having Richie on side also means that I have one less front to worry about. I had begun to fear that he had suspected foul play (rightly in fairness) on my part with regards to Charlie, his beloved Jack Russell, but a chance encounter with Richie outside the chipper, led to the allaying of any trepidation I may have borne with regards to that little incident, and the forming of our alliance over bags of greasy fried potatoes and battered sausages. It turned out that Richie had no suspicions about his pet's untimely death and even better still was able to confirm my belief that Peter and Paul Smith were embarking on an illegal substance selling venture and were hoping to eliminate all possible competition from the Whitefield area, namely us. In an even more serendipitous development, Richie's sister's continuing relationship with Stevie Smith means that Richie bears an even greater hatred, if that is indeed possible, towards the entire Smith family and willing as he was to aid our side in any way he could, offered his services to our Sentry Roster which was duly accepted under the above outlined conditions. So although circumstances seem to be running a little on the negative side of things, I do have some extremely positive developments to report. Aside from all the difficulties that I am currently encountering on the street so to speak, perhaps the most exasperating challenge I am facing is the persistent presence of my brother in my house, a situation so egregiously harmful to my mental health, that a serious degree of pro-activeness is called for, so I can at least alleviate this one burden on my conscience and I think I have just the idea to do it.

It is the Wednesday before Easter and we are sitting down for a full family meal to celebrate the homecoming of my brother, even though it seems to me that every dinner we've had since he came back has been eaten in his honour. Perhaps the fact that Dwayne is in attendance this evening, gives the proceedings that extra special touch and for me, I've decided that it will be extra special too. The table is adorned with two bottles of wine, one white, one red, or "both flavours" as my father has so perceptively pointed out. Dwayne is for some reason drinking Budweiser straight out of the can and judging by the fact that he is currently consuming his fifth beverage, I'm guessing that he's planning to stay the night and considering we're a good Catholic family and Dwayne, although a welcome guest to our household, is still not permitted to share a bed with my sister, I'm presuming space will have to be made somewhere so, no prizes for guessing who will have to give up one's bed and spend another sleepless night on the couch in the front room. My brother is pompously holding the wine glass to his nose, taking long, exaggerated nasal inhalations while swirling the ruby dark liquid around so that it looks as though it may spill out from the top of the glass, but never does; a feat my mother seems to admire with the awe of a member of a lost Papuan tribe, observing for the first time in their lives, the striking of a match. "Tell Dwayne here James, what you're doin over there, now don't hold back now whatever ye do, let him know the full shebang" my father orders my brother, refilling his glass of white wine as he does so, drowning the initial scepticism with which he perceived the substance at first, as he slips into a comfortable position on his seat at the top of the table, because we have company (Dwayne) his prosthetic limb remains fully attached. "Well dad as you know, I don't like to go on about these things, but if you insist!" "Oh but I do James, oh but I do" my father drawls, half closing his eyes as he does so. "Well basically Dwayne, I'm working in the city, investment banking if you really want to give it a title. Basically I work for extremely wealthy clients, advising them on what they may wish to invest their money in. Stocks and shares, all that jazz you know . . . . really it's not terribly interesting, I'm sure you'll agree." "Ah don't be so modest now James" says my mother, "tell him how many men ye have under ye, go on now, don't be shy. Tell him there . . ." "Oh Brigit" says my brother, calling my mother by her actual first name, thus demonstrating one of the annoying habits he has returned from London with, including saying "yaw" instead of "yeah", insisting on drinking coffee instead of tea at every possible occasion even though we only ever have the cheap instant variety, and referring to Britain as the mainland, as though Ireland were some offshore island of the United Kingdom and not a sovereign independent nation in its own right. What's worse than all of this is that however horrific these developments in my brother's already dubious personality may be, my family's complete obliviousness towards and even acceptance of these irritating mannerisms is completely incomprehensible. I sometimes have to pinch myself when I observe the admiring glow on my family's faces as my brother launches into one of his stories about meeting Phillip Schofield at a charity event he organised for autistic rabbits in Devonshire or somewhere, when clearly it's all a complete load of bollocks. I don't know why everyone else is blind to his obvious deception, but I'm not going to worry about it any longer, and as I've said, I'm going to make sure tonight really is *special* so I've taken the liberty of adding a little something extra to the wine that my brother so astutely pointed out, had a "smashing bouquet". "Well I don't mean to brag Dwayne my man, but I have *fifteen* men working on my team at the moment, and I can tell you in all honesty, that each one of them looks up to me like a father, and I look at them as though they were my very own sons." Even Dwayne is now looking at my brother with that same admiring glow as the rest of my family and I have to stop myself from breaking into all out laughter as my humour changes from one of annoyance to one of great mirth as I notice some tell tale signs that things are starting to take effect from my brother: A rapid blink of his eye here, a long drawn-out exhalation there, not blatantly obvious to the layman, but to the expert eye, this is gold dust. "Fifteen Dwayne, would ye believe it" my father states more than asks, pointing at an unopened bottle of white wine on the counter while nodding at my mother, who duly gets out of her seat to see to her husband's whim, "enough for a bloody football team, fif-feckin-teen". My brother then continues where he left off "Seriously Dwayne, you and Siobhan should seriously think about coming over. I could set you up with a nice gig over there no problem. We could always do with a guy like you, guys that have spunk; I like guys that have spunk." I should probably also tell you that my brother James is a raving closet homosexual, if that's not a contradiction in terms, and I actually do burst out laughing at this point, because like every other aspect of his ridiculously false life, I'm the only person who's able to see this. It's as if as though I've been given this special power in life, or like I'm the child in *The Sixth Sense*, whereby I'm able to see people's ghosts as they walk around the living world without anybody else noticing them. My sister gives me a look of intense hatred, because she naturally assumes that I'm laughing at the prospect of Dwayne living it up in London high society, even though I'm really laughing at how incredibly gay my brother is, although the image of Dwayne trying to function in any place that isn't Whitefield is rather hilarious. It gets to the stage where I just can't help myself so I say "I don't know if London would really suit Dwayne Jimbo, he only leaves Whitefield if he absolutely has to. Didn't you have to deliver a pizza to Rathfarnham once Dwayne? God, that must have been quite the expedition. But I'm sure it was nothing to my ever intrepid future brother in law, eh?" "Yeah I did have to go up there before, bleedin mad kip it is . . . ." Dwayne's reply is unfortunately cut short, as my sister elbows him in the ribs eyeing me with the contempt that I just love to elicit from her as a means of colouring the otherwise dull palette of our family life. "No messin outta you now ye pup ye" my mother says, clipping me jocularly over the ear as she replenishes my father's glass with an increasingly unsteady hand. We finish our main course as I sit with the smug prescience of an omniscient prophet and wait for our dessert to arrive. My masterful scheme continues to proceed as planned. My mother and father are as predicted, drinking luke-warm white wine, Dwayne is enjoying cans of Budweiser, my sister is just about stomaching large glasses of white wine and lemonade, I am partaking in the customary lactic secretions of a cow's mammary glands, leaving only my brother with his bottle of red wine. My brother is currently demonstrating the inner workings of his digital camera, to the utter astonishment of my family who may as well be looking at a Martian showing us how to flush the toilet on his flying saucer. He's flicking through all the pictures in his camera, stopping at one of a blue jaguar and saying "This is the old run around" even though it's blatantly just some random car he took a photograph of on the side of the road. Everybody's gathered around him like little kids, oohing and ahhing as he flicks through different pictures of an apartment that he's clearly just downloaded off the internet or something when he suddenly jolts back into his chair and says "What was that?" looking like a startled turkey, that's just realised it's somehow wandered into the middle of an Ethiopian village on Christmas Eve. "What's that James?" my mother asks, slightly taken back by the rather sudden and noticeable alteration in my brother's mood. "The walls, the walls on the kitchen . . . they . . . they've changed colour. They're green now and they used to be kind of cream didn't they? Why are they green? And him, who the fuck is he?" "Who are ye talkin about?" my father asks, looking at his son like, well he's under the influence of a mind altering substance. "That guy there, him there with that stupid look on his face." My brother extends his arm out and points a finger in the general direction of Dwayne who understandably seems unsure of what exactly to do in this situation, where his girlfriend's brother has clearly gone insane and is pointing at him and calling him stupid, so he does what he does best and opens up a can of Budweiser, drinking it as though he's just been told he has five minutes to live, which fingers crossed might be the case. "But that's Dwayne James, he's Siobhan's boyfriend, remember?" my mother asks almost soberly. "Are ye feelin all right son?" my father asks, as my brother suddenly rises to his feet and backs into the cooker behind him, knocking over a pot of hot custard as he does so. "No, not fuckin Dwayne, the bloke behind him! Yer man in the bee keeper's outfit! He's just after comin through the window, like it wasn't there. It's like he's a ghost or somethin. A big, bee keepin ghost!" My brother by now looks properly crazy, and I finger the piece of evidence in my pocket that finally proved to me what I'd suspected for so many years; that my brother is a complete fraud and borderline mental case, as well as being a roaring homosexual and possible sexual deviant, although the piece of evidence I have in my pocket doesn't necessarily substantiate all of those claims, but if I'm right about one thing then who knows? "Ah Jesus me feckin custard!" screams my mother, briefly oblivious to my brother's disintegrating, mental condition. "The custard, the Jaysus custard? Would ye give over about the feckin custard woman, can't ye see your son's gone bloody loopy!" My father grabs my brother around the shoulders, as his eldest son begins to shake in a fit of panic. My sister begins to sob hysterically. She turns to Dwayne in search of some moral support, but instead finds Dwayne looking at the scene in the same way I imagine he would have looked at a maths teacher who tried to explain to him how to do long division and she simply runs out of the kitchen screaming like a banshee who's just stepped on a thumb tack in her bare feet. Dwayne is awoken from his catatonic state as my father screams "Dwayne will ye help me for God's sake. Ye can't expect a one legged man like me to control an athlete like this fella. Fifth, fifth he was in the semi-final of the 400 metres in the community games back when he was a young fella. Strength of an ox and speed of colt he has. Jesus will ye help me!" Dwayne eventually stumbles forward, dropping his can on the ground as he does so, and the two of them manage to wrestle my brother into the living room as he screams "Don't let him let out the bees! Don't let him let out the bees!" while my mother seemingly oblivious to the entire shemozzle, busies herself cleaning up the spilled custard. Eventually my father and Dwayne manage to wrestle my brother onto the couch in the living room and as he persists in struggling against them, they are forced to sit on top of him in order to prevent him from any erratic movements. The atmosphere in the room is one of complete panic, and I can see that Dwayne is taking long, deep breaths, clearly trying to prevent himself from getting sick all over the living room carpet. Next of all, my brother begins howling like a deranged rhinoceros, emitting the most inhuman wail I have ever heard, and even I have to admit that it is slightly chilling, and for a moment I almost begin to feel sympathy for my brother. But then I snap my fingers in order to bring myself to my senses. My brother is a complete nuisance and always has been. I think about all the years we had growing up together, where every little insignificant achievement he had was lauded to the point of nausea. His alleged ability on the sports field which was probably similar to the athletic prowess displayed among ping pong players at the Special Olympics, his supposed academic genius, which didn't even qualify him to study in any college in Ireland and his lengthy tenure as head altar boy in the parish church which is a very obvious indication of his perverse sexual nature. But the thing that really annoys me most about my brother is the fact that he never stood up for me when I was in primary school, getting picked on nearly every day of my pre pubescent life by all manner of juvenile delinquents. No matter how many times I went to him to ask, even beg for his assistance he was always too scared, or even worse, too lazy to come to my aid. It's not that any of those experiences still bother me, luckily I've managed to elevate my social standing to one where I enjoy a great degree of relative respect, but the fact that his cowardly head never deigned to look in my direction when I was under very serious physical and emotional strain is something that I could never truly bring myself to forgive, so fuck him and everything he stands for.

He makes another attempt to wrestle his body away from Dwayne and my father, crying out "I told you not to let him let the bees out, they're gonna sting me in my eyes, I know they are, Jesus Christ I feel them crawlin all over me!" After a few minutes my father shouts at my mother to ring an ambulance which she duly does. I check my pocket again to make sure that the evidence I managed to find in the pocket of one of my brother's jackets while searching through his travel bag is still there, even though I know that it would be impossible for it to have gone anywhere. When the ambulance arrives, two paramedics take over from where my father and Dwayne had been restraining my brother and they administer a sedative which takes effect amazingly quickly, and I'm wondering if I'd be able to get my hands on some of that shit myself. They bring in a gurney to put my brother on, as long drips of saliva congeal on the edges of his mouth. The paramedics ask my father for assistance in putting his favourite first born son onto the stretcher, but he is physically exhausted and points at me in order to convey his wish for me to take his place. It is the moment I've been waiting for, so I happily leap to the two paramedics' assistance and grab my brother roughly by one of his legs as we lift him onto the gurney. We start to wheel him out through the hall towards the front door and as the paramedics try to fix some kind of drip to my brother's arm, I slide the evidence out of my pocket and lean my head down to his sedated yet still noticeably conscious face. I put my mouth to his ear and whisper "You're going to be fine by the way, have no fear. But as soon as you're discharged from the hospital I want you gone out of this house and straight back on the next flight to London. I might even visit you over the summer if that's ok? As long as you can hook me up with a free Big Mac and chocolate milkshake, that's all the hospitality I'll ask of you, brother." With that, my brother's eyes awake from their induced slumber, and focus on me with the burning glow of an epiphany leaping in his mind. I slip the evidence into the pocket of his jeans, taking care to ensure that the pin on his McDonald's name badge is safely fastened so it won't prick him in the leg, or worse. Well, he is my brother after all.

Tarzan's story (Number Three)

Normally having a free gaff is class, but the way things are going at the moment I actually wouldn't mind having my ma and da around because I'd feel like they'd almost give us some extra protection from the shit that's going on at the moment. Last night was fucking crazy, and The Beast been wrecked like that, is definitely the worst thing that's ever happened to me, no doubt whatsoever. It all just happened so quickly, it just came out of nowhere, like in one of those films when a meteor just lands on Earth, killing a load of people and causing total havoc in some big city or whatever. I'm literally still shaking with the anger and even the shock I suppose, but at least I've come to a definite decision. I'm taking that money from the greenhouse and I'm getting the fuck out of this place for good, it's the only option I've got at this stage and I'm fucked if I'm waiting around any longer. First, the greenhouse in school, today The Beast, next it'll be my fucking gaff or something, and I seriously don't want to be around when all of that kicks off. Knowing my ma and da, I'll probably get the blame for it and all so fuck it, it's goodnight Whitefield for me and hello the beautiful sunny beaches of Australia, where finally I'll get to do whatever I want with my life, without having anybody breathing down my neck and telling me what to do all the time. Now don't get me wrong, it's not that I won't feel any like, guilt about Dosser and Gobber and all, but I just don't see what else there is left to do. I can stay around here in this boring old dump, constantly looking over my shoulder to see if Peter and Paul Smith are coming after me and having to listen to Dosser's bullshit all the time, or I can go and make something of myself, get a fresh start away from all this stupid childish crap. I suppose if I'm to be honest, I've been feeling this way for a while, just waiting for the right time to make my move, trying to decide what'd be the best way to go about things and all, but I suppose everything that happened last night kind of made the decision for me.

Last night Gobber turned up at my gaff with this big grin on his face and when I was like "What are you so happy about?" He was all "Ah just basking in the warmth of fraternal love Taz, that's all" and I was just like "whatever". Anyway, at that stage Richie Grimes was sitting up on my back wall, the part where we didn't put any broken glass or anything, because he's helping us out now with our Sentry Roster, which is a bit of a godsend because it means I don't have to stay up all night and he's a top man anyway so it's a bit of a relief having someone sound to talk to for a change. Anyway, Dosser asked if me and him could go into the greenhouse to do a bit of work and have a bit of a chat and I was like "Yeah no problem". Dosser was just asking all the usual bullshit about how the plants were getting on and if I'd been keeping up with my bagging and portioning of the Catnip and Dagga, just basically checking up on me as usual and I was just like "Yeah of course your lordship", just trying to annoy him as usual and generally trying to wreck his buzz. Then he pointed, kind of like with his eyes, down at the secret compartment where the Running Away Fund is kept and he was like "Is everything still in order down there?" and I'd only checked it just before he came over and I was like "Yeah still hangin a little to the left, dangling over my massive set of balls" and he just laughed in this like, sarcastic way, and I could see that he was beginning to look a little nervous or something, and I could tell that the stress of everything was starting to get to him too. I didn't want things to get too bad between us so I said "Here man, let's get a smoke goin" and I started rolling one of my new cocktail cigarettes, just to kind of like, relieve, the tension. I said "Will I get Richie involved in this?" because as I said Richie is a sound cunt and I didn't want him to be stuck up there on that wall while me and Dosser were getting fucked up together and Dosser was just like "Naturally". I gave a tap on the greenhouse glass and waved Richie in with my hand. Richie stalled it in to the greenhouse and we were having a good old chat and at that stage I was actually thinking that we should probably get Richie involved on a permanent basis, especially seems as Gobber's after going AWOL and we don't know where the fuck he is or if he's ever going to come back. For all we know he could have fallen into the canal while he was out on the piss or something, or maybe he got agro with the wrong punter in some chipper, but I suppose we'll find out sooner or later. Anyway, I was just after sparking up the smoke and Richie was telling us about this bird he's been texting, who apparently has a load of mates, and he was saying that we should try and meet up with them and all when next of all, all we could hear was this massive smashing noise, like someone had after setting off a bomb right beside us or something. I dropped the cigarette and burned myself on my finger in the process and Dosser literally fell to the ground and covered his head with his hands like we were under attack or something. Then we could hear this other kind of bang, and Richie opened the greenhouse door and said "I think it's comin from outside". Well as soon as he said that, all I could think of was The Beast and I started panicking like that time I took Alpha Chlorolose and ended up in the middle of the St. Patrick's Day parade in town. But after a minute I got myself together and legged it through the house and out onto the road and I couldn't believe the like, vision, that was in front of me. My beautiful Beast was on fire, with all this horrible black smoke streaming out of it, and blowing into my eyes so I started coughing and spluttering, as my chest filled up with the horrible smoke. I hate to say it, but I seriously sunk to my knees and I just stayed there, watching The Beast burning, like I was hypnotized by the horrible black smoke or something. I must have stayed there for I don't know how long, but after a while I turned around and all I could see was Gobber, and he looked like a little kid that was about to start crying because I could see his lips trembling like he was holding back the tears. I think it was then that I realised what I was going to have to do. I just looked at him and roared "Just get the fuck out of here! Get the fuck" and I stood up and started walking towards him and I don't know what I would have done if he hadn't backed away and said "You're upset, I understand that. I'll ring you tomorrow, don't forget to keep an eye on the greenhouse" and he just ran away, off down the road like a frightened cat. I walked back into my gaff, and after a few minutes I could hear sirens wailing outside but I couldn't have been bothered dealing with any firemen or coppers, so I just turned off all the lights in the house and locked myself in my room. I'd a fuck load of fauxcaine up in my room and I just lashed it out of it all night, listening to music through my ear phones, just trying to drown out the noise of the banging coming from downstairs. When I woke up this morning I was in a heap. The first thing I did was look out the window and the first thing I could see was this black patch on the road where The Beast used to be. I checked my phone and my ma had left a message saying that she'd had a call from the coppers, telling her about what had happened and that she was coming back from my granny's tomorrow to see if everything was all right. She was asking me to call her, but I just couldn't be dealing with any of that, and that's when I came to the decision. It has to be tonight, that I go; I can't leave it another minute. In a few hours' time, I'm getting the fuck out of here, forever.

The Life and Times of Gobber Gilsenan (Continued)

Holy Thursday drinking has its ups and its downs, but the way I'm feeling at the moment, it's more an act of survival than anything else, as I try to stop the demons of a week-long bender from bringing me to an early grave. I have to say that I actually feel like a fucking tramp or something, I haven't seen a bed in days and I'm starting to disgust even myself by the smell coming out of every part of my shaking body. But what can I say, when you've gone this far there's only one cure I know of, and only one cure I want to know of at that. It's early evening at some stage and I'm literally holding myself up against the bar in Brogan's on Dame Street. I don't know what time it is exactly because my phone went dead a couple of days ago and if I try to focus my vision on the clock on the wall, my eyes start to go blurry and my head starts spinning so that I feel like I'm about to vomit, or pass out, or both. I suppose I could ask someone for the time but I'm in no humour whatsoever for any human conversation bar the necessity of ordering another drink. I've had my fill of beer at this stage, and I'm pissed off having to piss every five fuckin minutes so I'm on the Jemmy neat, cut out the fucking middle man and all of that, just cut straight to the chase I suppose would be the motto for today's proceedings. I spy across the bar, some other punter who's sitting on a bar stool, tipping away on his Sweeney and I don't know what it is but there's something familiar about the guy's face. I can't for the life of me remember where I might've seen the cunt before but I'm thinking that maybe I know him to see from years back, back in the old Rathmines days when I used to head out with a whole gang of us every Saturday night. I think I must be just imaging it all because I've noticed that he hasn't taken a peak over at me at all, so if he doesn't recognise me, I must not know him; every fucker from back in those days would deffo recognise me. Come to think of it, the bloke actually looks like a bit of a head the ball, bit of psychopath vibe off him or something. He's just sitting there on his own, staring straight ahead of him into space, almost like he's oblivious to everyone around him. The pub's actually fairly busy, and there's plenty of suits knocking around, after-work-crowd type players, I suppose getting their fill in before tonight's early close and tomorrow's archaic fucking embargo on the selling of all alcoholic beverages. I can tell that some of them are pure amateur status though, and even though there's a couple of potential lookers tagging along with the suit crews, it pisses me off that just because the pubs aren't allowed open on Good Friday, every fucking spastic in the country, most of whom probably haven't set foot in a boozer for weeks feel they have to come in and annoy the fuck out of proper professionals like me, by bumping into me while I'm barely able to keep myself balanced on my feet, and shouting orders right beside my ear when I've a pain shooting through my brain like I've got a knife stuck in my head. But fuck it, I'm not going to let them get to me tonight, I've got enough on my fucking plate as it is.

It's just when I saw the expressions on the two boys' faces when they were watching their precious little greenhouse go up in flames I had to say to myself, Gobber, what the fuck are you seriously doing with your life? I mean, I'm 22 years of age and I' running around with a couple of bloody teenagers, complete fucking weirdoes at that and it's like, I need to get my life back on track before I end up a total waste of space like too many lads I know have. I mean, it's not that I don't enjoy myself with the lads, it can be a bit of crack sometimes for deffo, plus it's a nice little earner, on top of what I'm making myself with the nixers, but it's nothing worth getting into any bother over. My fighting days are well and truly over, and I don't have the belly for a fight with a bunch of kids. No, from now on, it'll be Gobber Gilsenan goes solo and that's that. Back to basics and all the rest, and I'll be the better off for it, nothing fucking surer.

The aul barman in Brogan's is starting to give me a few dodgy looks, even though to be honest, I'm almost drinking myself into a state of normality, so I decide to head onwards and upwards because I don't want to suffer the indignity of being refused a drink at this time of the evening, especially in front of all those suit crews; I wouldn't give the fuckers the satisfaction of seeing a Serie A stalwart like yours truly suffer such an ignominious rebuff, no, no, that wouldn't do at all. I decide to nip down the road towards The Foggy Dew, checking if I've got any readies left in my wallet while I'm walking. I'm struggling down the path, trying to weave in and out of what seems to be an endless stream of massive groups of tourists and I can't believe my eyes but who can I see only Kieran O' Connor, or Cock as he was affectionately known, for obvious reasons, an old mate of mine from back in the day. At first, I'm hoping that he's not going to notice me and I try to avoid making eye contact with the cunt. Then out of the corner of my eye I notice that he's definitely clocked me while simultaneously I realise that I've not got a fiver to my name, and I can't believe my own luck. Normally, I'd rather castrate myself with a length of rusty barbed wire than have to talk to someone like my old mate Cock, but as I remember, he's as soft as a eunuch in a bath tub full of strippers, so if I can tap the cunt up for a few shorts to see me through the next hour or so, I suppose I'll have to put on a brave face, and subject myself to having to have a conversation with the prick.

"Ah Kieran me aul mucker, what's the story with you kiddo?" I say to him, all nice and friendly like because I don't want the cunt getting the upper hand in this one, and I don't want him to think that I was trying to avoid him either. "Jaysus Gobber, I thought it was fuckin you man but I wasn't sure like, you're lookin a bit different to the last time I saw ye. What's the story with the head? Ye shavin it all off before it falls off of its own accord is it?" The cheeky bastard says this while rubbing his hand across my head, and I've to bite my tongue, not to mention rein in the old fists to stop myself from absolutely leathering the prick. "Ah yeah, something like that man, something like that all right. Here, have ye time for an aul brewski? Just about to nip into the Foggy up here if ye fancy it. Catch up witcha an an all that, what do ye say?" "Ah ye know me Gobber, never one to turn down an offer of a scoop, it'll have to quick though, have to get back to the missus soon enough. She's up the duff an all man, so what ye gonna do, can't be out till all hours anymore, those days are well an truly over for me I'm afraid." "Fuckin rather you than me Kieran, never heard of contraception no?" I can't resist saying this but in fairness to him, he can't help but laugh and it's all best mates 2002 time as we walk into the boozer. We grab a table in the corner of the pub and I say "Here what ye havin?" and Kieran says "Guinness". "Fuckin aul fella ye are" I say to him as I make my way to the bar and I prepare myself to put on a bit of a performance. I decide I'll have to order a Heineken for myself as I don't want to be seen necking straight whiskeys by this cunt at this hour of the night so I order the two pints off the barman. Once the barman leaves the Guinness to settle and sticks my scoop up on the bar, I take out my wallet, open it up and look inside. I turn around to my drinking partner and I'm like "Man, I can't fuckin believe it, but I've actually got no spons on me. I thought I had a nifty in my wallet there but I was obviously mistaken. Is there a bank machine around here do ye know?" Obviously it's polite to ask this question but I mean, what cunt is going to make an old mate he hasn't seen in years walk back out of the out of the boozer to go looking for money so really the fucker's only got one choice. I can see in his eyes that he suspects that I've stitched him up but because he can't be sure he has to give me the benefit of the doubt. "Not at all Gobber" he says, I'll sort us out with these man, don't worry" as he gets up out of his seat and whips out a twenty fresh from the back pocket of his jeans with a slight air of resignation. I'm like "Ah cheers Kieran. Sure I'll sort ye out with a few scoops soon enough. Might head up to The Millers for a Dublin match over the summer, we could get a few of the old crew back in action what?" "Deffo man" he says, even though we both know there's about as much chance of that happening as there is of Kieran getting out of here without buying me at least four pints, but we'll just go along with the whole charade, just to keep the peace for the time being. Sure enough, after we neck the first pint, Kieran insists on getting a second round in, and I can tell he's getting a taste for it now himself, so I suppose we'll see how it goes. We talk about the old days, mostly shite about nights out we had with all the old crew, I suppose making them seem more enjoyable than they really were but it's weird how you really convince yourself that you're life was better in the past when really at the time it probably seemed just as hard going and mind numbingly boring as it is now. After four pints, Kieran's beginning to show tell tale signs of the lightweight, or at least someone who's not at match fitness due to lack of training and not to mention first team football. He's beginning to get really energetic and talkative, and although it's annoying the shit out of me, I kind of have to put up with it because the cunt's supplying me with drink. He's starts telling me about this job he's working on, telling me his bricklaying when I know for a fact that the lying bastard never served an apprenticeship and is more than likely making tea for all the lads on the site. But as I said before, I can't start laying into the cunt because he keeps getting the rounds in. I feel like I'm a writer who's after compromising his artistic integrity in order to satisfy the whims of his patron, but what can I do? Whoever pays the piper calls the tune, and at the moment the song is shut the fuck up and keep nodding along like a bloody donkey because it's not worth the hassle getting rowdy with the bloke, especially now that he's hitting the shorts, so we're getting to the business end of things fairly rapidly. After a while of listening to this load of shite, he looks at me real sincerely and says "So you still hanging around with those little kids from around my way? Your man, the half caste guy and the little Doyle youngfella?" It knocks me back a little and I hate to say it, but I'm actually embarrassed by the question and I think I might even be going a little bit red. "Nah, it's not like that" I say to him. "I just do a bit of work for them now and again, that's all. It's all strictly business, nothing else to it." "Yeah I here they're selling a bit of something or other, well fair play to them I suppose, but to be honest man, I hate cunts who go to St. Leonard's. I mean, what's wrong with their local fuckin school d'y know what I mean? I mean it did us fine didn't it? Don't understand why cunts have to go to St. Leonard's; fuckin snobbery is all it is." I nod in agreement, as I'm eager to steer the conversation away from this topic, but then Kieran says "Here, between you an me man, Stevie Smith's little brothers are supposed to be turnin into mad little fuckers, just so ye know. I hear they're supposed to be sellin a fair amount of shit now, and they're tryin to get your mates to stop doin whatever it is they're doin. Just a heads up like, whatever ye do, don't tell anyone ye heard it from me." I tell Kieran that I know all about it and that I'm finished working with the two lads anyway, which is true and all so it's no big sweat. I reckon I've managed to get us away from this topic, and I ask him what he reckons about Ireland's chances in the World Cup, but it's like the stupid fucker doesn't even hear me and then he hits me with a fucking bombshell. "Here, I know ye haven't been with her for a couple of years now, but I'm sorry to hear about all of that." As soon as he's said it, I regret the very moment I ever came into the place with him. Why didn't I just keep on walking and find a fucking ATM, for the sake of saving sixty or seventy quid. I should've known the conversation would eventually get around to *her*. I look at him with what I'm guessing is a kind of stupefied expression if I'm to be honest, but the stupid idiot just keeps babbling on. "You know, what happened to Shauna man, I know yous haven't been together for ages but, first love an all that man, I'm sure she musta meant something to ye. I don't know if yous broke up on bad terms or whatever, but for that to happen to her. Nobody fuckin deserves that. Fuckin animals that did it to her should be fuckin shot." All I can bring myself to do is nod my head in agreement, and I can't believe it, but I can feel the tears starting to rise up in the back of my throat, flowing up to the back of my eyes so that I have to fight to make stop them from streaming down my face. My only fucking weakness, my only ever weakness, was *her*. "She's basically on a life support machine I hear" the stupid insensitive prick continues, "there's machine breathing for her, and they don't know if she's ever gonna come out of the coma. What a thing to happen to a girl, gang raped and fuckin beaten to a pulp like that. They say it took her aul fella, four days to recognise her after she was brought into hospital; the swelling was that bad around her face. And the worst part is, only three of the six lads got sent down for it, the rest of the scumbags walked away scot fucking free, unbelievable. Justice system in this country is fucked. But here man, dunno if ye head or what, but the three lads who got off? Every one of them has taken a hiding since the judge let them walk, seriously. Two of them had their legs broke an another one ended up losin an eye after he was beaten up walkin home from The Millers. They don't know if it's just a coincidence or what, they reckon maybe it was the da, but they can't pin anything on him anyway. Sure you woulda known him Gobber wouldn't ye? What was he like man, was he the type of cunt that could do somethin like that?" I'm actually left speechless by what Kieran's saying to me, and I start to feel nauseous, even like I'm about to get sick. I knew I should've kept walking. Why would I come in here with him when I knew he'd mention *her*? How could he not mention the bird I spent three blissful years of my young life with, three blissful years that I ended by being an absolute piece of dirt bag shit, treating *her* like shite when all *she* ever wanted to do was love me, and for me to love *her*? How could I've known that the lads I sold that shit to would end up meeting her down a lane, in the middle of the night, off their tits and do that to *her*. I couldn't possibly have known that that would happen. My beautiful Shauna, my beautiful, beautiful, baby girl Shauna. Suddenly it all comes over me in a hot sweat, I feel my stomach heaving like it's trying to escape from my body through my mouth and I vomit uncontrollably all over the floor, right in the middle of the pub. I fall to my knees and I can hear people laughing all around me, and when I look up, I can see that even Kieran is laughing at me, and when I try to get back up on my feet, I slip and fall on my face straight onto the vomit-soaked floor. Next thing I know I'm being hauled out of the door by two barmen. I look at Kieran as he shouts after me

"Make sure ye bring your own money witcha next time Gobber ye slimy prick" and I try to shout back at him but before I know it, I'm back out on the footpath, shouting at a brick wall as people shuffle around me, trying to ignore my presence, just like I've tried to ignore so many things about myself all through my life. I sit down with my back to the wall and try to compose myself. I tell myself to put it all out of my mind, but in my heart of hearts I know I can't do that. I know I've got to make a new beginning for myself and I know exactly how I can go about it. I've waited long enough for the chance, and fuck me but there's no time like the present. Those two little shits must think I have the brain power of a fucking mentally retarded squirrel if they think I never noticed the obvious irregularity in the floorboards in Tarzan's greenhouse, or that I never noticed the way they're shifty little beady eyes keep looking down at the same spot in the floor whenever I walk into the place, as if the power of their eyes could guard their little secret. I know where that fucking money is, and fuck me but I need that more than they ever will. They have their whole lives ahead of them, mine is dying a slow and painful death and I need to get out of her fast. Unbelievably some old bloke walks by me on the path and chucks a two euro coin into my hand, obviously thinking I'm some kind of down and out, well how wrong could you be pal, how wrong could you fucking be. Gobber Gilsenan is no down and out. Gobber Gilsenan is moving up and out of this festering corrupted cesspit of a place with the speed of a young Paolo Maldini shutting out an attack from an impertinent winger who would dare to attack the Rossoneri goal. I look up and see the last 19A bombing down Dame Street and I leap to my feet, re-energised with a fresh sense of purpose in my life. I manage to get to the bus stop just in time, jump on and take a seat downstairs. I spy that punter I saw in Brogan's earlier on, sitting across from me. I'm wondering where the fuck I know him from, but again he's not looking over at me so I must just be mistaken. By now, I can hardly contain my excitement. All that shite, all that crippling nausea I got out of my system and spilled all over the floor of The Foggy Dew. Tonight no matter what's already happened is going to be a special night for Gobber Gilsenan. Tonight is a night for new beginnings.

The Thoughts of Dosser Doyle
(Conclusion)

I've been trying to ring Tarzan for the last few hours and his phone's still turned off. He's supposed to be on security duty tonight according to the Sentry Roster, so I've been forced to call around to his house in order to ensure that he is still carrying out the duties that are expected of him. It's unusual for me to leave the house at such a late hour on a Thursday night, but my parents are thankfully rather too preoccupied with my brother's temporary insanity, to be overly vigilant of my activities so I've managed to set upon my journey without anybody noticing. I'm cycling through the lane in the dark at a rather rapid pace, and I must admit that I am feeling rather anxious about everything. Gobber's whereabouts remains unknown, Tarzan has now become impossible to contact and I seem to have developed this general feeling that all is not right on this night, but I'm sure it's just because of all the excitement of the events of recent days. Although Tarzan seemed greatly vexed by the destruction of his automobile in last night's inferno, the second to have erupted among our collective property in a matter of days, I know he possesses a great amount of resilience, not to mention his unsurpassable sense of Esprit de Corps, and that's why I'm so surprised, and admittedly a little perturbed as to the potential reasons as to why his phone is turned off and why he hasn't attempted to contact me in order to allay my worsening fears.

I arrive at the back of Tarzan's house and I'm very disappointed to see that he is not seated at the regulation lookout position and affirm that I must not allow such reckless disregard for the safety of our produce to go without reproach and conclude that I will have to verbally chastise my comrade for his lax attitude towards our Sentry Roster. On the positive side, at least the gap in the wall where Tarzan ought to be will allow me to gain access to the garden easily, a serendipitous development I must be grateful for as I'm respiring and perspiring at quite a rapid rate after my exertions on bicycle. I lean my bike against the back wall so I can use it as a climbing frame to assist my endeavours to enter Tarzan's back garden. I climb atop the wall and before I jump down into Tarzan's back garden, I notice the small lamp is on in the greenhouse and I can see a number of figures huddled in the middle of the glazed edifice; a sight which I find most perplexing. I land roughly on the patch of grass next to the wall and as I approach the greenhouse, I cannot quite believe my eyes. I pull across the door and look inside to see Tarzan, Gobber and Mister Johnson all glaring back at me with rather a menacing air of hatred emanating from them. I'm admittedly, a little taken back by the entire scene. Gobber steps forward and I attempt to say "Ah, the prodigal son has returned to the fold" when I feel the thundering power of his right fist, smash against my nose like a Tiger tank crashing against a crudely constructed barricade in a lightly defended village in the middle of the Ukraine. The force is so strong it sends me flying backwards and my flight through the air is stopped only by the cold, indifferent stone of the back wall. Gobber shouts in my face before I have time to even contemplate trying to make sense of the situation, "Where's the fuckin money you cunt?" Just as I realise the meaning behind his venomous outburst, he continues shouting the same sentence at me with the vitriolic regularity of an MG34 machine gun, mowing down wave after wave of hapless Red Army conscripts. "What do you mean, where's the money?" I retort, managing to comprehend the general thrust of his vocal assault, and finding my own voice again, after what must have been minutes of a paralysing breathlessness. "Don't pretend you don't know where it is" he says, "It'd be typical fuckin you to take it for yourself without tellin any cunt." Mister Johnson and Tarzan emerge from the greenhouse and stand behind Gobber who appears to have lost the requisite energy required to continue his verbal and physical assault on my person. "I keep tellin ye, he doesn't have it. I mean, why would he turn up like this if he'd already taken it? Anyway, he doesn't have the heart to take it himself. I know he's a cunt sometimes, well, most of the time, but he doesn't have that in him, no way." Mister Johnson delivers this somewhat perversely complimentary speech and it seems to placate Gobber slightly, who although he's certainly managed to clam himself down, is still shaking like someone caught out in the cold, even though it's positively mild out. Tarzan nods knowingly and affirms "Nah he wouldn't do it, he's not like us, and he doesn't have the balls." At this stage, I'm really starting to wonder what in the name of Jove is going on. I raise myself to my feet and ask "Would someone kindly tell me what in the name of Jove is going on here?" Gobber immediately backs away and lights a cigarette, Mister Johnson simply sinks to his knees and surprisingly, Tarzan steps forward to enlighten me as to the nature of the current circumstances vis a vis, me getting punched in the face by a former associate who has been inexplicably missing for nearly a week, the reasons as to why Mister Johnson is standing in Tarzan's back garden, and why Tarzan himself has not answered his phone all day, thus requiring my attendance at this impromptu gathering. "The Running Away Fund is gone Dosser, we don't know where it is, but it's gone." Tarzan delivers this rather pithy synopsis of recent events in such an even tone, that it takes a few seconds for the literal meaning for this collection of words, placed in that particular order and articulated vocally by my alleged friend, to register in my brain. "Sorry, gentlemen if it seems I'm a little confused, I've just been rather viciously punched in the face as you may have noticed, but do you mean to tell me that the Going Away Fund, as in all of the money that I, or should I say, we have collected over the entire course of our operations has gone? Disappeared into thin air? Is no longer physically present in a state of matter, occupying space in the vastness of our entire universe, is that what you mean by 'gone'? And sorry again for perhaps appearing a tad foolish, but would you mind telling me as to why the fuck all of you are here on this Good Friday morning, in Tarzan's back garden, without informing me of your respective presences in our main base of operations?" The silence which meets me, and the sorry expressions of guilt and desperation written on the faces of my companions, tells the story of an epic poem. "Judas and Brutus had nothing on you collection of fucking untrustworthy reprobates! Who the fuck has the money, who the fuck has my fucking money?" For the first and probably last time in my life, I completely lose control of all my faculties, both mental and bodily, as my arms and legs start flailing, kicking and punching at my alleged comrades, my supposed associates, my so-called friends. Without any conscious thought, I am screaming through the black Whitefield night, cursing and condemning, proclaiming the death of all that is good and pure in this world, as I crumble once more to the earth. Tarzan shouts "Relax will ye for Jesus' sake. Peter and Paul musta took it, they have to have. Who else would take it? I'm tellin ye now they have it. Let's fuckin tool up an go after the bastards!" Mister Johnson shoots Tarzan an evil look and shouts "That's a load of bollocks and you know it. It's your fuckin house for God's sake. You have it, I know you do. You're just not tellin us where it fuckin is!" Tarzan spits at this idea, erupting in rage, he points practically with his whole body towards Gobber. "What about this cunt? He's been gone for days, well enough time for him to hide the cash somewhere, or stick it in the bank, or spend it all on fuckin booze you alco cunt!" Gobber screams again in my direction "I'm tellin yis, he fuckin has it. The little shite has always only ever cared about himself, he has the cash put away somewhere, I know he has!"

Suddenly, our accusatory deliberations are interrupted by the sound of smashing glass, followed by the louder puff of a small explosion and the now familiar sight of deathly flames, as the greenhouse, the tabernacle of our existence as an organisation, descends to hell from its earthly tomb. "It came from over the wall" shouts Gobber, as Tarzan runs to the back gate and pulls back the latch as we, en masse file out into the lane. Although it is dark, it is possible to make out two figures running down the lane away from the fire, and when you are familiar with their form, it is possible to affirm that the two fugitive figures are those of Peter and Paul Smith. Without a word being spoken, our recent enmity is completely forgotten as my associates and I are once again united in the face of a common enemy, and we tacitly agree to pursue our fleeing foes.

I run not so much towards my enemy, but away from my friends. In this moment, I do not feel as though I am chasing after Peter and Paul Smith, I feel only that I am running for its own sake. I feel a cooling breeze invade the mild night air as I run, caressing the warm extremities of my body. In this moment, I am running; without any knowledge of where it will lead me, nor do I care as much. In this moment I feel a freedom, I feel the freedom of a lost child, who has no need or want to go home. And as I run, I wonder what kind of child could be lost, and still feel no fear or no desire to return from whence they came? What kind of love or hate must make the bed of a child who is content to scatter themselves like golden grains of sand on a stony beach? For at this moment I run because I have nowhere else to go. In this moment I run to seek another space in heaven or earth, in which to rest my weary mind, because there is beauty only in the unknown and I know this is the only truth I can be sure of. I find that I have run so far, that I am in a lane I may never have walked down before.

It is still dark, but an almost full moon has slid away from behind a benign cloud, to give a hue of white to the patch of the world that I call home. I cannot see Peter or Paul Smith, nor can I see Tarzan, or Gobber Gilsenan, or Mister Brian Johnson; the only three people in this world that I could even begin to call friends. At this moment I am alone, but this solitude does not last for long. Soon, I feel the breath of life behind my back. I do not turn around to bear witness to the face of this life, because to feel its presence is enough. I am struck to the ground with the force of gravity, and it does not allow me to rise again. I can feel a repeated thumping on the back of my head but there is no pain. My legs and arms also experience this force of life, my bones break and the blood begins to leak from my punctured veins, and pour from my body, onto the concrete ground on which I lie. Although I do not want to look up, my face is turned upwards so that I now face the sky, as stars begin to appear above me, beneath the rushing clouds that are being blown away by the cool breeze that had so recently touched my skin. My view of the sky is obscured once again by the face of a man. He says his name is Revenge and that I must pay for what I have done, just like all the others. He continues to crush my bones and tear my flesh, but still I do not feel pain. As I lie on that grey ground, I feel only one thing, and that is the truth that I belong where I am. I, in much the same way as the moon is the child of a celestial being whose power we cannot hope to understand, am the child of something else. I am the child of a different being whose power is no greater or no less than the progenitor of the moon, but has its beauty all the same. And as I lie on this grey concrete ground, the man named Revenge is still standing over me, and I don't know whether I'm going to live, or die.

Epilogue

Easter Sunday morning is a beautiful day for some. As chocolate faced children, rip to shreds with delight, the boxes of Easter eggs consumed too early in the day to ever be a good idea. "You'll make yourself sick if you eat anymore" counsel worrying mothers, who secretly laugh at the merriment of houses full of children, behind half open kitchen doors where roast lamb dinners are cooked with love and potatoes. The church is busy too today, as the fine weather guides troops of worshippers, marching towards the open gates of God's house to celebrate his resurrection from the dead. For today is the second most joyous day in the calendar, if you consider Christmas to be the most, and not everyone does, and the church they say is dying, is still pulling in the crowds after all these years; kind of like Frank Sinatra, but in this case the tickets are cheaper.

For others Easter is just another day, barely worthy of a title. As men lost at sea awake in foreign homes, not speaking the tongue of the natives and possessing only vague memories of a life spent in a dream. Young women also, search the sounds coming through their bedroom windows for a love whose song they once thought they heard, but turned out only to be the disheartening din of passing traffic. They scan the horizon with their eyes as well, to seek a glimpse of a fleeting falcon they might once have seen, before they are kissed on the shoulder by the only man they ever found who had his own cage, and content but not enraptured, they move away from the light of the window, until that sometime lover they so recently sought, can no longer see her young smile on the breeze, as the brightness of her ghostly form becomes indistinguishable from the colour of her bedroom wallpaper.

Others wish they could have the chance to sink their bodies into the sepulchral background of suburban life. There are those whose lives have been touched by a light so darkly vibrant, that they will live forever among the onlookers and passersby as people who are beyond the pale. These figures must spend the time of every day, seeking a sanctuary away from prying eyes, so marked are they by events from their past, carrying memories with them, like crosses on their chastened backs.

One person, who is not burdened with such a cross, walks the streets of Whitefield this morning. He is surely in fine fettle and a chirpier lad you never did see. Although he is evidently contented with his life, he does not feel it prudent, or indeed mannerly, to impose his relatively good fortune on other people's misery. The boy whose name is Richard Grimes, or Richie to his friends, is wearing a brand new pair of white adidas shoes. So white are they, that it almost hurts his eyes to look upon them, but look Upon them often, he continues to do, simply because he cannot stop himself. The boy is nearing the local newsagents and as he approaches the shop he produces a large roll of used notes from his pocket, its sizable mass fortified by a tough elastic band. It is not the only large roll of notes that the boy owns, indeed there are many, many more, but he has carefully concealed the others in a secret place he is sure nobody will ever find. He strips a solitary ten euro note from the roll, in order to purchase some light refreshments for himself. He buys a coke and a chocolate bar and as he leaves the shop, a smile appears across his face. He is laughing at the stupidity of others and the splendour of chance, and he is thinking about what a great view of the world you can have when you sit on top of a high wall and watch the people below you, especially when those people below you forget you're there, and you can see all the secrets of their lives. He walks past the church and he takes a big bite from his chocolate bar, watching the crowds of people leaving as mass comes to an end. He wonders aloud what he might buy with his recently acquired fortune, "I think I'll get myself a new dog" he says.